MW00565213

Midnight Men

The Supernatural Adventures

of

Earl and Dale

Kevin David Anderson

A
Grinning Skull Press
Publication
PO Box 67, Bridgewater, MA 02324

ISBN: 1-947227-42-4 (paperback)
ISBN-13: 978-1-947227-42-2 (paperback)
ISBN: 978-1-947227-43-9 (e-book)

DEDICATION

To Hope,
my favorite person for twenty plus years and counting

CONTENTS

ACKNOWLEDGMENTS

Thank you to editor, author, Danielle Kaheaku for her editor's eyes. Thank you to Richard W. Goldsmith and William Anderson for their reading and unbiased opinions. Thanks to Lana Holt whose transforming cosplays inspired a character. Thanks to Danielle Kaheaku again and to Kristina Grifant for starting the San Diego Chapter of the Horror Writers Association, which has been a great source of encouragement and support. And thank you to the Fiction Writers Workshop and Night Writers for helping me tune up my creativity. Also, thanks to Jonathan Maberry for creating the Writers Coffeehouse, a monthly networking session supporting writers at all stages of their career. Big thank you to the talented Jason Hill who first brought Earl and Dale to life in his amazing audio adaptation of "Green Eyes and Chili Dogs," and to Craig Groshek who released that adaptation upon the world via his Simply Scary Podcast on the Chilling Tales for Dark Nights Network. A great big thank you to the fine folks at Grinning Skull Press for taking a chance on two heavyset truckers, to Jeffrey Kosh for his fantastic cover art, and to Hope Anderson - Earl and Dale's number one superfan.

Green Eyes
and
Chili Dogs

Dale stared down at death. It wasn't the first time, and until his arteries finally petrified from a lifetime of truck-stop cuisine, it wouldn't be the last.

No more than twenty, the girl lay on an autopsy table. Not the modern stainless steel variety, but a porcelain antique with aluminum legs and a drain similar to the kind found in the average bathtub.

Dale hovered over the grisly scene. For a few seconds, he thought he might be dead, too, just a disembodied apparition. Then the chili dogs he had wolfed down a few hours ago started doing unpleasant things to his insides. Even though he gazed down at a young woman frozen in death during what he assumed was a premature autopsy, it was the chili dogs causing waves of nausea to ripple through him. Swallowing back the discomfort, he reached out for the poor girl.

Despite a thick layer of makeup, her face had an innocent, endearing quality. He wanted very much to close those green eyes, give this one some peace, and let the ferryman know she was ready for the final journey. But his hand disappeared into her cheek, emerging out the other side.

That's when Dale knew it was merely a dream. It made sense. Most everything was grainy, out of focus, black and white, except for those piercing green eyes. He took a deep breath and willed himself to consciousness. *Damn it, Dale. Wake the hell up.*

He opened his eyes, then shut them again, stunned by the glare of oncoming headlights. Bringing a hand over his brow, he opened his eyes slowly, like a child cautiously opening a closet door, unsure of what's inside.

"Hey, hey, welcome back sunshine," a husky voice to his left said.

Glancing over, Dale saw Earl in the driver's seat of the eighteen-wheeler. His friend and sometimes partner, unshaven, grinned at him with tobacco-stained teeth. Earl's gut would have done Santa Claus proud. It pressed up against the steering wheel, and his stretched-to-the-limit t-shirt could barely contain it.

"You get enough beauty sleep, partner?" Earl said.

Dale yawned.

Answering his own question, Earl said, "Nope, didn't think so. Still look like three-day-old road kill."

Dale heard a feminine laugh behind him. He turned around and looked behind his seat. A young woman bent forward, hand over her face, giggling.

"Oh, Dale, this here is Katy. Picked her up about twenty miles back."

Katy offered her hand. "Hi. I really appreciate the lift. Was out there for hours. Thought I'd have to sleep next to a cactus."

"Uh, yeah. No problem," Dale said, taking her soft hand, and gazing into her green eyes. Without letting go, he turned to Earl. "Pull over."

Earl frowned. "What's wrong?"

Dale let go of her hand. "Just pull over."

"Damn, if you need to drain the lizard, put your knees together for a mile or two," Earl said. "There's a chew and choke just up the—"

"Now, Earl," Dale said. "I gotta go now."

"Fine." Earl started to downshift. "I swear you got the bladder of a ninety-year-old woman. Hell, we oughta invest in some of them adult diapers so we could get a haul in on time."

The tires rolled over the gravel along the side of the highway, and before the rig had stopped, Dale opened his door. He jumped out of the cab, his boots touching down in the Utah desert.

At half past midnight, it was pitch-black outside, but the lights from the rig did a fair job of chasing away the darkness in a ten-yard perimeter. Dale walked straight for the point where light faded into night, kicking up dust under his heavy footfall. He wasn't a fat man, but no one had ever accused him of missing a meal. Dale unzipped his fly and pissed into the breeze.

"What the hell is so damn urgent?" Earl took position next to Dale. "I swear, sometimes you're jumpier than bull's testicles on snippin' day."

"Why'd you pick her up?"

"You're not gonna give me the 'Never pick up hitchhikers speech,' are ya? She can't be more than a hundred and ten pounds. Hell, I think we can take her."

"No, it's not that."

"What then?"

"I... I just saw her."

Earl shook his head. "You couldn't have. You've been sawing logs since Barstow, buddy."

Dale looked down, tapped, and sighed. "No. I saw her in a dream."

A grin curled up Earl's cheeks. "Yeah, I dream about young things like that all the time. Once there was this—"

"Not that kind of dream, you cradle-robbing shithead," Dale snapped. "I mean she was...stripped naked. Cut up like a high school dissection project."

Earl lowered his voice, glancing back at the cab. "You saw her naked?"

"Old man, will you please focus?"

"Sorry." Earl zipped up.

"I think she's in danger or...something." Dale sighed. "Just a feeling."

Earl didn't respond for a few moments, distant crickets filling the silence. "Oh Lord, how I hate it when you get a feeling," Earl said. "Well, if she stays with us, we can look after her."

"Yeah, I suppose. I hate this kind of crap."

Earl leaned close to Dale. "Did you get a chance to check out the headlights on her?"

Dale could picture them, but not at all like Earl probably was. In Dale's vision, her round breasts were no longer held in place by firm, uncut skin. They had flopped to either side of her chest and rested on blood-soaked porcelain.

"Jeez, Earl. You're old enough to be that girl's estranged, drunken, perverted, unshaven, don't-even-invite-him-over-for-Thanks-giving-no-more grandfather."

Earl raised his voice. "Unshaven?" He turned his head so Dale could see his face in profile. "This is trimmed and deliberate stubble." Earl ran a hand over his cheeks and double chin. "I think it makes me look like that Ethan Hawke. What do you think?"

Dale felt vile rumblings deep in his belly and splashes of vomit burning his throat. "Hell, I don't know, Earl. When Ethan is in his late fifties and puts on seventy pounds, I'll let you know."

If he got moving, he might be able to quell the need to puke, so Dale started walking back to the truck.

"Jeez, Dale. Can't ya ever say anything nice to me?"

Dale stopped. *Damn, he's needy.* Without turning around, he said, "You don't smell god-awful today. How's that?"

"Now, was that so hard? Swear to God, good buddy, getting a compliment out of you is like pulling Siegfried off of Roy."

Before Dale could take another step, he felt a massive

belch ascend his esophagus. He tried to swallow it, but it burned like raw jalapenos. He instinctively bent forward, just in time to avoid puking on his boots.

Earl placed a hand on his heaving back. "Ya see, that's why you're not supposed to eat more than one of them chili dogs at that place. Hell, even the waitress said so."

Katy yelled from the cab. "Is he all right?"

"Oh yeah," Earl said. "If puking yer guts out ever becomes an Olympic event, my friend here will win that gold medal faster than you can say. 'Ohhhweee, what's that smell?'"

Feeling a great deal better and ten pounds lighter, Dale wiped his mouth. "Well, that was fun."

"If you're all done redecorating Utah, I suggest we get this show back on the road."

Dale held out his hand. "I'll drive."

Earl pulled out the keys. "All right, but be gentle with her this time. My rig's a Peterbilt lady, unlike that Mack whore you tool around in."

Earl was baiting him into another smack-talking session over whose truck was superior, but he wasn't in the mood. His throat burned like hell, every breath he took reeked of chili, and there was a girl in the cab he could easily picture with her chest cracked open. He just wanted this run to be over.

Dale sparked the engine back to life while Earl let out a long belch. The unwelcome odor of chili filled the cab. Earl rubbed his belly and made a sour face.

"How many of those chili dogs did you have?"

"Just one," Earl said.

"Well," Dale said, pulling back out onto Interstate 15. "It's probably gonna take a little longer."

"No, sir," Earl shook his head. "I ain't puking. Only girls puke. No offense ta either of ya."

Katy chuckled behind them.

"So where are ya headed, Katy?" Dale asked.

"Back home," she said. "Salt Lake City."

Christ, Dale thought. Few places on the planet gave Dale the willies, but Salt Lake City always made his hair stand on end. Even in broad daylight, the city just seemed off kilter. All the streets spun out from the cathedral, like the spires in a web, trying to snare a meal for some unseen spidery god.

"So do you guys drive together all the time?" Katy asked. "I mean, I've seen truckers ride together before, but it's usually a man and wife team. Oh, unless you guys are..."

Detecting apprehension in her voice, Dale said, "Are what?"

"Well, I don't judge or anything." Her voice quivered. "And not that there's anything wrong with that."

Dale finally got her meaning. It must have hit Earl at the same time because they both responded with a deep and masculine, "No!"

"God, no," Dale continued.

In the rearview mirror, Dale saw Katy wave her hands as she said, "Like I said, not judging."

Earl laughed, then belched.

Dale fanned the smell of regurgitated chili with his hand. "Will you stick a cork in it? Jeez."

Earl rubbed his belly. "Better out, than in." He turned around. "See, Katy, we're just doing a double-haul. Did ya notice we got two trailers hooked together?"

"Uh, yeah," Katy said.

"The one on the end is his." Earl gestured to Dale. "Sometimes cargo needs to get from L.A. to Chicago in an awful hurry. With just one driver, that can take near three days iffen the driver is obeying the law. With two drivers, Dale and I can go straight on through, cutting the time in half."

"Get there faster," Katy said.

"And pays triple." Earl grinned.

The headlights lit up a sign, which Dale squinted to read.

Salt Lake City 12 miles.

Earl leaned toward Dale. "She thought that you and me—"

"I got it, Earl," Dale snapped.

Earl sat back up straight. "Iffen I swung that way, I could get someone prettier than you." He turned to face Katy. "Don't you think I could get someone prettier than him?"

Katy laughed. "I don't know. Maybe."

"What do you think of this stubble?" Earl said. "Think I look a bit like that Ethan Hawke?"

"Yeah, a bit," Katy said.

Earl turned toward Dale. "Told ya."

Good God. Dale contemplated driving into a set of oncoming headlights. "So Katy," he said, catching her gaze in the rearview mirror. "What brings ya home?"

"Oh..." She slumped back into her seat. "My mom called me. Wants me to help with Billy, my younger brother."

"He sick?" Dale asked.

"No, just acting funny."

Earl turned around. "Funny, how?"

"Ever since he graduated from high school, couple months back, he just sleeps all day."

"Oh hell," Earl said. "That's just being lazy. Post-graduation syndrome."

"It's not just that," Katy continued. "Mom said he never eats anymore. He's turned pale and thin. And when he does go out, it's only after dark."

A chill crawled up Dale's spine. He glanced over at Earl, who was looking back at him. Dale could tell they were thinking the same thing.

"Mom says his whole personality has changed—like he's a different person. And he has this new group of friends Mom has never seen before." Katy paused.

Dale met her gaze in the mirror. The luster of her green eyes faded.

9

Katy shrugged. "I don't know. Mom thinks that I can talk some sense into him. We used to be close."

Mentally, Dale kicked himself. There was a silver cross in the glove box of his truck, kept for just such an emergency. But they weren't in his truck. They were in Earl's. Dale had no idea what implements Earl kept on hand, beyond a Bowie knife—one as big as a machete.

Katy rested her elbows on the back of their seats. "Hey, listen. You guys have been real nice to me, and I'm sure my mom wouldn't mind if you wanted to come in for a minute. Use the facilities, grab a bite to eat."

Earl let go with another belch, patting his stomach. "Nothing to eat, thank you, but I could use a quick shower."

"Sure," Katy said, turning toward Dale. "How about you?"

Dale sighed, wishing he were still asleep.

"Well, how about it?" Earl said.

"Sure, why not," Dale said, putting on the turn signal. He eased the rig over, taking the first exit into Salt Lake City.

A few minutes later they parked on a faintly lit suburban street. The houses were big—two and three stories—and even in the night, Dale could see finely manicured landscaping.

Katy hopped down. "Just let me go in first and say hi. Then I'll wave you in, okay?"

"Yeah, sure." Earl closed the cab door. Turning to Dale, he lowered his voice. "Think we should let her go in alone?"

"I think her story has already been written, my friend."

"Huh?"

Dale shook his head. "Never mind."

They both watched in silence as Katy crossed the street and followed the walk to a two-story Victorian. The dark porch seemed to swallow her petite form. She had been out of sight for a full minute before either of them spoke.

"How long we gonna sit here?" Earl rubbed a hand over his stubble.

Dale looked up the street. The ghost-white steeples of the Mormon temple rose like watchtowers, keeping a vigil on its flock. The looming spires added to Dale's discomfort, reminding him that there were a million places he'd rather be about now. "Guess that's long enough." He turned to Earl. "Whatcha got?"

Earl reached under the seat and pulled out a heavy vinyl carrying case rolled up like a sleeping bag. As Earl unfurled it, Dale was pleasantly surprised to see that Earl was better prepared than he'd imagined. Throwing-knives, a handgun, bullets—some silver, some not—and several sets of brass knuckles were all tucked in to form-fitting pouches.

"I'll take the thirty-eight," Dale said, removing the revolver. He flipped open the carousel, checking to see if it was loaded. It was.

As he tucked the gun in the small of his back behind his belt, Earl pulled out two throwing knives and shoved them in his back pocket. He reached under the seat again and came up with a Bowie knife cradled in both hands.

Dale smiled as he read the large inscription on the blade. BETSY.

"You ready to go to work, old girl?" Earl said to his knife.

Dale slapped Earl's arm. "Come on, old man."

As they crossed the street, Earl let go another chili-laced burp. Dale frowned at him. "More stealth, less belching."

Earl feigned a salute, and they moved up the walk. The wooden porch creaked under their considerable weight. In the stillness of the night, it seemed thunderous. Dale put his hand on the door. It was ajar. He took a deep breath and pushed.

The door swung inward, and they both stared for a moment. There were only two sources of light in the house. One came from upstairs, very faint, distant—probably escaping from underneath a closed door. The other was bright and glaring.

Dale got the impression that it was a light bulb hanging

free with no lampshade to soften the glow. It shone upward, and although Dale couldn't see the source, it was coming from a cellar.

Gesturing with Betsy, Earl said, "Age before beauty."

Dale moved inside. His boots made no sound as he stepped onto a thick throw rug. Following his instincts, he headed toward the cellar, motioning Earl to follow.

The cellar light, at the end of a wide hall, illuminated family photos on the wall. Dale recognized images of Katy, with someone he assumed was her younger brother. The siblings were pictured at different moments in their lives—elementary school, soccer team pictures, proms. As he moved down the hall, taking in the images was like watching them grow up.

When Dale reached the cellar entrance, he glanced back at Earl before he started his descent. He had no doubt that Earl would always be there, covering his back, ready to take on whatever horror awaited them, but he still felt the need to check. They both took a deep breath and then descended.

Midway, Dale hunched to get a better view and caught sight of four aluminum table legs sitting dead center on the cement floor. With one more step, he saw the white porcelain of the autopsy table. He paused for a moment and closed his eyes.

"You okay?" Earl put a hand on Dale's shoulder.

Dale nodded, swallowed hard, and opened his eyes.

Stepping onto the cellar floor, each moved to opposite sides of the porcelain table. They stared down at Katy and her green eyes.

"Oh, sweet Jesus." Earl wiped his brow.

Dale knew this is what they would find, but a small part of him, now crumbling into disappointment, wanted to be surprised. She looked cold, and he wanted to cover her somehow. But her days of feeling cold were long gone.

"I don't get it," Earl said. "This couldn't have happened in five goddamn minutes. This took hours to do."

Dale nodded. "I know."

"And if she's been lying here—" Earl paused, swallowing. "Who the hell did we have in my rig?"

Dale just shrugged.

Earl shuddered as if a ghost had just moved through him. "How in the hell does this creepy shit always find us? I mean, it's not like we go looking for it."

Dale examined the two small puncture wounds in Katy's neck, very round and deep. "We're just lucky that way, I guess."

"So, what now?" Earl said. "Get outta here? Make an anonymous call to Johnny Law?"

Dale shook his head. "Katy didn't bring us here just to find her."

"Afraid you were gonna say that." Earl sighed. "So what's the plan?"

"Check the rest of the house. If we don't find nothin', then we wait."

"Great," Earl said. "I always wanted ta—"

They both jumped as an old rotary phone mounted on the wall began to ring.

Dale pointed the 38 at the phone; his finger wrapped tight around the trigger guard. Upstairs, at least four other phones were ringing in unison, some with electronic bleeps, others with a traditional ring.

After the fourth ring, Earl said, "Are ya gonna shoot the phone?"

Dale rolled his eyes and lowered the pistol.

"You want I should get that? It might be our bad guy calling to say hey." Earl grinned.

Before Dale could respond, the ringing stopped. It didn't stop because the caller had given up, terminating the connection. It stopped ringing because someone answered it.

Dale and Earl exchanged silent, wide-eyed glances.

Someone upstairs, possibly on the second floor, had picked

up, and Dale could make out a male voice, filtering down through the still house.

"No. I was just getting a little rest," the voice said. "I can't wait to be with you again, my beloved."

Dale heard feet slap down above as if someone was getting out of bed—or a coffin.

"Yes, it did take a long time," the voice continued. "Mother, too. But it was well worth it. They tasted divine—like black roses harvested from graveyard soil."

Heavy steps moved above. The voice got louder as the footfalls began to descend the stairs.

"You did?" The voice sounded excited. "How delicious."

Dale motioned for Earl to take position under the stairs on the right. Dale stood to the left.

The voice was now at the top of the cellar stairs, and the words were crystal clear. "Until we are together again, my dark princess. For I am but only half a demon without you."

Dale had the nauseating feeling of listening to a horror romance novel on tape, complete with cheesy goth dialogue. Worst of all, he was almost sure what the creep would say next, and he cringed at the thought. *Don't say it, please don't say it.*

"You complete me," the voice said at the top of the cellar stairs.

God, I can't wait to kill this son-bitch.

Dale heard the soft beep of a cordless phone being switched off, and then heavy footsteps shook the wooden stairs as the man descended. Dale pressed himself against the wall, sucking in his gut. Earl did the same, with little effect.

A dark figure stepped down onto the cellar floor, a black silk cape trailing behind him. Shoulder-length hair the color of midnight swayed with the creature's movements as it approached Katy's body. He reached out a bony hand and caressed her dead cheek.

"We still have so much more to do, my sister." The monster

was Katy's younger brother, Billy. He moved to the other side of the table, his ebony eyes aimed at Katy's dead green ones. "We've only just begun this journey, you and I. Together we will explore passions only dreamt about in the—"

Earl interrupted the bastard's monologue with a loud, unrestrained belch.

He looked over at Dale and said, "Sorry."

The dark figure stood erect, about five and a quarter feet tall. Dale registered a hint of surprise on the creature's face. Billy wore a dark pinstriped vest with a tuxedo-style collar. Blood-red jewels dangled from a choker around a milky-white neck streaked with veins.

Billy raised his arms dramatically, flinging the cape off his shoulders. He bared one-inch fangs that gleamed ivory under the naked light bulb.

Jeez, Dale thought. *Somebody's got Dracula envy.*

"Foolish mortals," Billy said. "Rushing down into a dark lair, knowing not what you'll find."

"Yeah," Dale said. "We're kind of stupid that way."

Billy, now a blood-lusting thing, stepped away from the table. "Do you know whose presence you're in?"

"Enlighten us." Earl brought up the knife.

Billy narrowed his gaze, and his black pupils were just visible between slits of pale skin. He tilted his head down, revealing a Bela Lugosi hairline. "I am a God of Death."

Dale chuckled.

"You mock me, sir?"

"Sorry," Dale said. "I just thought that iffen I ever met a god, he'd be... ya know." Dale looked at Earl. "Help me out, buddy."

"Taller?" Earl said, raising an eyebrow.

"Yeah." Dale agreed, taking aim with the .38. "Taller."

Billy hoisted his arms like a Shakespearean thespian demanding the audience's attention. "Like the night, I am forever. Long after this earth has reclaimed your bodies, I will continue in the darkness, forever employed by death, draining the living for my unending journey through time. I am eternal. I am the night. I am forever—"

Dale shot Mr. Forever through the forehead.

Billy fell back against the rear wall and slid downward. Like a slug, he left a thick, pulpy trail. Astonishment chiseled on his dead features.

Earl moved fast for a man his size, approaching Billy's body. He knelt and looked as if he were going to poke the boy with Betsy.

"Easy, Earl." Dale kept the pistol trained on Billy's unmoving chest. "That ain't always the end of them."

"Careful is my middle name." Earl brushed the blade across Billy's cheek.

Dale lowered the gun. "Your middle name is Marion."

"Now, I told you that in confid— What the hell?" Earl rotated the blade, revealing a dull white substance on its edge.

A flesh-colored spot had appeared were Earl had scraped the knife. Earl rubbed his thumb across Billy's neck, smearing the stenciled-on veins. His thumb glistened with makeup.

"You gotta be kidding me." Earl opened the dead boy's mouth. He yanked out one of the fangs. Holding up the dislodged prosthetic tooth, he shook his head. "You crazy son-bitch." He turned to Dale. "What the hell is wrong with kids today?"

Dale sighed, putting the pistol back in his belt.

Earl stood and tossed the porcelain fang onto Billy's chest. "I mean, why can't they just raid their parent's liquor cabinet and smoke pot like we did?"

Dale moved forward, looking down at Katy's green eyes. They were the prettiest shade of forest he had ever seen.

"I swear, Dale, video games, social media, reality TV—it's rotting their little brains." Earl's voice rose. "Get up, you son-bitch. It's my turn ta kill ya."

"You about through?"

Earl rubbed his forehead. "Yeah." He joined Dale at the table. "Sure was a sweet thing."

Dale said, "An angel if ever there was one." He closed her eyes with his fingers. "Sleep now, child."

Earl crossed his hands over his belly, and both men stood silently with only the sound of their breathing between them.

The sound of the front door closing echoed upstairs. Dale froze. Footsteps moved over the ceiling, heading for the cellar stairs.

Dale and Earl turned to face the door. Within moments, a set of long female legs encased in thigh-high patent leather boots came into view. They seemed a bit unsteady, as if the owner was carrying something, making the journey down the steps awkward. When the woman reached the bottom level, she froze, surprise showing through a pound of goth-styled makeup.

She held a bundle two feet long, limp and unmoving. It was a child. The bright pink *Dora the Explorer* pajamas contrasted sharply with the woman's Vampira outfit.

"I'll be dammed," Earl said. "There's a Missus Son-bitch."

Without a word, the woman dropped the child. Dale lurched forward, arms outstretched. He missed the child's body but caught her head, keeping it from hitting the cement floor. The woman scrambled up the stairs.

Dale pulled the girl to his chest as he felt something pass over his head, nicking his hair. One of Earl's throwing knives stuck in the thick black heel of Vampira's boot.

The blade didn't slow her down.

Earl grimaced apologetically.

"Get that child-stealin' bitch," Dale yelled.

Earl rushed past Dale and mounted the stairs. "Look out, wide load coming through."

Dale held the child out in front of him. "Please don't be dead." He placed a thick finger on the small neck, holding his breath.

The child was breathing, and he felt a strong pulse in her neck. He gasped with relief. "Thank you."

He leaned in and caught the familiar scent of chloroform. "Goddamn sons-a-bitches."

The child stirred. He brushed her beautiful auburn locks away from her eyes and stood up. "You just get some rest, sweetie. Ain't nothing gonna hurtcha now."

Dale looked back at Katy, now understanding why she had brought them here. "You done real good, girl. Real good." Then he headed up the steps.

In the living room, Dale found a loveseat close to the entry-way. He gently deposited the sleeping child and pulled an afghan over her. "I need to go help Uncle Earl, but I'll be back," he whispered.

Dale hurried through the open front door. He took out the pistol, looking up and down the street for any sign of Earl or Vampira. On the last porch step, he felt something slick under his boot. Both feet went out from under him. He braced for impact. Ass first, he hit the brick walkway.

"Goddammit." Dale rolled off one cheek, the stench of chili assaulting his nostrils.

"Oh hell, Dale, I'm sorry." Earl strolled across the lawn.

"What'd I slip on?"

Earl stood over him, rubbing his belly. "I come up them basement steps so darn fast it jarred something loose. That chili dog just did a Mount Saint Helens on me."

Dale realized what he was sitting in. "Aww, man..." He sat back down. "Well, did ya get her?"

Earl shook his head. "Sorry, buddy. Twenty years ago, maybe." He slapped his gut. "This body was built by Bud."

"Dammit, Earl."

"Hey, I ain't no Mark Spitz or nothing."

Dale furrowed his brow. "What?"

"Ya know, that Olympic running guy."

"Mark Spitz was a swimmer, you idiot."

"Oh." Earl scratched his head. "Who am I thinking of? Olympics, fast running fella."

"I have no idea." Dale thrust his hand up at Earl.

Earl grasped Dale's hand and pulled him up. There was a wet sound as Dale's butt departed the walk.

Dale stood, slapping regurgitated chili off his ass. "Exactly why am I friends with you?"

"Because I'm so damn pretty." Earl grinned. But looking back at the house, his expression turned solemn. "Is the little one, I mean is she—"

"No," Dale said. "Just sleeping. Chloroform."

Earl let out a long breath. "What now? Can't call the local cops. We'd be here for the next few days trying to reckon all this."

"Yeah, and I'm not looking forward to explaining how we come to be here, neither."

"What then?"

Dale thought for a moment. "I still know a few folks at the FBI. One I know would keep my report of what went on here anonymous. At least the info would get filtered down to the locals."

"What about the little one? Can't leave her here."

Dale gazed out across the yard, seeing the enormous white spires in the distance. "I got an idea."

"The FBI, huh." Earl slapped his belly. "I know you don't like to talk about it, but one day you're gonna have to tell me more about this life you had before we met."

Dale slapped Earl's back. "Now, you know my life didn't really begin 'til I met you." He moved up the steps.

"As much as I appreciate the sweet talk," Earl said, "I know you're just trying ta change the subject. Again."

* * *

After depositing the sleeping child on the top step of the temple, Dale looked back only once. When security guards swarmed around the bundle, he said a silent goodbye.

Dale made his way to where Earl waited in the truck, engine humming. He hopped into the cab.

"Everything go all right?" Earl said.

"Just fine."

Earl turned the lights on as the truck began to roll forward. "If I might make a personal observation, good buddy?"

Dale buckled up, sighing. "If you must."

"For a man as religiously void as you is, that was a very spiritually insightful thing you just done."

Dale folded his arms and sank into his seat. "Will you please just get me out of Utah?"

"That suits me, and there's this all-night diner on the other side of the state line, fries up the best—"

"You just puked," Dale said, looking at Earl in amazement.

Earl patted his belly. "I know. Now I got all this room. Ya see..."

Dale shook his head, tuning out Earl's annoying drone. He wanted so badly to go to sleep. He wanted so badly for this run to be over. Shutting his eyes, he attempted to will himself unconscious. It didn't work.

He gazed out his window and imagined that he saw green eyes dimly reflected in the glass.

Good Night, Katy.

Night of the Spider

October 2:23 a.m. California Highway 99, Northbound...

"Get your butt down here and visit your boy. You ain't seen him in near a month," the voice screamed out of the little cell phone speaker.

Dale held the phone away from his ear with one hand and kept an iron-clad grip on the steering wheel of his Mack truck with the other. His ex-wife's rant was going into overtime, and he wished he knew enough about his new cell phone to know if it had a volume control. "I go where the work is. Dammit, Velma, you know that."

"Don't give me that crap. That's the same excuse you used to spend time with that whore in..." Her voice faded, and when it roared back, it was punctuated with a static pop. "...kill me."

Dale brought the phone back up to his ear. "What'd you say, Velma."

"Don't pretend you don't know who I'm talking about. I know all..." The signal faded again, then came back, the voice panicked. "I don't want to die. Can anyone...me. Please."

That didn't sound like Velma. His ex-wife would cut off her tits before she asked anyone for help. Dale held the phone out, glancing at the little screen. The words "Weak Signal" flashed. He brought the phone back to his ear. "Velma, what the hell are you talking about?"

"Please, help me." It wasn't Velma. This voice sounded younger and terrified.

23

"Who is this?"

The voice dropped in and out. Dale was only getting fragments. "...Sandra Cl...please...gonna kill us. I can't move."

"All right, calm down. Tell me where you are."

"End of Route one ninety-four in...cave...drag race."

"Come again."

"...raced a red Spider down Route one ninety-four...can't move my...dead bodies all over."

Dale's heart skipped a beat. He held the phone away from his ear as a familiar feeling rumbled in his gut. It felt like standing in front of a large, ominous door that was opening slowly, creaking on old, tired hinges, leading to places Dale never looks for but always seems to find.

He sighed and touched the phone back to his cheek. "I'm northbound on the ninety-nine. Which way are you on the one ninety-four? East or west?"

No answer.

"Hey, Sandra, east or west?"

Silence.

Dale pulled the phone away, looking at the tiny screen. No Signal. "Goddamn Chinese piece of crap." Dale pressed a few buttons on the phone trying to get the call back, but he didn't really know what he was doing. After a few seconds, Velma's voice popped back in, loud and clear. "...that best friend of yours is so dumb he couldn't find his ass with both hands in his pockets..."

"Jesus," Dale said, then pressed the red button, hoping it would send Velma's voice back to whatever cellular hell it had come from. The connection was cut with a chirp, and Dale tossed the phone toward the passenger seat, where it landed in the box it had come in.

Well, that was that. Route 194 stretched across California for miles. Without any hint of direction, he didn't have a chance of finding, Sandra Whatshername. He let out a long breath, somewhat relieved that the doorway to places filled with cries for help, dead bodies, and whatever else that always found him between the ungodly hours of midnight and dawn was closed.

Still, as the miles rolled by, he couldn't let it go. Maybe he'd feel better if he told someone.

Dale reached down for the CB mic and was thinking about switching to the emergency channel when—

"Hey, Twilight Man, you got your ears on? Come back."

Dale grinned at the sound of his friend's voice, Earl, coming out of the CB speaker. He brought the mic to his lips, pressed the call button. "This here is the Twilight Man, how you doing, Night Crawler."

"Well, my butt is rawer than a two-dollar pavement princess's you know what. Other then that, I'm just ducky. I'm backsliding down the grapevine on the rebound, looking to make camp in Bakersfield. Knew you were in the area. Wondered if you wanted to gather the wagons at a chew and choke for some breakfast. Come back."

Dale looked at his watch—half past two. "Sounds good, but hey listen. I got this call on my cell I'd like to run by you."

"Stop the presses! You got a cell phone?"

Dale groaned softly. "Yes, let's not make a big deal out of it."

"Damn, I need to alert the media. Dale got his-self a phone. It's like you're joining the human race and everything. Welcome to the twentieth century, good buddy," Earl said.

"It's the twenty-first century, numbnuts." Dale glanced over at the phone laying in its packaging. "Picked this thing up about an hour ago. Thought I'd try and give my boy a holler since it's his birthday tomorrow. But of course, Velma picked up."

"You have my condolences," Earl said. "How is bitch-zilla?"

Dale chuckled. "Still Queen of the Harpies. Anyway, someone's voice broke in on the call."

25

"That can happen, especially if you go cheap," Earl said. "Let me guess, you got a flip phone. One that cost 'bout eleven ninety-nine? Swear Dale, you pinch pennies so tight you can hear old Abe Lincoln squealing."

Dale sighed. He hated how well his friend knew him. "It was nine ninety-nine, and the guy at the truck stop threw in a box of Red Vines. Now, do you want to hear this or not?"

"My ears are on. Come back."

Dale quickly recapped what he'd heard before the signal faded. "So, what do you think?"

"Well, that's stranger than Liberace at a football game. I assume she was talking about a car, say like an Alfa Romeo Spider?"

"Could be, but I don't know. Didn't get that kind of detail."

"I wonder if she meant mines?"

"What was that? Come back," Dale said.

"Yeah, you said something about a cave. Maybe she is held up in those mines off the one ninety-four. About two miles west."

"How do you know about mines way out there?"

"I know lots of things. I'm not just pretty. They's Copper mines. Closed I think. Don't you remember there was that college kid last year that died while...spelunkerin'?"

"Do you mean spelunking?"

"Yeah, sounds right. No idea what it is, but apparently, you can die doing it."

Dale's eyes followed an exit marker. He just passed the turnoff for Route 193 and knew 194 wasn't far away. *Just keep on trucking* he told himself. In a few minutes, he could be in Bakersfield, enjoying food guaranteed to hurry him along toward an early death. He was getting too old for this shit.

"So, what you gonna do, Twilight Man?" Earl's voice popped over the CB.

Dale took in a deep breath, letting it out slowly. He was trying to push the terror in the girl's voice from his mind, but as he exhaled, he realized just how much she had sounded like his youngest niece in Knoxville. The girl's call for help wasn't something he could just drive on by.

Goddamn, son-bitch. He always felt nothing good could come from buying a cell phone, and damn if he wasn't right. With a sour expression on his face, Dale put his turn signal on and steered the rig toward the approaching exit—Route 194.

"What's your twenty?" Dale said into the CB after exiting the freeway.

"'Bout thirty-five miles from your back door. Guess breakfast will have to wait? Come back."

"Well, drop the hammer, Old Man. It's too goddamn early for breakfast, anyway." Turning on his high beams, Dale exited, then turned west. The dual beams of lights cut a path through the darkness, revealing field after field of agricultural endeavors. After two miles, the farmland fell away and rolling hills silhouetted in the soft moonlight rose up on either side of the road.

The truck began to vibrate as the tar-covered surface disappeared. Gravel took its place for a few hundred feet, then that dissolved, leaving just a dirt path. Dale was just about to throw in the towel when at the edge of his high beams he could see a sign.

Hope Mine
1/2 mile

The sign had a painted arrow indicating a right turn onto another dirt road running south. He brought the truck to a stop in front of the sign and gazed down the southbound path, dark and nameless. Although the sign appeared to be a half-century old, there were a dozen tire tracks, maybe more, some very recent.

He steered south, finding that the new dirt road was not

much smoother than the other one. His truck shook and vibrated over every hole, kicking up dust. After he had gone the length of several football fields, he could see taillights glinting in his beams. First one pair, then two. Then about a dozen flickered in the darkness, like distant stars.

Cars lined the dirt road, and although they looked abandoned sitting in the dark, some caked with dust, they all appeared to be new. Modified street racers, tediously tricked-out, resting silently in the night. Their owners, who had obviously spent considerable time and money to make these vehicles look ridiculously fast and furious, were nowhere to be found.

"What the hell?" Dale said. "Where's the party?"

The road ended, and Dale eased the truck over, parking alongside a racing green Acura with a rear foil on it big enough to be used as a surfboard. Not the kind of car likely to be found on a rural dirt road.

Just ahead Dale could see the entrance to the mine. It wasn't what he'd expected. All the images of mines he'd ever seen were products of Hollywood—big railroad ties framing the entrance to a dingy looking cave with some kind of a sign that usually read, "Danger" or "Keep Out."

The Hope Mine was more of a hole, and from Dale's point of view, high up in the cab, he could see it burrowing down into a blasted hill at an angle steep enough to make walking difficult. But doable. Dale was already picturing himself sliding on his ass down the gullet of the hole into the waiting arms of god knows what.

He fumbled under the seat and reached into a compartment so concealed no scale inspector, Border patrol, DEA, or cop would ever discover without completely dismantling the cab. He pulled out a Christmas gift from a few years back—a sawed-off double-barreled shotgun with his CB handle carved into the stock. His mom always knew what to get him. After stuffing a half-dozen shells in his pocket, he reached behind the seat and grabbed something else he was sure he was gonna need. A rope.

The CB crackled to life. "Twilight Man, this is Night Crawler. Come back."

Dale picked up the mic. "Yeah, what's up, Earl?"

"Good buddy, you ain't gonna believe this. Guess what just blew my doors off?"

Dale sighed. "I'm a little busy right now. Can we play this game later?"

"It was moving like a bat out of hell. Thought it might even leave the ground."

"What was?"

"A red Spider."

Dale swallowed. "Come again."

"It could have been scarlet, but I swear to god it was redder than a Catholic girl on her wedding night."

"Your eyes on straight?"

"Hell, yeah. I'd say it was a nineteen sixty-five Alfa Romeo hardtop. Did I call it, or did I call it?"

"Yes, you called it. You're very wise."

"And pretty."

"I'm willing to bet it wasn't solo?" Dale said.

"No, sir, it was not," Earl came back. "How'd you know?"

"You're not the only one who's more than just pretty. What'd you see?"

"Looked like a yellow, could have been white, Honda Civic, all souped-up, racing alongside. You know them street-racing, life-size Hotwheels kids are spending all their coin on?"

Dale looked over the graveyard of cars, any one of which could have been owned by the late Paul Walker. "Yeah, I have a pretty good idea of what you're talking about. Everybody wants to be Vin Diesel."

"What's a Vin Diesel?" Earl said.

"Forget it," Dale said. "Which way they go?"

29

"Heading North. I bet my left nut they're heading your way."

"Yeah, that's a big ten-four. And why the left nut?"

"Well, I'm extra partial to my right one. Have been ever since I discovered what they were."

"Very sorry I asked. What's your twenty?"

"I just passed Route one ninety."

"Jeez, Earl. You move slower than turtle shit."

"Bitch, bitch."

Dale told Earl what he had found and what he planned on doing, even though he hadn't really convinced himself yet.

"You really going down there?" Earl said.

Dale scratched his head, pondering the wisdom of his plan. He brought the mic up to his lips. "You didn't hear that kid's voice. If she were my kin, I'd sure as hell want someone to go after her." He leaned over and removed a flashlight from the glovebox.

"You ain't even sure she is down there."

Dale turned the flashlight on, shinning it over the dust-covered cars. "Well, she ain't up here, that's for sure. If you don't find me when you get here, call in the cavalry."

Before Earl signed off, he urged Dale to take his cell phone. Dale reluctantly agreed and gave his friend the number.

Dale slung the rope over his shoulder and stepped out of the cab. He buttoned up his leather vest, then stepped to the front of his rig. He secured one end of the rope to the bumper, then strolled toward the mine. Upon reaching it, his boots knocked a few rocks down into the darkness.

He scanned back up the road that brought him here, checking for approaching headlights. Nothing. Darkness. He wasn't worried about the driver of the red Spider. Dale could deal with some young punk street racer turned serial killer, if that's what this was. Running cargo across the United States in the dead of night for a living allowed Dale the frequent opportunity to meet a wide variety of assholes. Mr. Alfa Romeo Spider was nothing special. But as he gazed back down into the opening in the Earth, the hair on the back of his neck stood up, and he couldn't extinguish the feeling that something was looking back up at him. Something cold, unfriendly. Something ugly.

"I'm coming, kid." Dale tossed the rope down, and the blackness seemed to swallow it. He turned on the flashlight, chasing away the dark, and was relieved to see that the floor seemed to level out about twenty feet down into the mine. He gripped the rope and began his descent, boots sliding in loose earth. His two hundred forty plus pounds of muscle and well-fed trucker's physique created an avalanche of gravel, limestone, and thick dust. If there was something down there waiting for him, he had made enough noise to let it know he was coming.

With each step, the air got colder, and something else assaulted his senses. A thick stench started to rise, pungent, adding weight and a foul color to the air. It was a recognizable aroma. One Dale had taken in more times than anyone ever should. But his familiarity with the smell didn't desensitize him to it. He gagged, tasted vomit, and his eyes watered as he moved closer to the source of decay and rot.

He reached into his back pocket and pulled out a handkerchief, tied it around his mouth and nose like a train robber. The thin material did a piss-poor job, but it filtered the stench enough so that his eyes stopped tearing up like a little girl.

Preoccupied with not puking, he almost didn't notice that the texture of the walls had changed. He shinned the light on both sides and up onto the ceiling, seeing a silky thread weaving its way around the rock. *Wonderful. Bugs,* he thought.

The thread seemed to get thicker the deeper he went. It even started to spread onto the floor, winding over long, horizontal boulders pressed up against the wall. He had passed a half-dozen of these elongated rocks wound up tightly in silk before he realized they weren't boulders.

They were bodies.

Ahh, crap on a cracker.

Dale knelt down next to one, peeling away some of the strands with the barrel of the shotgun. It was a strange-looking corpse. It looked like the mummies in the Chicago Museum he got to gawk at as a kid—all dried up, shriveled. But no mummy he ever saw wore a Raider's cap.

The light glinted off the NFL logo, and as Dale tapped it with the shotgun, the corpse's jaw dropped open with a crack. Dale stood back up, watching a spider the size of his hand crawl out from the shriveled body's throat. He noticed others crawling about, none larger than his palm. They moved over the bodies, feeding, their fangs pumping up and down, drinking in their meal.

Dale narrowed his eyes, his blood beginning to boil. He turned on a heel and started heading deep into the mine. When he could, he adjusted his steps so that each one was followed by a crunching sound, bringing a satisfied grin to Dale's face as spiders died under his alligator skin boots.

"Sandra," he began to call, not giving a crap about being stealthy. If there was something down here wanting a fight, he was in the mood to oblige.

Sandra's name echoed down the passage and Dale could hear it reverberating for miles. He checked every body he passed for signs of life, knocking spiders to the ground with the barrel of the gun. The bodies were in varies stages of decomposition, some looking very fresh, but none were alive.

He stopped to deliver an occasional twist of the heel as arachnids died underfoot, but he began to notice that the further he went into the belly of this nest, the more eight-legged bastards there were to crush.

He burped out a sigh, beginning to feel defeated. If he went much deeper, they might grow so numerous he wouldn't be able to dispatch them with a simple twist of the boot. They were already starting to drop onto his arms and shoulders from the ceiling.

Damn it.

On the verge of turning back, his flashlight caught something silver and metallic on the ground.

A smartphone.

A hand lay on the dirt floor, still, and close to the phone. Dale followed the arm up to its silk-cocooned body hanging from the ceiling. Enough silk strands had been torn away that an arm had managed to get free. Even beneath the wrapping, Dale could see that this body was fresher than the rest. Dale stepped over and pulled at the tightly wound silk around the torso. Big, glittering letters on the girl's t-shirt read, "American Idol." He placed two fingers on her jugular. Nothing. He checked again. Still nothing.

He bent down and retrieved the phone. A name was printed on the protective case. Sandra Cleveland. *Damn.*

"I am sorry, Sandra. Just not quick enough."

Dale swatted at the spiders that had their fangs in her, then crushed a few under his boot, cursing. He was just twisting his heel on the last one when he heard the sound of engines. At least two.

He wiped his feet in the dirt, grinning. "Now, let's go deal with Mister Serial-killin', Spider-lovin', Son-of-a-bitch."

With the shotgun over his shoulder, he began to jog back toward the entrance. The sounds of the cars were getting louder, engines revving. By the time he reached the rope near the entrance, one of the engines had been killed.

A voice drifted down the hole as Dale climbed up. "I beat you, bitch. Now, get out of that historical artifact you call a car."

Dale reached the mouth of the mine and stepped up into the night. The first thing he saw was a teenage male, just old enough to shave, wearing an oversized sweat suit, an unnecessary amount of gold chains around his neck, and a cap with the bill pointed backward. He was jumping up and down, and every few seconds he would perform some ludicrous dance move that the white kid clearly believed he had mastered.

"Beat you fair and square," the teenager said, moving away from his modified street racer—a Honda Civic with a chrome blower rising from the hood. He walked and sort of danced over to the Italian car—a red Alfa Romeo Spider. "Come on out, let's see you're losing bitch ass."

The Spider just idled patiently as if it were waiting for something. Its black-tinted windows seemed to be keeping all its owner's secrets, and as Dale stared at it, a chill moved through his body.

It suddenly occurred to him that there may be more than one shit-head in the Spider. Two, maybe three, he could deal with, but if there were more and they were armed... He decided to conceal himself, watch a while, and see what he was up against.

He crouched down behind a pile of rocks just outside the mine's entrance as the teenager continued to taunt the driver of the Spider. "Hey, you gonna show yourself or what? It's time to pay up, bitch. Let's see the pink slip." The teenager kicked the front tire of the Alfa Romeo.

The Spider's engine revved, and the kid took several steps back. The engine roared again, and the car began to vibrate, violently, looking like a rocket moments before leaving the launch pad. Dale felt the ground trembling beneath him.

The teenager held up his hands as if he suddenly realized where he was, in the middle of nowhere surrounded by derelict street cars. "You know what? Just keep it, man." He took two more steps back. "I don't want that antique roadshow anyhow."

Before the kid took another backward step, the engine suddenly switched off. The roar faded with a suddenness that took

Dale by surprise. And then, the Spider was still.

Dale stared at the car's windows, looking for movement. Nothing.

"So all right then," the teenager said, tugging at his cap. "I'll catch up with you on the road, biotch—"

The hardtop roof of the Spider began to move. Accompanied by a high-pitched mechanical whine, the roof opened like the hood of a car.

Dale rubbed his hairy chin. *No idea Alfa Romeos could do that.*

The roof continued up and back until it lay flat on the trunk—the machinery that moved it cut off with a choke, creating a cold silence.

The teenager took a step forward. "That is sick. You trick that yo'self?"

Out of the opening in the Spider, a female head started to rise like a disembodied apparition. Long hair spun over her scalp, so black in melted into the night. A slender, creamy skinned neck bled into smooth, naked shoulders. Her hands rose, gripping the top of the windshield.

The teenager smiled at her. "Hey, babe. You know I don't really want this time machine." He pointed at the Spider. "Maybe we could work something else out, y'know what I'm saying?"

The woman smiled back, her black lips framing white teeth. She ascended further, revealing round, naked breasts, nipples hard and gray.

"Oh, yeah," the teenager said, stepping forward. "I like a woman that drives commando."

"Watch yourself, kid," Dale muttered softly.

She rose up even more, as if being lifted on a hydraulic platform.

The teenager suddenly stopped moving forward. "What the..."

Another set of breasts hung beneath the first. And another

under them. The woman's engorged chest looked like a sow that had recently given birth, with gray nipples descending the length of her torso.

The teenager pointed a finger. "You freaky bitch. Stay the fu..."

Something else emerged out of the Alfa Romeo—long, thick, hairy.

"Oh, shit," Dale said.

One by one, eight hair-covered legs, each with the girth of an adult python, uncoiled from the car's interior. They stretched out as if waking from a long hibernation, then began to plant their arachnid feet on the dirt.

The creature lifted itself out of the car, looking like something out of Greek mythology gone haywire. From the waist up, it resembled a human female, but everything else was arachnid. With multiple leg joints and thick brushes of hair, it scurried away from the Alfa Romeo, its dark eyes, at least eight feet above the ground, peering at the teenager.

The boy who had been so animated only a minute ago seemed frozen in place. Paralyzed in the creature's Medusa-like gaze, he didn't attempt to run, even when it scurried toward him.

Its front legs bucked up, enveloping the boy. He was lifted off the ground, and four hairy legs began to spin his body. Silk shot out of the ass-end of the creature, and within a few seconds, the boy was mummified, cocooned for her children's consumption.

The eight-legged monster then began to move toward the mine, its wrapped-up prize dragging behind. Dale hunkered down as much as his large body would allow, gripping the stock and barrel of the shotgun so tight his knuckles were pearl white. He knew the shotgun's kill range was less than ten feet, but he wasn't looking forward to getting that close.

Goddammit, Earl. Where the hell are you?

All eight legs came to a stop at the mouth of the mine. Its human half started to lean forward, and for a second Dale thought she was just crouching to fit through the entrance. But he was wrong.

The creature bent all the way forward, its human hand picking up something off the ground. It was Dale's rope. Her head and torso came back up, the rope gripped in both hands. Her black eyes seemed to follow the length of rope tethered to Dale's truck.

Well, shit. Dale readied the shotgun. *So much for a surprise attack.*

Anger, vile and terrifying, consumed the creature's face. It started moving toward the truck, its human hands coiled into fists. After only a few yards it stopped, the anger melting away to what Dale thought was concern, as if she just realized the rope also descended into her burrow, her nest. She sniffed at the air, like a wolf catching the scent of blood on a wounded animal. She cut loose her latest prize, lowered her head, and scurried down into the mine.

The teenager's wrapped-up body rolled down a slope and out of sight. Dale waited a few seconds for the hair on the back of his neck to relax, then stood up, letting out a long breath he wasn't even aware he'd been holding.

He stepped from behind the pile of rocks and made for his cab, already picturing himself sitting safely within its confines. He'd much rather shoot down at the thing from inside his truck—better yet...catch the beast in a crossfire from high up with Earl and his thirty-eight on one side and him on the—

A bloodcurdling scream that was only part human exploded from the mine. Dale whirled around, shotgun at his hip as the anguished cries echoed behind him.

Damn it, Earl, I could use some help here.

Okay, nothing to panic about, Dale told himself. *The bitch didn't see me up here, so she probably thinks I'm still in the hole somewhere. Just keep quiet and—*

A loud chirping noise shattered Dale's thought. He spun around, looking for the source, which seemed to be behind him. After spinning a half-circle, the chirping was behind him again. He did another fast one-eighty, scanning the entrance of the mine for a few tense seconds. Then he finally realized what it was.

Goddamn phone.

He pulled the cell phone from his back pocket, desperately trying to make it be quiet. He flipped it open, and after pressing several buttons, finally hit the green one. The screen lit up. The chirping stopped. He was about to whisper something into the phone when he realized that whispering was no longer necessary.

Eye-shine glinted deep within the gullet of mine, and it was moving toward him.

"Dale, you there?" Earl's voice squeaked out of the tiny speaker.

Dale didn't answer, just took several steps back, shotgun leveled at the mine's entrance in one hand, cell phone in the other.

"Hey, good buddy, I'm at your back door," Earl said. "Find anything?"

Dale held the phone in front of his face and said. "A bug. A big, fucking bug." He threw the phone into the mine and saw it bounce off the beast's chest. He gripped the barrel of the shotgun, anchored the stock on his hip, just as the eight-legged monstrosity exited her lair.

Pausing as it emerged, its back legs still lost in the mine's entrance, the beast seemed to know what Dale held in his hands, and it stood still, hissing, contemplating. She tilted her head, lowered her chin, and glared deep into Dale's eyes.

The creature cast no visible shadow in the thin moonlight, but Dale felt himself being enveloped by it anyway, cold and scurrying up his spine. They stood motionless, like two gun fighters waiting for that undeniable moment demanding split-second reactions.

"My god, you're five hundred pounds of ugly," Dale said.

The creature slowly began to circle and hissed in a low guttural tone, sounding not unlike his ex-wife.

"Jeez, if I want to hear a woman hiss at me all night long, I'll go visit my boy."

Dale rotated with her, keeping the shotgun aimed at her chest. He judged her to be about fifteen feet away, just a bit too far to do terminal damage, but he wasn't about to take a step forward. As it turned out, he didn't have to.

"Whatcha waitin' on, Christmas? Let's dance, bitch."

The eight-legged beast lowered her head like a bull, thrust her human hands forward, and charged, howling like hellspawn.

Dale counted to two, held his breath, then let go with both barrels. The explosions echoed down the mine as the beast pitched back, hands clasping her chest. When her hands fell, Dale could see one of her upper breasts was gone, and an arm hung by cartilage and sinew. Blood splattered her torso, flowing down onto hairy legs.

She thrust a raised hand forward, clawing at the air, looking more enraged than ever.

Dale took quick steps backward, pulling two more rounds from his pocket. He had to lower his eyes for a split second as he popped the shells into the chamber. When he brought them back up, a hairy leg struck him in the jaw. He felt his feet leave the ground and heard his gun go off.

He sailed several yards through the air and then hit something hard. What he'd landed on bent inward under his weight, and it took a hazy second to realize he wasn't on the ground.

He had landed on the hood of the Alfa Romeo.

The she-bitch scurried toward him, rising up on her back legs, teeth bared.

Dale pointed the shotgun, not really aiming, and pulled the trigger. The soft sound of the hammers falling atop the empty chambers was, at that moment, the worst sound in the world.

Shit.

Dale sat up, digging into his pocket for more shells. He saw her hand reaching toward him, and he swatted at it with the stock of the gun. She blocked his blow, knocking the shotgun from his grasp.

She reached down and clasped Dale around the neck, lifting his ass off the hood. She pulled his face to hers, opening her mouth. For a second Dale thought she intended to sink her teeth right into the bridge of his nose. He could taste her breath, foul, rank with rot.

Then something seemed to catch her attention. Her eyes moved past Dale, and he felt her grip loosen. He wasted no time. He brought both fists down on her wounded arm. The creature howled, and Dale fell from her grasp, landing back on the hood with a thud. Pain rocketed through the back of his head as a familiar sound echoed in the night, rumbling, growing close.

Dale rolled off the hood just as Earl's eighteen-wheeler plowed into the Alpha Romeo like a freight train, horn blaring. The crash was deafening. Sparks flew as big as muzzle flashes, metal-tearing screeches exploded into the night.

Dale kept rolling in the dirt as Earl's trailer rushed by. He got a quick glance of the arachnid bitch raising her human hands in a vain attempt to slow down fifteen tons of speeding metal.

With the Alfa Romeo as a hood ornament, Earl's truck bulldozed into the creature, its hairy legs leaving the ground. The eighteen-wheeler began to slide as the brakes were applied, but it didn't stop before smashing into a rocky man-made hill piled high with unwanted material excavated from the Hope Mine.

The creature was pinned between the rocky hill and the crumpled frame of the Alfa Romeo. Earl's truck seemed to stand guard over the scene, pushing forward enough to keep the arachnid in her place, crushed in a tangle of broken black legs and twisted metal.

Dale propped himself up into a sitting position as Earl stepped out of the cab. He had never been so happy to see his friend. "Took you long enough. You cruise the granny lane all the way here, did ya?"

Earl walked over to Dale, hand extended. "You never could appreciate a proper entrance."

Dale grabbed his friend's hand and allowed himself to be pulled up. "Thanks, old man."

Earl stood a few inches shorter than Dale, but many pounds heavier. "Well, I was in the neighborhood."

Dale smiled and walked over to get his shotgun.

"Can I assume breakfast is on you?" Earl said.

"Yeah." Dale gathered up his weapon.

"And not the usual cheap Denny's grand slam, neither. A real fine and proper breakfast."

Dale walked back, slapped an arm around Earl's shoulder. "I'd take you to the Russian Tea Room 'bout now if I could."

Earl tugged on his black Harley Davidson t-shirt. "We're a bit underdressed."

They both stared for a few silent moments at the carnage on the far side of Earl's front bumper. The creature squirmed in front of them. Two of its long legs still moved just outside of the crushing pressure of Earl's truck. Its female head lay over the top of the rocky hill, blood drooling down the sides of her mouth.

Earl stepped forward, taking a hard look. "Christ, Dale, you sure do have a knack for finding the meanest, ugliest women."

"It's a gift."

"Well, you ought to think serious 'bout giving it back." Earl scratched his head. "What the hell is that?"

Dale had heard of these creatures. Mostly just whispers in

the night, really. "Think their called Homo-Arachnes. Part people, part bug. Werespiders, if you want. Think the last one on record died off in the fifties, along with them giant desert ants. Military took 'em out. At least, that's the rumor."

"Well, that rumor is in need of a status update." Earl looked over at the mine entrance. "Anyone alive down there?"

"Nothing on two legs." Dale pointed down the slope. "There's a kid down there in a silk wrapper, probably just napping. Looks like spider-bitch liked to stun its prey."

"I'll go take a look," Earl said, then pointed over at the crushed beast. "Why don't you go and say goodnight to Gracie?"

Dale nodded and strolled toward the rocky hill. He pulled two shells from his pocket and loaded the shotgun. Closing the chamber, he climbed up and around to the uppermost part of the hill, where the creature's head lay.

Its black hair spilled out onto the dirt like crude oil, and Dale placed a boot on a few healthy strands, inches from her scalp. She tried to raise her head up, but Dale's boot held it down by its midnight-colored locks. She looked at him and hissed, blood spotting his jeans.

In these final moments, Dale could never despise these things. Not much anyway. It was just an unnatural thing doing what unnatural things were made to do. But now it was time for Dale to do what Dale was made to do. He leaned over, placed both barrels up against her forehead. "Say goodnight, Gracie."

He pulled the trigger.

The Greatest Fear

"What the hell is eatin' you?" Dale said while pushing the desk up against the barricade. "You're more irritable than a de-fanged rattlesnake."

Earl grabbed an oversized chair and carried it to the desk. "I just had my finger sewn back on. Ain't that reason enough?"

"No, I mean before that, and don't act like it's the first time you've had an appendage reattached." Dale reached for an end table. "Last couple of days you've been pissin' and moanin' about something or other?"

Earl pulled out his knife, an ungodly looking bowie-styled blade named Betsy. "I guess it's the thing with my nephew." With lightning speed, Earl slashed off the undead fingers that were trying to pry the door open. There was a moan as the detached digits bounced down the barricade of office furniture like stones in a rock slide.

"Little Joe-Joe?" Dale piled on the end table.

"Yeah, but he ain't—"

To Earl's right, the glass began to crack. Pressure from the corpses pushing inward was starting to have an effect. The office window that looked out into the hospital hallway frac-tured. Thin, spiderweb-sized cracks streaked down the center as dead faces and hands pressed against the outside.

Earl sighed at the ugliness on the other side of the glass, then reached over and pulled the blinds shut.

"That's probably not going to cut it," Dale said, looking

around for something to board up the window.

"Jesus, we're going to die!" shouted Mr. Kanye, the hospital administrator who, earlier in the day, wouldn't accept Earl's insurance. He huddled on the floor of his office as far away from the door as possible, along with three hospital employees in different colored scrubs, a woman in street clothes, and an elderly woman in a wheelchair.

"Calm down," Dale said, moving toward a coffee table.

"Don't tell me to calm down. This is my office, and you're not in charge here."

"No, sir, I am not," Dale said, lifting the table, then moving to the window. "But it doesn't help the situation to lose your head. Best way to get through this is to stay calm."

"That is true enough," Earl added. "You'd be surprised what Dale and I've managed to survive just by keepin' cool." Earl helped Dale slap the coffee table against the window.

"Bullshit," Mr. Kanye said. "Neither one of you know what you're doing or what is going on."

As Earl dragged a faux leather loveseat over to prop against the coffee table, Dale looked back at the panicking administrator. He grinned, knowing that the moment in which he would be required to bitch-slap Mr. Kanye was not too far off. He told himself he wasn't going to do or say anything to hurry the moment along, just stay polite, calm, but when it did come, he knew most distinctly that he would enjoy it.

"True enough," Earl said as the glass finally gave way. Hands pushed through the gaps that the coffee table did not cover. Glass hung down like teeth on a jack-o'-lantern, cutting into unflinching dead flesh. Earl hacked at a few, splitting the palms down the middle, letting each half hang on either side of a useless boney wrist.

Dale turned to Earl. "What thing with your nephew?"

Earl wiped the blood from Betsy on the loveseat cushion. "I just got his invite in the mail. Joe-Joe is—"

"Somebody needs to do something," Mr. Kanye shouted. He jumped to his feet and moved toward the barricade Dale and Earl had constructed. For a brief moment, Dale thought Mr. Kanye was coming to help. Seeing as how this tiny group of survivors hadn't offered to lift a finger thus far to help secure the room or fight off the undead, it would have been a nice change. Up 'til now, they mostly whimpered, some cried or cowered on the floor, which Dale didn't mind a whole lot. It made it easy to order them around, get them to move, keep them alive for as long as there was sufficient reason to.

But now Mr. Kanye was up, moving purposefully, his paisley tie flapping about his sizable belly as he moved. Dale was about to tell him where he could help as he and Earl had both sets of hands on the barricade. But in a flash of disappointment, Dale realized the hospital administrator was not rising to their aid, but was on a mission of his own.

He pulled a key from his pocket and quickly stuck it in the keyhole of the desk drawer, the same desk Dale and Earl had slid up against the door, without anyone's help. He wrenched the drawer open so fast it almost fell to the floor. Mr. Kanye retrieved a pistol, a hammerless revolver, and immediately pointed it at the window.

Without any hesitation or aim, Mr. Kanye fired. The bullet went through the coffee table, missing Earl's hand by inches.

Dale grinned. The bitch-slapping moment had arrived.

Mr. Kanye fired again as Dale quick-stepped to the side, spun on a booted heel, then brought up a practiced hand. But before he could bring it down in what would have been a most satisfying blow, a lamp slammed into the back of Mr. Kanye's head. His out-of-shape form went limp, and then dropped like a weighted body tossed off a pier.

Dale looked at the crumpled pile on the floor. "Goddammit!"

"Don't you mean, thank you," said the woman wearing street clothes who had just put down Mr. Kanye.

"Yeah, that, too," Dale said, trying not to sound disappointed.

"I could use a hand or two over here," Earl said.

Dale snatched the pistol up, identified it—Smith and Wesson M&P 640—then moved back to the window. A dead face pushed its way through a gap, glass cutting into the cheek deep enough to expose bone. Dale placed the muzzle on its forehead and fired.

"Dammit," Earl shouted, stepping away from the window. "Said more hands, not gunfire."

"Sorry," Dale said, realizing he had fired the revolver a little too close to his head. Another walking corpse filled in the spot at the window Dale had just cleared. This one was naked but shuffled oddly as if the body bag it had been in was now crumpled and dragging around its ankles like an oversized pair of pants. Dale stuck the pistol deep into its mouth, attempting to muffle the blast a little. Dale fired and blew out the back of its neck. The head snapped back, like it had taken a baseball bat to the face. The corpse fell away.

A few hands rose to take its place, but no more faces. Dale wondered if they were learning. The dead, for the moment, staggered back a bit and gave the barricade some breathing room.

He turned to check on his friend. Earl had a finger in his ear and seemed to be massaging it.

"Hearing bells?" Dale said.

"A-ring-a-ding-ding," Earl said. "Put that away before you make me deaf."

Dale tucked the pistol away as the woman who had wielded the lamp held out her hand. "I'm Hanna," she said, and that's Mema over there." She gestured to the octogenarian in the wheelchair. "Afraid I don't know these other folks."

"That's all right," Dale said, looking over at the hospital employees—one male, two female. "Can one of you check on our hero here?"

The employees looked at one another for a few indecisive moments, then a heavyset Asian woman in blue scrubs started to get up. She used the armrest of the wheelchair to steady herself as she rose. The old woman occupying the chair didn't try to hide her disgust. She moved her hand and leaned away so she wouldn't have to come in contact with the nurse, and Dale swore he could see loathing in the old crone's eyes.

"I'm Kathy," the nurse said, kneeling down to check Mr. Kanye's vitals.

"Will he live, Kathy?" Earl said.

She nodded, then helped Mr. Kanye into a sitting position. His eyes fluttered, and he reached for his head. Blood dripped down the back of his hairless scalp, and as he touched it, anger flashed across his face. Dale was pretty sure Mr. Kanye was about to start spouting off again, and he thought he'd nip it in the bud.

He hunkered down in front of the hospital administrator, close enough to get a deep inhalation of his musky cologne, and took a fistful of his silk tie. Dale pulled him close. Mr. Kanye reached up with one hand and touched it to Dale's forearm, a forearm that was as thick as a brick and as soft to the touch as a cinderblock. In an instant, Kanye's anger melted away, and sweat glistened on his forehead.

"Now listen up, pencil dick. You do anything that stupid, something that puts me or my friend in danger again and I'm gonna put you on the other side of that window." Dale paused to make sure it was sinking in. "Do we understand one another?"

Mr. Kanye nodded enthusiastically.

"And to revise my earlier answer," Dale added, "Yes, I am in charge."

"Why," Hanna said. "Because you have the gun?"

Dale stood up slowly, feeling extremely underappreciated. "No, not because I have the gun, but that is normally a pretty good reason."

"Why, then?"

"Because my friend and I know a thing or two about a thing or two. Do you?" Dale said, realizing that he sort of sounded like Dr. Seuss in an insurance commercial.

Hanna didn't respond, uncertainty on her face.

"If it makes you feel better..." Dale removed the pistol from his belt and held it out to Hanna.

She stared down at it, clearly debating the situation. Before she made up her mind, the male orderly stepped forward and took the gun from Dale.

Dale looked at the tall, beefy man in salmon-colored scrubs. "You know how to handle that?"

"Eight years in the army, two of them on the DMZ," he said, tumbling out the carousel to eye the ammo.

"That's all we need up in here," Hanna's grandma said. "A spear-chucker with a gun."

"Mema!" Hanna scolded. "We talked about using that kind of language in front of the..."

The orderly looked up from the gun and turned to meet Hanna's uncomfortable gaze. "In front of the what?"

Hanna swallowed. "The...the people. All the people in the... public. Generally."

The orderly aimed his brown eyes at the woman in the wheelchair. "Yo, Mema, my name is Duane. Feel free to use it. You can also feel free to roll your own ass around from now on."

Dale put a hand on Duane. "Let's all just calm down a minute."

Duane pulled his arm away. "Get your redneck hands off me."

Dale felt a burst of anger radiate from his chest to his fist, but he smacked his lips and did his best to ignore the impulse to act on it. With a deep breath, he transferred the angry energy into a smile, which he had been practicing with Earl's encouragement, one he hoped was not too creepy but at the same time sent the message that he wasn't one to be pushed around.

"Now, Duane," Dale said. "I'm gonna let you have that one." He held up a finger. "But just that one. Temperatures are all running a bit hot right now, and that is reasonable. But we're all in this together. And for the time being, we're stuck with one another. So, let's stay civil. Am I being understood?"

Duane's eyes seemed to register that he knew he'd pushed Dale as far as was safe, and he nodded, slowly, calmly.

"Okay," Hanna said, clearly happy that the focus wasn't on her anymore. "What's the plan?"

Dale nodded. "Let me consult with my larger half here, and I'll get back to you. In the meantime, everybody relax. Be civil."

Dale didn't pause to see if anyone had suddenly decided to ignore all their instincts by relaxing and stepped over to Earl. "So, what do you think?"

Keeping one hand on the barricade, Earl said, "Well, I think Mema might be a racist."

"Reached that conclusion all by yourself, did ya?" Dale said.

"Hey, I pay attention."

Dale pushed up against the barricade. "Yeah, definitely a few tiki torches in her closet."

"You get a holler back yet from those a-holes in gray?"

"Not yet," Dale said. He reached down and picked up the receiver on Kanye's office phone that somehow managed to stay on the desk during the hasty relocation. He listened for a dial tone. Checked several lines. Nothing. "Hardline communications are out, so we know they're on site. Assholes."

Dale pulled his smartphone from his inside leather vest pocket. No signal. "And they've taken out the towers."

"How they gonna hit you back?"

"Well, I got a message through before it went dark. If they

want to holler at me, they can; I just can't call out. That's part of the protocol," Dale said. "Shit, it was probably my call that got us stuck in here. Dumb, dumb."

"Well, at least you're pretty."

Dale snickered. "So, what were you saying about your nephew."

Earl looked like he just remembered he forgot to take the garbage out. "I got his invite the other day."

"Invite?"

"Joe-Joe is getting. He's getting gay-married."

"Earl, it's not gay-married; it's just married."

Earl shook his head like someone who had just stepped in the place a dog had done his business. "I know, I know. I don't mean to sound like a jackass."

Dale's phone rang. "To be continued."

"Dale here."

An overworked female voice said, "Hold for Captain Major."

"Yep," Dale said, then pulled the phone away from his ear. "Getting married, huh?"

Earl nodded. "Seems like only yesterday I was bouncin' him on my knee and building him that kid-size kitchenette. Had a real working microwave, y'know."

"I know. You roped me into helping you."

"That boy could make the best muffins on the reservation by age six."

"Dale, Captain Major here," came a deep, stoic voice from the phone. "What's your situation."

"I think you know my situation," Dale said. "I'm stuck in here smack dab in the middle of your quarantine zone."

"I am very sorry to hear that. Earl in there as well?"

"Yeah, his luck tends to run parallel with mine," Dale confirmed. "He sliced his finger to the bone on a hitch this morning when we were switchin' up trailers. Took near half a day to get it sewed up proper. Swear we were almost ready to leave when all hell broke loose."

"Did the rising originate from inside or outside the facility?"

"I'm pretty sure it came from inside. The morgue is downstairs, and I'm guessing it was pretty full. As you probably already know, this hospital's morgue serves as several county's Grand Central Station for the dead. Earl said he saw a few rise in the ICU, but we're pretty sure most came up from the morgue."

"Are you a hundred percent certain on the point of origin?"

"Captain, I'm not a hundred percent on anything other than we're up a creek at the moment and all the paddles want to kill us, including you," Dale said.

"Dale, we're gonna do all we can to get you—"

"Don't piss on my leg and tell me it's raining," Dale said. "I know MIG protocols. I know you're following them. But I got to let you know, Captain, there is something odd about this particular rising. I can't, as of yet, put my finger on it, but there is something wrong with this one."

"I concur. Our lab has identified some abnormalities. We obtained two samples from the infected hospital, one from the parking lot, another from the maternity ward. It had eaten its way through some of the infants before we secured it."

Dale hated how Captain Major could discuss the most horrific of details with clinical and utter desensitization.

"Though clearly deceased," he continued, "neither sample contained any of the known pathogens, indigenous or otherwise, known to raise the dead. We also tested for trioxin and all other known toxins. All negative."

Dale knew it was a long shot, but he took his best swing anyway. "Well, then we're dealing with something that is outside MIG protocols. You have containment, and I didn't spy more than twenty or thirty, give or take. You can contain this.

Cleansing is not necessary."

"Our spotters put the number of reanimates at forty-three, and you know that the lack of a known cause does not negate the necessity to cleanse the zone. We have protocols for situations that fall outside of protocol."

"Of course, you do." Dale felt like he was talking to a damn recording. "Just tell me it wasn't my call that got us trapped in here."

Captain Major didn't respond.

"Crap on a cracker," Dale said. "All right, when do you go?"

"At dawn," Captain Major said. "We need daylight for damage assessment."

Dale looked at his watch. That gave them about three-and-a-half hours to figure something out.

"Again, I am sorry, Dale," Captain Major said. "Can I pass a message to Velma and your boy?"

Dale ended the call. It wasn't that he didn't have anything to say to Velma and his son, he just couldn't imagine his last words to them being delivered by an ex-military pencil-neck MIG agent who had all the warmth of a dead jellyfish.

A hand reached through the broken office window and grabbed Earl's wrist. "Give it to me straight," Earl said, twisting his hand free from the undead grasp, then swung Betsy, cutting off the offending attacker's appendage at the wrist. "How're we doing?"

"Our usual," Dale said, nudging the severed hand on the floor with his foot. "We got three hours."

"That's just ducky. What do you want to tell them?" Earl nodded toward the small group on the other side of the office.

"No point in sugarcoatin' it. Just need a minute to gather my thoughts and figure how to phrase it." Dale leaned up against the barricade. "So, what do you got against Joe-Joe getting married?"

Earl held up his hands in surrender. "Nothin'. Nothin at

all."

"Hell, his family is okay with it, the tribe is okay with it, why can't you be?"

"I am, I swear. I just feel for him, you know. All the extra crap he and his partner will have to put up with. The judgment, the bullshit."

Dale put a hand on his friends' shoulder. "He's got you to protect him from the world of assholes. Besides, it ain't like when you and I were his age. Things have changed. More people believe that folk's internal wiring about who we want to be with is set by the Powers That Be. Hell, you think I'd be attracted to Velma if I had a choice in the matter? I am wired for crazy. It ain't a choice."

"Not everybody believes that," Duane said, stepping over toward the barricade.

"Hey, private conversation over here," Dale said.

Duane grimaced. "There're eight people trapped in a one-room office. There are no private conversations."

Dale nodded. "Fair enough."

"My sister is a gay," Duane said. "My Baptist parents spent a lot of money trying to fix her at those pray-the-gay-away camps. Didn't work. And now, no one in the family speaks to her anymore, especially after she announced she was getting gay married."

"It's not gay married," Earl said. "It's just married."

"Whatever you call it," Duane said, "they're hard to get cakes for." He turned to Dale. "Now you gonna tell us what that call was about, and how it is that you can even get calls when none of our phones can get a signal?"

Dale looked around the moderately sized office and absorbed the fact that everyone had been listening. "Okay, here is the situation. We're in a Class A quarantine zone that has been deemed unrecoverable."

"What does that mean, unrecoverable," Kathy said, standing up.

Dale took a deep breath. "It means at around sunup those keeping us inside will retreat to a safe zone and a low-yield nuclear device will be dropped on this facility."

"How does that help us," Kathy said, "If they're keeping us in..." Her words trailed off as the cold realization clearly hit her. She fell back against the wall, and the other nurse, a very senior-looking Hispanic woman, took her hand.

"Let me talk to them," Mr. Kanye said, holding out his hand.

Dale stared at the chief administrator. "There's nothing you can say that will sway them."

"The Mayor is a good friend of mine. If I can talk to him."

"Won't make any difference," Earl said. "Once MIG decides to cleanse, it's game over."

"Just give him the goddamn phone," Kathy shouted.

Except for the clawing at the door, the room fell silent. All eyes fell on Kathy, visibly shaking.

The awkward silence was broken by a cackle. The old woman shifted in her wheelchair and said, "You gonna let a gook talk to you like that?"

"Mema," Hanna said. "Please behave."

"Yeah, Mema," Duane said. "Do yourself a favor and shut the fuck up."

Mema looked away from the scowls in the room and started mumbling under her breath. Her incoherent rambling reminded Dale of those old Popeye cartoons he'd seen as a kid. Dale never knew what the old sailor was saying under his breath, but even as a kid, he could tell it was salty.

Mr. Kanye held his hand out to Dale again. Dale slapped the phone into his palm. "It won't call out. If they want to talk to us. It'll ring."

Clearly not believing Dale, Mr. Kanye continued to try and get the smartphone to work, even held it up to the light like a cashier checking for counterfeit bills.

What an idiot.

"Who the hell is MIG?" Duane said. "The government?"

Dale shook his head. "It's more like a black ops arm of the W.H.O."

"The what?"

"World Health Organization," Kathy said. "And they're going to kill us?"

"Erase us is more like it," Earl said. "When they're done, no one will even remember this place or us."

"Earl," Dale said, with a glare.

Earl lowered his voice." You said not to sugarcoat it."

"Little sugar never hurt anybody," Dale murmured. "Okay, listen up. We got about three hours to get as far away from this hospital as possible. I haven't met a quarantine zone I couldn't get in or out of. So, let's take a look at where—"

"How many quarantine zones you been inside of?" Duane said.

"Counting this one?"

Duane nodded.

"One."

Duane threw up his hand and spun away.

"I'm just trying to stay positive. I'm familiar with quarantine protocols, and if anyone is going to find a hole in them, it's me. So, the air is covered, supported by chinooks running silent. The main exits, windows on the first and second floors should be sealed up by now."

"You thinking about shimmying down a third-story window," Earl said, gesturing to Mema's chair. "'Cause that'll be fun."

"How about underground?" said the nurse who hadn't yet spoken. She stepped away from the wall. Dale guessed her to be in her sixties; her once-black hair had only a remnant of its former glory, now fading in thick strands of gray. Dark lines in her skin were carved deep into a Latin complexion.

"What is your name?" Dale said.

"Maria."

"Typical. Half their women are named Maria," the old woman hissed. "Mariaaaa, I just met a girl named Maria—"

Hanna bent down and got in her face. "Stop it, Mema. Right now."

Mema waved a dismissive hand, then went back to mumbling under her breath.

"Go on, Maria," Earl said.

"There are tunnels under the hospital."

"That's right," Duane said. "Steam tunnels, I think."

"But they are closed. Have been for a long time," Maria said.

"They're not that closed," Duane said.

Dale turned his attention to Duane. "What do you mean?"

Duane looked over at Mr. Kanye. "Certain employees go down there from time to time to partake in some relaxing activities."

"Sex, drugs, rock 'n' roll?" Dale said.

"Sex, drugs, not so much rock 'n' roll. More Barry White, Lou Rawls, little Snoop Dog."

"That area is off limits," Mr. Kanye chimed in. "Are you admitting to participating in these activities, Duane?"

"I am not admitting to anything," Duane said. "I just want to get the fuck out of here."

"As do we all," Earl said. "Mister Kanye, iffen we're all alive tomorrow, feel free to write Duane up. But at the moment, we got bigger fish to fry."

"A steam tunnel isn't gonna take us much farther than the property, which might get us under the quarantine in the immediate area, but we'd still have to cover a lot of ground on the surface," Dale said.

Mr. Kanye swiped sweat from his forehead. "The tunnels go further than the property. Much further."

"How do you know this?" Dale said.

"Uh... Part of the county's new emergency evacuation plan. They're expanding the tunnel to evacuate patients in case of a flood. The hospital is less than a mile from a major waterway, which makes this a flood zone."

"They want patients to be evacuated underground during a flood?" Earl said. "That sounds about as smart as scuba diving in quicksand."

Kanye shook his head, obviously flummoxed. "Not just flood. Tornado, earthquake, any natural disaster."

"How come we haven't heard about any of this?" Kathy said.

"Do you attend town meetings?" Kanye said.

"No," Kathy said.

"Then don't act surprised when you don't know what's going on."

Dale was pretty fair at smelling lies, but he didn't need to be to smell the line of bullshit Kanye had just pulled from his ass. He didn't know why he was lying, but he also didn't have the time to look a gift horse in the mouth. It didn't matter why the tunnel was there, as long as it was really there.

"How far does it go?" Dale said.

"Far enough," Kanye said.

Dale looked over at Earl. "What do you say, old man?"

Earl shrugged. "Feels like we're about to jump off a cliff into an itty, bitty stream, and I can't swim."

Dale slapped a hand onto Earl's shoulder. "No matter. The fall will probably kill us." Dale turned to Kanye. "So, where's the entrance to this tunnel?"

Kanye didn't answer, and Dale glanced over at Kathy and saw dread on her face.

"Far end of the hospital. Downstairs," Maria said. "In the morgue."

"Well, that's just ducky," Earl said.

"How far?" Dale said.

59

"A hundred yards, give or take," Duane said.

"We'll never make it," Mr. Kanye said. "We're better off staying here."

"In case you've forgotten recent events," Dale said, "there will be no *here* in less than three hours. Staying is not an option."

"We can make it," Earl said. "Hell, there ain't that many of 'em."

Dale looked at his friend as if to say, *You sure?*

Earl shrugged.

"Okay," Dale said, slapping his hands together. "We're making a run for it."

Kathy said, "What if the tunnel is locked or doesn't go far enough, or we get lost down there, or—?"

"One catastrophe at a time, please," Dale said. "We'll pole-vault those hornet nests when they sting us in the ass."

"What?" Duane said.

"Nevermind," Dale said. "For those of you that don't have a gun, find yourself a weapon."

"Like what?" Maria said.

"Chair leg, lamp, paperweight, scissors," Earl said. "There is lots of stuff in here. Hell, Mister Kanye's cologne is strong enough to put the dead off."

"Hold on," Mr. Kanye said. He stepped over to a closet and opened the door. He reached in and dragged out a full set of golf clubs.

Excitement glinted in Earl's eyes. "Now we're talkin'. Golf is my game."

"You hate golf," Dale said.

Earl stepped over to the bag, pulled out a nine iron, and took a practice swing. "Yeah, well, that's cuz I never played full-contact golf before."

"All right." Dale lifted a driver from the bag. "Grab a club and then step over to the door."

The small group of survivors single-filed to the bag, except for Duane. Hanna grabbed a sand wedge and gave it to her grandmother, setting it in her lap. The old woman pushed it away and let it fall to the floor, clearly unwilling to defend herself.

Mr. Kanye picked it up and stroked it as if it were a long-lost pet. He gently returned it to the bag and took out a five iron.

"Okay, Earl and I will go out first and clear the doorway. Then once we start moving, we will pair up to watch each other's back. Earl and Duane will take point and clear as they go."

"Why the hell am I up front?" Duane said.

"You wanted the gun, and you know the way," Dale said.

"No worries," Earl said. "You lead, and I'll watch your back like fleas on a dog. Just try not to shoot me."

"No promises."

"All right, Kathy and Maria follow Earl and Duane, then Hanna and Mema behind them." Dale looked over at Mr. Kanye, cradling his club to his chest. "And you and I will bring up the rear."

Kanye swallowed, then nodded.

"We move fast, we move together, we watch each other's butts. Duane, lead us straight to the morgue, fastest way possible. No stops at the gift shop. Any questions?"

Dale glanced around at scared, uncertain faces. It was a good bet that they were not *all* going to make it. In fact, in these kinds of situations, it was almost necessary that some don't. The fallen often provide a needed escape window. How does that old joke go? *You don't really need to outrun the bear...* Dale just wished he could pick who would stumble and fall and who would benefit from the time-delaying sacrifice. He wasn't the type to encourage those kinds of outcomes, but if he were...

No one helped Earl and Dale take down the barricade. Not

surprising since no one had helped them put it up. When the door was clear, Dale put his hand on the handle and Earl stepped over to the still partially covered window. He peeked out.

"How we lookin'?" Dale said.

"Well, most of the ugliness is over here by the window." Earl waved playfully at the dead. "Looks like we have four to deal with. Three are making googly eyes with me, and one is at the door. It seems to be teetering. If you wait ten seconds, I think its back will be to ya."

Dale looked back at the room full of survivors, most holding a club to their chest as if it were a life preserver. Dale only hoped that when the time came they'd use them instead of just hug them. "Be ready," Dale said. "When we say move, beat your feet. Anyone that doesn't gets left behind."

There were a few nods, one grimace, and a lot of trembling hands. Dale wished he had something inspiring to say, like his high school coach would at halftime when he knew damn well they had to go back out on the field and take a beating.

"Now," Earl said.

Dale pulled the door open and was immediately presented with an ass, bare, sagging, and way too wrinkled for his liking. Hospital gowns flatter nobody, not even the dead. He swung the club down and buried the head of it into the back of a blonde hair-covered skull. Its knees buckled, and it fell forward into the wall, but it didn't go down. Its hands slapped on the wall, and it started to push itself up.

Dale yanked his club back, but it was hung up on the broken edges of the skull. Gray matter and bodily fluids started to spill down the rear of the hospital gown, changing its color from hazy white to a gooey mix of black and chunky crimson. He put his boot on the corpse's back to pull the club free. He drew back too hard and fell off balance, stumbling toward Kanye's office door. He whirled around, hoping the corpse was on the floor. It wasn't. The corpse took steps trying to move forward, but since it was nose to paint with a wall, it wasn't making a lot of progress.

Dale felt Earl move behind him. He just caught the glint of Betsy as Earl went to work on the walking corpses still clawing at the window. They didn't lunge at Earl, just kept pushing on the glass. Earl grabbed the nearest one by the scalp and pulled it back into Betsy. The large bowie knife sunk into the corpse's spine, cutting into the cervical vertebra. Earl twisted with his characteristic kill move, severing nerve, muscle, sinew, and bone. The body went limp but remained standing until Earl let go of the scalp.

With one crumpled at his feet, Earl moved to the next.

Dale was torn between helping Earl and keeping an eye on the one with an open skull trying to walk through the wall. Earl stuck Betsy into a temple, and to Dale's mind, Earl seemed to have his business in hand. Dale turned back to his corpse at the wall. He was going to take another swing at its head but had the strangest urge to look into its eyes. He grabbed the loose fabric on its shoulder and whirled it around, discovering that it was female, or had been. Besides its sex, Dale noticed that her eyes didn't seem right. They were sunk deep in her head, not a facial feature Dale concluded, but because her cranial area had been opened up, releasing internal pressure and matter, causing a slight tug from the optic nerve toward the rear. It was times like these when Dale wished he hadn't been so intensely schooled in human anatomy. But as dislocated as the eyes looked, it wasn't where they were setting that bothered him about the eyes; it was their intensity.

The carnivorous undead tended to have a vacancy to them that was unquestionably the product of instinct and need. But these eyes had spark. Dale didn't want to call it life, but there was something, and Dale got the unshakable feeling that something alive was looking at him. It may not have been the former owner of this dead woman's body, but something, someone was glaring at him.

Shaking off the feeling, Dale swung the club again, forcing the body to the ground. Before it tried to get up, Dale brought his boot down on its head, crushing what was left of the skull. He'd put too much force into it, and he lost his footing on the slick, glazed floor.

Earl seized his shoulder and pulled him upright.

"Thanks," Dale said, glancing around. Except for the two girthy truckers, nothing moved. He looked at the three still corpses under the hall window. "It doesn't appear that I am doing my fair share of the work."

"Yeah, you're 'bout as useful as a steering wheel on a mule."

"It's been a long day. And I did get one."

"Don't exert yourself. You need to take a sit down?"

Dale shook his head and pointed to Earl's pile under the window. "You notice anything odd about those three?"

"Just that they didn't seem all that interested in eatin' me," Earl said. "Not sure if I should be relieved or insulted."

Dale lowered his voice and patted Earl's belly. "Maybe they just didn't have that big of an appetite."

"Fat jokes," Earl said. "Funny. You think maybe it's time you looked into getting some new material?"

"I'll put it on my Ta Do list," Dale said and started to walk down the wide hospital hall, motioning Earl to follow. They tiptoed down the hall and glanced around the first corner. Twenty yards down the hall, an elderly zombie, its back to them, crouched over a very dead hospital security guard laying in the center of the passage. The dead security guard's skin was very dark, and the whites of his eyes, open, frozen in horror, were a haunting contrast.

They walked back to the office. Dale glanced in. None of them had moved, not even Duane. They huddled against the wall farthest from the open door.

"You sure you want to be in the caboose with that pencil pusher?" Earl asked. "He really makes my ass itch."

"Me, too, but if somebody has to be thrown off the train, I think I'm the best man for that job."

"Hey, that reminds me," Earl said, a little too loud. "Guess who Joe-Joe asked to be his best man?"

"You?"

"Sure enough," Earl said. "Imagine that, me, a best man."

"The balance of my imagination is occupied picturing you in a tuxedo."

"Not that hard to imagine," Earl said, looking down at his belly, then immediately tried to suck it in. An attempt that was scarcely noticeable.

Dale motioned to the survivors. "Time to go. Everyone stay with their apocalypse buddy."

Duane was out first. Earl joined him and said, "Don't fire that thing unless you have to."

Maria and Kathy emerged next. Maria held her six iron as if it were a sword and she a knight of the realm, but Kathy gripped her club by the head and held it to her chest. Dale grabbed it as she stepped by and handed it back to her in a way in which she had to grip the handle.

"We're going to be all right," Dale said.

Tears fell down her round cheeks, but she didn't remove a hand from the club to wipe them away. "You don't know that," she replied.

She was right, and Dale was a terrible liar. His mother once told him that a lie isn't believable unless someone wants to be lied to, and it didn't seem that Kathy was interested in having smoke, even well-intentioned smoke, blown up her ass.

"Why you let all them darkies walk ahead of us?" Mema said to Dale as Hanna pushed her out into the hall.

"Grandma, please."

Dale hunched a bit. "Those people are going to help clear

your way to safety."

"I'd rather die than let a chink and a wetback save me."

"That can be arranged," Dale said.

Hanna trembled at the threat and quickly pushed her grandmother down the hall.

Mr. Kanye walked out of the office, then closed the office door and removed a set of keys from his pocket.

"What're you doing?" Dale said.

"Locking up?" Mr. Kanye paused, clearly realizing how ridiculous that was. "Sorry, I'm not thinking straight."

"No need to apologize. You're allowed a brain rattle now and again in stressful situations." Dale started walking after Hanna and Mema.

"I don't think stressful quite covers it," Kanye said.

"Amen, brother."

As Dale turned the first corner, with Mr. Kanye close enough to be his shadow, he found Hanna stopped in the middle of the hallway. Dale peered around her and could see Earl down the hall. Earl brought Betsy up, then stabbed it into the corpse feeding on the dead security guard. It jolted as if a bolt of electricity coursed through its dead body. Earl pulled the blade back and quickly stuck it through an eye socket. The dead went still, then slumped over its meal.

Earl knelt down and picked up the gun in the dead guard's hand. After a quick examination, he said, "Crap," then started searching the guard's body. It took Dale a second to realize he was looking for ammo. After a few seconds, Earl stopped and set the gun back down.

Dale scanned their party. Kathy was sobbing. Maria was shaking. Mema was mumbling nonsense to herself, and Hanna was gripping the handles of the wheelchair so tight her knuckles were pearl white.

"Dale," Kanye said in a whisper. "Did you hear that?"

He didn't at first, but then, there it was—a shuffling of

bare feet.

"I think, behind us." Kanye stepped closer to Dale, his cologne as pungent as ever.

Dale stepped around Kanye and went back to peer around the corner they had just turned. He could see Kanye's office door and the bodies on the floor in the hall. It was a long hall, with doors on either side. Lots of places to hide. But what had made the noise wasn't hiding.

Ten yards past Kanye's office, a man stood in the hallway. Except for a toe tag, the man wore nothing. Wrinkles and sagging skin didn't hide the Y-shaped autopsy incision, stitched up with thick, dark sutures, a stark contrast to the pale, dead skin. Its hands were by its sides, and its feet were positioned a bit wider than shoulder width. The head, sporting a thin layer of salt-and-pepper hair, tilted slightly, eyes wide, staring, locked on Dale.

Dale held his breath and waited. Waited for it to move. Waited for it to blink. Charge. Dance a jig. Anything. But it didn't. It just stood there. Looking at him.

Dale slowly let his breath out. As he did, he got a familiar feeling. The feeling that he had earlier when he had put down the corpse in the hallway. The feeling that he was being watched. Not by the corpse in the hall. But by something else. A presence. It was like that irrational moment when you looked beyond yourself in a mirror, beyond your own reflection, and just for an instant you thought you saw something looking back. Something on the other side of the mirror.

A chill moved through Dale as the corpse then did something he couldn't believe.

It grinned.

The walking dead groaned, moaned, staggered, shuffled, and sometimes they even slobbered as they attempted to ingest copious amounts of human flesh, but never, ever, did they... grin.

KEVIN DAVID ANDERSON

A scream, shrill and terrifying, boomed behind Dale. He spun around so fast he knocked Kanye to the ground. Hanna frantically pulled her grandma backward, and Dale nearly collided with them. He shuffled to the side in time to see Maria swinging her golf club into an open doorway. The head of her club had swung all the way to the ground, clearly hitting nothing. Dale could not see Kathy.

Following the screams, Dale and Earl got to the open door at the same time. Dale shoved Maria from the doorway and stepped inside the room. Three of the undead had Kathy sprawled out on a hospital bed. Her scrubs had been torn apart and hung threadbare on the woman as the dead went to work on her flesh. Dale got there just as teeth tore open Kathy's neck. The jugular severed, blood gushed upward, then fell back, spraying the floor, a grotesque fountain.

Dale swung his club as hard as he could. The driver thumped deep into the skull of the dead that had just ripped out Kathy's throat. Before he could pull the club back, he heard boots sliding on linoleum.

"Goddammit!" Earl shouted.

Dale turned as he pulled his driver free. Earl lay flat on his enormous back, the bottom of his boots slick with Kathy's blood.

"You on vacation!" Dale yelled as the zombie he'd buried his club in fell to the ground. The two others were on the far side of the bed, where Earl had slipped. Both momentarily stopped tearing at Kathy's flesh to peer down at Earl. Before either of them could attack, Earl kicked at the closest one. There was a loud crack as Earl's boot snapped a knee, and the now-crippled zombie fell on top of him.

Earl propped the dead woman's corpse off his belly, holding her as far away as his arms would allow. Dale stepped around the bed and swung his club upward, teeing off into the corpse's face. The blow snapped the zombie's head back like a PEZ dispenser. It went limp.

Earl pushed it off him.

Dale turned, expecting the third and final zombie to be attacking, but it had gone back to feeding on Kathy's bleeding body.

Duane burst into the room and fired a series of rounds into the zombie's body. The force of the bullets stood the corpse up and drove it back. But it did not fall.

"In the head," Dale said. "The head!"

Duane adjusted his aim and fired.

The bullet exited the head, removing a fair amount of the coroner's stitching that held its face, which had been peeled away during the autopsy, in place. Once again liberated from the head, its face fell forward and hung like a bib around its neck. The body careened into a wall, then slid down the surface with a sickening sound as bare skin skidded across the decorative tiles.

Dale held a hand out to Earl. "You break anything?"

"Just my pride."

As Dale helped Earl up, he saw Maria in the hall. She was speaking Spanish, making the sign of the cross, and backing away. And before Dale realized it, Maria backed into another open door across the hall.

"No, wait," Dale said, moving past Earl, then stepping around Duane. "Maria."

Maria was several feet into the examining room across the hall before she stopped, then panicked as she realized where she was. She looked to her left, and her mouth fell open. Dale stepped into the hall, intending to reach forward, grab Maria, and yank her back into the hall, but his boot got hung up on Mema's wheelchair, and he stumbled. Off balance and barreling forward, he slammed into the wall across the hall just a few feet from the doorframe. He pushed himself up in time to hear Maria scream. Then the door slammed shut.

Mr. Kanye was at the door a second later, his keys out.

He thrust a key into the lock and twisted as Maria's cries of pain reached a fever pitch. Dale grabbed Kanye by the scruff of the neck. "Opened the goddamn door."

Kanye just stared back at him, frozen, the gaze of a true coward.

Dale snatched the keys. There were more than twenty keys on the ring. Dale picked one and tried to put it in the lock. But before he made contact with the lock, there was a loud crash from inside the room. Maria stopped screaming. And the only sounds that Dale could hear now indicated that Maria was no longer alive. Chewing. Tearing. Eating.

"I did the right thing," Kanye said, backing away from Dale. "That's a few more we don't have to worry about. You're welcome!" Kanye backed into Earl's belly.

Dale took a deep breath and pushed from his mind the pleasing image of Kanye being dragged behind his eighteen-wheeler from here to the Mississippi.

"Earl, did you clear these rooms when you went by?"

"Yeah. Tapped the doorframe. Took a peek."

"A peek?"

"Well, we didn't go in and vacuum and dust, but we took a gander. Duane, back me up."

Duane nodded. "The rooms were empty...unless..."

Dale turned to Duane. "Unless what?"

"Unless..." Duane said. "Unless they were hiding."

"Horse hockey," Earl said. "A reanimated corpse can do some remarkable things, but hide-and-seek ain't in their wheel-house."

Dale looked back into the room where Kathy died. It was a moderately sized exam room, two beds, and two sets of curtains on rollers to offer patients privacy. There were no windows and no other doors.

"Fuck," Dale said. They were hiding. The sons-a-bitches were hiding. And that's when Dale realized why the zombie he had locked eyes with didn't attack. It never was going to attack. It was there to hold Dale's attention, to turn it away from the group. While he was occupied with their rear, the attack came from the sides. It was a trap. The zombies had laid a goddamn trap.

"Okay," Dale said. "New plan. No more peeking in rooms. Kanye."

On hearing his name, Mr. Kanye took a step back. "Yes."

"When we reach a room, you lock it. Understood."

Kanye nervously nodded his head.

"You in front with Duane, Mema, and Hanna in the middle, Earl and I will cover the back. Duane, how much further?"

"Maybe a hundred yards to a stairwell that will take us down, unless you want to take an elevator."

Dale shook his head. "You never know what kind of surprise is waiting for you on the other side of an elevator door, and there is nowhere to run."

"Stairs then," Duane said.

"Let's get a move on," Dale said.

The new plan seemed to go well. Kanye stayed up front and locked doors every twenty to thirty feet. He was fast with the keys. If there were anything in those rooms waiting to ambush them, they'd have to be smarter than locked doors.

Turning a corner, the hallway narrowed. There were only a few doors left between them and a door at the end of the hall leading to the stairs. Duane opened the door a crack and peeked in, then looked back at Dale. "Clear."

Kanye locked the last door behind them, and they moved into the stairwell. It smelled of rust and old, unclean metal. Off-white paint peeled away on the steps and handrails, revealing several layers of different colors beneath, a metallic reptile shedding several layers of skin at once.

"What about Mema?" Hanna said.

Dale looked at the steep, narrow steps and then over at

Duane.

Duane got his meaning and immediately said, "Not a chance in hell."

"It's your job," Mr. Kanye said.

Duane unclipped his hospital ID from his scrubs and tossed it over the rail. "I quit."

Mema cackled. "Don't need no help from no nig—"

"Shut up, Mema," Hanna shouted. "We need help. I can't roll you down the damn stairs."

Not waiting for instructions, Duane and Mr. Kanye started down the stairs, and neither of them was looking back.

Dale met Earl's gaze and held up a fist. "Rock, paper, scissors?"

"Damn," Earl said, and held up his fist. "Ready."

They both called in unison. "One, two, three, shoot."

Earl threw paper, and Dale threw a rock.

"Goddammit," Dale said.

"You know what they say about good deeds," Earl said.

"They never go unpunished," Dale replied, stepping in front of Mema's chair. He hunkered down. "Lean forward, Mema."

The old woman did, and Dale threw her up on his shoulders like a sack of potatoes.

"Thank you," Hanna said.

"Let's move," Dale said, stepping down. The old woman weighed nothing, a feather pillow filled with hollow bones. The smell was not as easy to deal with. An adult diaper in need of changing was right by his face. Dale breathed through his mouth as he took the steps in careful strides, with Hanna and Earl a step or two behind.

Dale heard a door open in the stairwell below. Obviously, Duane and Kanye were not waiting for them.

"We gonna make it?" Hanna said.

"Heck ya," Earl said, scooping up the wheelchair. "I feel our luck changing already."

"Earl," Dale snapped.

"My friend is superstitious," Earl said to Hanna. "Just having a positive mindset, Dale. I believe it's gonna be smooth sailing from here on out."

And then the lights went out.

Plunged into darkness, Dale clenched his teeth. "Dammit, Earl."

"Sorry."

"Nobody move," Dale said. "Emergency lights should kick on in a few minutes."

Although it was irrational, the darkness seemed to bring more than just a change in visibility. The air seemed colder. Mema seemed heavier. And her mumblings seemed less incoherent. Dale tuned in and tried to understand what she was saying, but before he discerned anything, there was a gunshot.

"Christ!" Dale started moving down the stairs, one hand on the metal rail attentively like a blind man reading brail. By the time he'd reached the next level, there was a flicker of lights. The distant hum of the generators somewhere on this level echoed off the walls. In another few seconds, the lights stabilized. Nowhere near as bright as the hospital's normal lighting, but better than darkness.

Earl set the wheelchair down, and Dale placed Mema back in the saddle, trying very hard to ignore the aromatic moisture on his shoulder.

Dale grabbed the handle of the stairwell door. "Earl, hang back with the ladies. I'm gonna—"

Another two shots rang out in quick succession. And then screaming.

Dale moved through the door fast, bringing his golf club up like a batter at home plate. It was a wide hall; several gurneys could move down its length side by side. The ceiling lights were dark, but where the walls met the roof, there were floodlights evenly spaced down its length, creating a series of well-illuminated spots and dark areas.

"He shot me," came a voice from behind Dale.

Dale spun, saw Kanye huddled like a child on the floor clutching his shoulder, and knelt beside him. "Let me see."

Kanye shook his head and continued to keep the pressure on his wound.

"Duane shot you?"

"Yes."

"Let me see." Dale reached up and moved Kanye's hand. "It's just a scratch. You're not even bleeding."

"He is so fired."

"He already quit." Dale looked up and down the hallway. "Where is he?"

"They took him."

"They? Which way."

Kanye gestured to Dale's right. There was a blood trail, sporadic but detailed. Dale could almost read the struggle in the crimson streaks and smears. He was about to follow but suddenly felt something large looming over him. "Hey, Earl. Thought I told you to wait in the stairwell."

"I got bored. You know my short attention span."

"Fair enough." Dale stood and traced the blood trail with his gaze. "You three wait here. Earl and I are going for a walk."

"He's dead," Kanye said. "Let's just get to the morgue."

"If it had been you dragged down the hall, I'm sure you'd want someone to check on you," Dale said. "But by all means, feel free to continue on your own."

"We'll be right here," Hanna said.

Mema cackled, then hacked up mucus.

With Betsy and a golf club at the ready, Earl and Dale moved down the hall, each with one eye on the blood trail and the other cast as far forward as the backup emergency lights allowed. Their footfalls on the floor were near silent, an effect they had mastered through more practice than either would like to remember.

"If I had a dollar for every blood trail we've followed down a perfectly civilized hallway..." Earl muttered.

"You could afford to buy a decent truck," Dale finished.

"Leave my wheels outa this."

Dale stepped over a blood streak, clearly made from a flailing hand, red-soaked digits on white linoleum. "So, best man, huh."

"Yes, Sir," Earl said, sidestepping a metal tray and clipboard on the floor.

"Well, check my recall, but that is a first for you, I think."

"I would've liked to have been best man at your wedding, but you didn't invite nobody."

"Sorry about that, but when you are marring crazy, you don't exactly want to share it with the world." Dale brought a finger to his lips, and the two men fell silent. Ten feet ahead, the hallway turned to the right, and so did the blood trail.

The two men approached the corner. Dale took a peek. The lighting wasn't as good compared to the passage they had come down, but it didn't need to be. He could see Duane. Or at least what was left of him.

Three ravenous corpses knelt around his limp body, tearing out organs and breaking off bone. Blood-soaked hospital gowns hung loosely on the zombies like tattered curtains. The floor around the scene was no longer white, but a pool of crimson.

"That's the thing about blood trails," Earl said. "There's never anything pretty at the end of 'em."

"Nope," Dale said. "Let's make this fast."

The two men rushed forward, club and Betsy swinging. Before any of the dead even noticed them coming, their heads had been cracked open like walnuts. They all fell forward on top of Duane's body, a grotesque dog-pile of death.

Dale searched the scene and found what he'd come for. He knew Duane was dead, but it was the gun he wanted. It was still in Duane's hand. He grabbed it by the muzzle, pulled it free, then wiped it free of gore on the backside of a hospital gown. The owner of the gown didn't seem to mind.

"How we lookin'?" Earl said.

Dale checked the ammo. "Shit. One left."

"That was hardly worth the walk. You got plans for it."

"If it comes to it, I'll save it for Hanna."

"You're quite the gentlemen. What about the other two."

Dale started walking back. "I'd gladly strangle the both of them, whether it comes to it or not."

They turned the corner and could see the others right where they left them.

"Let's just stick to Plan A," Earl said. "Getting the hell outta here."

"Yep. Besides... I want to live long enough to see you in a tux."

"Well, who invited you to the wedding?"

"I got the invite same time as you, dumbass."

"Why didn't you say nothing?"

"I don't have to share my social calendar with you."

"Social calendar? The only things on your calendar are Jesus's birthday and the Superbowl."

"Well, now I got three things."

Kanye was on his feet when Dale and Earl met up.

"All right, Mister Kanye," Dale said. "It's up to you to show us the way."

Kanye stood up a bit straighter, stopped putting pressure on the wound that wasn't a wound, and said, "Okay, follow me."

The five of them moved down the hall, the opposite direction from where Duane had been dragged. As they turned the corner, a body lay on the floor. Blood pooled around the corpse dressed in faded green hospital scrubs. Kanye sidestepped it, and everyone followed. Everyone except Dale.

Dale hung back and poked the body with his golf club. Then

hooking the shoulder with his boot, he rolled it onto its back. The dead doctor or nurse was male, black, and had its throat torn open. He had bled out pretty quickly. His hands were soaked with his own blood, and Dale imagined him trying to keep pressure on the wound. A quick scan from head to toe revealed no other wounds.

Strange. *The zombie didn't eat their kill*, Dale thought. Interesting.

He looked back up the hall and saw Earl, a look of impatience on his face, holding open a door. "You need a personal invitation?"

"Don't get your panties in a bunch," Dale said. "I'm coming."

Earl stepped through the door that had the word MORGUE stenciled on it and lingered while Dale joined him. "You find something interesting?"

"Maybe," Dale said, more to himself than to Earl.

Dale had been in his fair share of morgues, but this was by far the largest he'd ever seen. At least fifty feet across and more autopsy tables than could be counted in a quick glance. Vertical freezers lined one wall, with many of the long steel draws open, revealing no occupants. Near the entrance, a body lay face down on the floor. Dale squatted near its hips and rolled it over. The body was male, wearing pale gray hospital scrubs. Its eyes were still open, dark brown, and its head was slumped at an odd angle. A gold chain had come loose and was draped across its face, a six-pointed star still attached to the broken chain was partially embedded into the man's cheek.

Dale searched for a wound, and when he couldn't immediately find one, he checked the neck.

Broken. Add that to the list of things zombies don't do.

Dale closed the man's eyes and stood, then joined the others.

Kanye led everyone to the very back of the room, where he paused in front of a large steel shelf unit on wheels. "Give me a hand," he said to Earl.

Earl stepped over, and together they rolled the shelf away from the wall, revealing an opening. It was clear that there had been some sort of door covering the opening, but it had been removed long ago. Rust filled the holes in the doorframe that marked the area where hinges had been. Kanye stepped inside, momentarily disappearing into darkness, then lights flickered to life.

Dale stepped close to the opening and peeked in. It wasn't what he expected. It was a steam tunnel all right. Furnaces, big and round, took up most of the floor space around the opening. They appeared to be in a state of disuse, and Dale figured they hadn't been turned on in decades. Steam pipes ran along the tunnel's length, and a makeshift lighting system had been installed. And Kanye knew instantly how to turn them on.

Kanye looked back at everyone, and Dale narrowed his gaze at him. "The lights?"

"Runs on a separate battery system," Kanye said. "Not part of the hospital system."

"You seem to know your way around here for someone who forbids people to come down here," Earl said.

"Off limits to everyone else," Dale said. He pointed down the tunnel. "How far does it go?"

"All the way to the outskirts of the next town, Honeywell Springs." Kanye waved everyone to follow.

They moved through the passage, and Dale could see that up ahead a new tunnel had been created. It veered to the north and used the same non-hospital lights as the steam tunnel. This new tunnel didn't look like an emergency escape route for patients. It had walls of earth and railroad ties for supports. It was not the first of its kind Dale had seen. It was all too familiar.

When they reached the new northbound tunnel, Kanye held his hand out in a polite gesture, ushering Hanna and Mema inside.

Such a gentleman, Dale thought. "So, Mister Kanye, what're you smuggling? Prescription drugs?"

Kanye looked like a man that was too damn tired to make up more lies. "Nothing that mundane."

Earl scratched his chin. "What then?"

Dale took a stab at it. "Organs."

Kanye started walking down the passage. "Our morgue is the largest in the state. So many bodies pass through here, and you would not believe how many of them don't have their organ donor cards filled out. It's a shame that all those lifesaving organs just get sent off to the crematorium, while patients die on waiting lists."

"So you provide a public service," Dale said.

"To those that can afford it."

Earl scowled. "Rich folks don't feel the need to wait in line like everybody else."

Kanye looked back at them. "I don't give a damn about the economic inequities in all this."

"What do you give a damn about?" Dale said.

"That I have three kids in college, and that a hospital administrator, even the head of billing, doesn't pay as well as I thought it would."

"Jeez," Earl said. "Everybody's got an angle."

"Everybody and their dog," Dale said. "Lead on, Mister Kanye."

Kanye stepped in front of Mema and Hanna and motioned everyone to follow. "If we keep a steady pace, we should be there in about eighteen minutes."

"You think we're gonna be able to slip under MIG's quarantine zone?" Earl said.

Dale lowered his voice. "It's a long shot. But even if we slip this noose, our lives will be very different going forward."

"How you mean?"

"Captain Major ain't gonna let this lie. He'll come after us, and with his resources..."

"Damn. Out the frying pan..."

"Into the fire." Dale finished. "But, on the bright side, I have noticed that in the past hour your mood has improved. Mostly since..." Dale snapped his fingers and grinned. "Since you found out that MIG intended to nail the lids shut on our coffins."

"Do you have a point?" Earl's voice sounded noticeably irritated.

"Yes, I do."

"Git on with it," Earl snapped.

"You're not upset about Joe-Joe getting married to a man."

"Course not," Earl said. "I'm not an idjit. I love that kid."

"I know you do. But you're scared, and what scares you the most, what's made you so damn irritable for the past week, and what caused your lack of focus this morning, which is what sent us to this damn hospital in the first place, the whole reason we are even in this fix, is..."

"Is what?"

"It's what you'll have to do if we survive this mess."

Earl sighed. "Go on."

"You're gonna have to stand up in front of everyone you know, everyone you love—hell, your entire tribe—and give the best man's speech."

"I know." Earl's shoulders slumped. "And I'm terrified."

"Of what?"

"You know I'm not good with words. I don't want to look like a fool," Earl said. "Not in front of Joe-Joe. I couldn't handle that."

"All the gays will be screaming in hell," Mema said, her shrill voice echoing down the tunnel. "When demon fire—"

"Old woman, will you shut the hell up!" Earl snapped.

Dale stepped close to his friend and put an arm around

his shoulders. "You can be pretty thick, sometimes."

Earl shrugged him off. "Thanks for your support."

"What I mean is, it doesn't matter what you say, or how you say it."

"What're you talking about?"

Dale laughed. "Earl, you mean the world to that kid. You're a father figure, older brother, role model, and weird uncle all rolled up into one. And there is no speech, good or bad, that is gonna change that."

"Yeah...I guess you're—"

"All immoral deviates will suffer the pain that they got coming," Mema said.

"Dammit," Earl said, then leaned down near Mema's ear. "Not one more word out of your demented mouth. You feeling me, Aunt Bea?" The woman fell silent.

Earl stepped back and took a deep breath.

Dale chuckled.

"What's so damn funny?"

"You," Dale said. "Scared to death of a speech."

"Hey, I'll have you know that public speaking is the number one fear. Death is number two."

Dale nodded. "I know, and it does explain a lot." Dale let another chuckle slip.

"I was once a gay," Mema said. "I knew the love and intimate touch of a woman."

"Mema, please be quiet," Hanna said.

"Now hold the phone," Earl said, rushing forward and placing a hand on Hanna's shoulder. "I think Mema wants to tell a story. Let's not interrupt."

Everyone seemed to lean a little closer to Mema as they walked. Even Mr. Kanye turned an ear back to listen.

"It was 1945. The boys were coming home from the war, and the factories we had kept running with our blood and sweat were firing all the woman. Most went quietly back to being the homemakers they wanted to be. I was one of them. But not Ester. No, sir. The foreman had to beat her and throw her out to make her leave. I saw it happen. I took her home, stripped her naked, and nursed her wounds. She was a sight to behold. Rosy the Riveter wasn't fit to be her shadow. She was a Greek goddess sculpted by heaven. We made love that night, and she touched me like no man ever could. Or ever has."

"Wow," Dale said. "Did not see that coming."

"But in my tortured soul I knew it was wrong," Mema said. "Even my beloved Ester will be torn apart by the agents of the devil. Revelations! Hellfire will consume the impure. The blacks, the chinks, wetbacks, the Jews will all be torn asunder."

"Back to our regularly scheduled program," Earl mumbled.

"Mema, enough," Hanna said, then turned back to Dale and Earl. "I know it's not an excuse, but Mema's head is out of sorts. It's gotten real bad last couple of years. With the dementia, I'm not sure she knows what she is saying."

"So, she wasn't always racist?" Dale said.

"Uhm, no, that is not what I mean. She is. Big time. It's just that she used to be...not as outspoken in mixed company."

"So more of a polite racist," Dale said.

"You can roll a zebra around in the mud to hide its stripes, but eventually the mud's gotta come off," Earl said.

"I guess," Hanna said.

Dale glanced at Mema. She had gone back to mumbling to herself and didn't seem to give a rat's fart that people were talking about her. She was beyond caring what people said or thought. Maybe it was old age, maybe it was dementia, or maybe it was something...

Except for Mema's mumbling, they walked in silence for the next ten minutes, and Dale was thankful for the quiet. He had a lot to sort out. Kanye turning out to be an organ smuggler was one of the only things about the last twelve hours that did make sense. The list of things that didn't make sense seemed to be longer than his arm, and at the very top of that list, Dale held the image of a corpse locking eyes with him and grinning.

Just as Dale got an idea, one that might explain what was going on, Kanye said, "We're here."

Kanye quick stepped to an iron rail gate. He pulled it inward, then grabbed two handles that were attached to a plywood wall. He seemed to be struggling, so Earl stepped forward and helped him slide it to the left. Fresh air from outside rushed in, smelling of pine.

Less than a minute later, they all stood under a night sky. Hanna shivered a little in the chilly pre-dawn air. Dale looked up at the stars and breathed deeply for the first time in a long while. Before Dale had exhaled, blinding floodlights hit the small group, seemingly from every conceivable angle.

"That is far enough," Captain Major said through a bullhorn.

"Hey, Captain, that you?" Dale said, knowing damn well that it was. Bringing a hand up to his face, he was able to make out a least a dozen silhouettes in the night. He didn't need to spy the details to know that they were wearing state-of-the-art zombie hazmat suits—a blending of Kevlar and lightweight chain mail, the kind in shark suits—and armed with a mix of military grade M4A1 carbine and lightweight flamethrowers.

"You get points for trying, but you know how this has to end."

Dale took a deep breath and hoped he wasn't wrong. "Yes, Sir, I do. But I think you owe it to yourself to at least hear my report."

A figure stepped forward and went from silhouette to a six-foot-tall, square-jawed man with a razor-sharp crew cut, wearing a suit that looked dated, but definitely gray. "You can't talk yourself out of this," Captain Major said, the bullhorn at his side.

"Not trying to," Dale said, holding up three fingers. "Scout's honor."

"I doubt you were ever a Scout, but you got two minutes."

"Thank you. But first, do you currently have eyes on any of the infected inside the quarantine zone?"

Captain Major pulled a walkie-talkie from his inside jacket pocket, depressed the call button. "Sargent, are you monitoring infected movement?"

"Yes, Sir. I've got nine on the south entrance, four on the lawn, and over a dozen in the parking lot. Do you need a clearing?"

"Tell him to just keep his eyes on them, and don't look away," Dale said.

"Sargent, maintain observation status, and standby."

"Copy that."

"Okay, Dale," Captain Major said. "You got some trick up your sleeve, I'd like to see it."

"So would I," Earl said.

"It took me a bit to reckon all this, but I think I got a handle on it now. You said yourself, Captain, that this one was different."

"I admit this one is outside normal parameters. Forty-five seconds."

"Tomato-tahmotto. Truth is, this outbreak doesn't fit normal parameters because it isn't an outbreak. It has been made to look like one, though." Dale stepped slowly to his right, mindful that firearms were aimed at his head.

"I need evidence?" Captain Major said. "Thirty-five seconds."

"The evidence I got is pretty much circumstantial." Dale continued to walk slowly, making no sudden moves. He was circling the small group of survivors. "It's more about behavior, observation, nothing you could've figured out in a lab."

"Twenty-five seconds."

"I appreciate you keeping an eye on the time," Dale said,

nearing Earl. "It's not at all distracting."

"My pleasure. Twenty seconds."

"So, like I said, behavior, not so much what they have been doing, but more what they haven't been doing, and who they haven't been doing it to."

"You don't know this about me, Dale, but I hate riddles. Fifteen seconds."

"I beg your pardon," Dale said, standing close to Earl. "The only way to prove this to you is to show you. Now Captain, please try not to react. Just watch."

"Whatever it is you're going to show me, now is the time. Ten seconds."

Earl looked at Dale, and his expression seemed to say, *I hope to hell you know what you're doin'.*

Dale gave him his best *Me, too* glance.

"Five seconds."

With lightning speed, Dale reached down and withdrew the pistol tucked in Earl's belt. He pivoted on a booted heel and placed the muzzle to Mema's forehead.

Hanna screamed, "Noooo!"

Dale fired, sending the back of the old woman's head into Hanna's crotch. Chunks of crimson, brain, and skull decorated Hanna from knees to tits, and she screamed.

Dale let the gun fall and threw his hands in the air as weapons took aim. "Now, everybody hold on." Dale had to shout over Hanna's screams as the red dots of laser scopes covered his body. "Everybody hold the phone one second." He met the Captain's perplexed glare. "Check it, Captain. Check it."

Captain Major slowly brought up the walkie. "Sargent, status update."

"Holy shit, Captain, they all just did a Phantom Menace!"

Captain Major's perplexed looked did not abate. "Come again, Sargent."

"Sorry, Sir. They all just dropped. The walking corpses,

all down. No movement."

Captain Major took a deep breath and looked hard at Dale.

Dale smiled the friendliest smile he could muster, one that hopefully said, *Please, don't shoot me.*

"Sargent, I want confirmation. Send squads into the Quarantine, full suits. Report back."

"Roger that."

"How?" Captain Major said.

Dale took a breath and lowered his hands. "Necromancy. The old woman was a necromancer, in the early stages of dementia, and I don't know what stage of racism, but she was not going to win any multicultural unity awards, that's for darn sure."

"Necromancer," Captain Major said. "Never came across one before. I would have liked to interview her."

Dale shrugged. "Sorry."

Captain Major glanced over his shoulder and raised his hand. "Stand down."

Dale looked over at Earl and saw the red dots disappear. "You okay, big guy?"

Earl let out a breath that he'd obviously been holding. "I need a change of britches."

* * *

More than forty-eight hours later, Dale staggered out of a very non-descript building. MIG had put him through vigorous decontamination, probing, interrogating, more probing, then even more decontaminating. Although Dale's reasoning had been sound, MIG wasn't taking any chances. Their job was to prevent, at any cost, an outbreak of the undead like the one in '68, and except for a few that got loose in Africa and the former Soviet Union, they had been pretty successful.

Dale wasn't sure what time it was, but looking at the sun

through squinted eyes, he judged it to be mid-morning.

"Hey, ugly," Earl said from across the parking lot, wearing the same gray-colored zip-up onesie that Dale had been issued after their clothes had been incinerated. Earl was leaning on his truck, a Peterbilt that he was as proud of as a little girl with her first mud pie.

"When you get out?" Dale said, making his way toward his friend and bringing a hand up to shield his eyes from the sun.

"Around sunrise," Earl said. "Why they hold you so long?"

"Spite, I imagine. Captain Major didn't seem all that happy that he didn't get to blow something up."

"Well, that's understandable," Earl said, tossing Dale a Mac Tools ball cap.

Dale snatched it and quickly put it on. "Thanks."

"But I tell you what... They spritzed parts of me I haven't seen in ages. I ain't been this clean since... Well, hell, I don't know when."

Dale reached the truck. "You smell like disinfectant." He took a whiff of his right armpit. "Me, too. Clean as a whistle." He leaned against the door. "You see the other two come out?"

Earl nodded. "Mister Kanya came out with me. He didn't say much other than I didn't have to worry about any bills from the hospital."

"What a generous son of a bitch."

"It was as close to a thank you as I was gonna git. So I took it."

"You see the girl? Hanna?"

"Yep. Wandered out about an hour ago."

"You know it skips a generation. Y'all have words?"

"That is one of the few things about necromancy that I do know," Earl said. "And yes, we had words."

"You explain both sides of the coin to her?"

"Gave her our card. Told her if she needed help with the dreams, finding some control, help with any of it, t'give us a holler. We'd put her in touch with people. Good people that can help."

"And the flip side?"

Earl nodded. "Also said that if we catch wind of her following in Mema's footsteps, that we'd be calling on her."

"Did you make an impression?"

"Like an elephant on a pogo stick," Earl said. "Hey, that reminds me. You don't often make an impression on me, but I got to hand it to you, you rolled out your big boy brain on this one. How the hell did you figure out what was goin' on?"

"Don't be too impressed," Dale said. "If I were a lot smarter, I'd have figured it out faster. First tip-off was the dead. Even you noticed they were different."

"Not until you pointed it out, I'm sorry to say." Earl folded his arms. "They staggered, moaned, and ate human flesh, just as expected."

"I think that was just for show, especially the eating flesh part," Dale said. "I found bodies that hadn't been chewed on. Old Mema was making it look like a rising to keep suspicion away from her."

"Crafty old hag," Earl said.

"Controlling the dead, seeing through their eyes takes a lot of control, even for a seasoned necromancer. I'm sure Mema had that control at one time. Probably hid her gift, just used it when it suited her. We'll never know. But what I do know is that her dementia did her mental control no favors, and it let that old-time bigotry out to play. It was who the dead went after and didn't go after that made it click in my mind. When I realized her mumbling wasn't mumbling at all, but incantations, well, there ya go, I guess."

"Raising the dead, dementia, and racism does not make for a fun evening." Earl got a very uncomfortable look on his face.

"You okay?" Dale said.

"It's just..." Earl took a deep breath. "Not sure I know how to feel knowing that the reason I survived is because of the color of my skin."

"Can't really feel one way or another about the cards you draw in life. I guess it's all in how you play 'em."

Earl groaned. "I think I have given you my opinion, more than once, on how I feel about your card analogies."

"Yes, you have," Dale said. "How about this? If you and I ever become mindless, flesh-eating zombies, we solemnly swear to eat folks of all colors, nationalities, religions."

"And sexual persuasion," Earl added.

"Sure enough," Dale said. "A smorgasbord of diversity."

"Amen," Earl said with a chuckle.

"Now, let's get the hell out of here."

"I hear that," Dale said. "And we need to get to the business of finding you a tux."

"Don't remind me," Earl said. "How about a drink first?"

"It's not even noon, Earl."

"Well, as the song goes, it's five o'clock somewhere."

Kandy with a K

Part One – Earl's Usual

"I thought you said we were going to Starbucks before heading out of town. We damn near passed 'em all."

"Turn in here. Park next to the Walgreens." Earl gestured for a hard right into a shopping center parking lot. "There's a nice little coffee shop right next door."

"That is not a Starbucks," Dale said, easing the eighteen-wheeler over.

"Said the place I was takin' you to was Starbucks-like...as in, I don't *like* Starbucks."

"Everybody and their toothless cousin likes Starbucks."

"Not me. No sir. They're all full of script-writing, skinny jean-wearing, vegan cupcake-eating hipsters rubbing on their Tibetan meditation beads."

Dale sighed, knowing Earl only went into an impromptu rant if he was trying to hide something, and Dale had a sneaking suspicion of what it was. "Ah hell, Earl. What's her name?"

"Who?" Earl said, trying to tuck in his t-shirt.

Dale put the rig with its two trailers into "Park," air brakes hissing. "The poor non-Starbucks barista I'll be watching you embarrass yourself in front of while I drink my coffee."

Earl ignored his friend and jumped out of the cab.

Dale instantly felt the absence of his three-hundred-plus pound friend as the bench seat tilted his way. He hopped out and met Earl at the front of the rig, grinned, and said, "Well?"

"Her name is Kandy, if you must know. Kandy with a *K*."

"And why do you think Kandy, Kandy with a K, is interested in talking to you. She blind, have a poor sense of smell?"

"No need to be hurtful. I have a relationship with the lady. She texted, asked me to stop on by before we head on up t'Fresno."

"Texted? What are you? Sixteen. Since when do you text?"

"Everyone on the planet texts, Dale. Everyone except you." Earl headed toward the small corner coffee shop, with Dale in tow. "You really need to keep up with technology."

"You can lecture me 'bout technology when you replace that eight-track player in your cab. You know we can get Johnny Cash on the CDs now."

Earl grimaced. "Won't sound the same."

"Progress never does," Dale said.

Earl stopped at the coffee shop door, put his thick digits on the handle, and took what seemed like a deep ceremonial breath. He looked inside through the door's porthole-shaped window.

Dale tried to see what or who Earl was spying on, but his friend's large head pretty much obscured the view.

"You gonna go in, or are you just going to stare at her from out here?"

Earl turned around and met Dale's gaze. "Please, Dale, don't embarrass me."

"When have I embarrassed you?"

Earl's brow hardened, eyes narrowed.

"I mean, recently?"

Earl took another deep breath and stared down at his boots. It was then that Dale realized that his friend was anxious. Nervous, even.

Earl, nervous?

This is a man who has driven an eighteen-wheeler straight through the shadow of the Valley of Death while drinking a beer and giving the devil a one-finger salute. And he was nervous about meeting a woman. A woman named Kandy. Kandy with a K.

Dale pulled a handkerchief from his back pocket. "Wipe your forehead. You're sweatin' like a stuck pig."

Earl took it and dabbed his brow.

Dale put a hand on his friend's shoulder. "I got your back, Buddy. Now suck in that gut and get on with it."

After one more deep breath, Earl nodded and opened the door. The two big men stepped inside one after the other, both removing their baseball caps. To the half-dozen patrons of the tiny mom-and-pop coffee shop, the two truckers in the door- way were not to be ignored. Earl stood a very full-bodied six foot two inches, and Dale, a bit leaner but by no means healthy looking, was at least a can of beer taller. Only a half inch of boot heel could take credit for their stature, and their road- weary attire seemed to tell stories of lost highways and dark destinations.

Earl ambled up to the counter, heading for a stool like he owned it. Not wanting to crowd his friend, Dale hung back a few steps and took in the place. It was nice. Not fancy, certainly not a Starbucks, but nice. Lots of tables, all dark wood. Cur- tains on the windows, and big, deep chairs next to a faux fire- place with electric flames burning brightly, if not repetitiously. The corners were shadowy. Dale liked that. A place to blend in. Disappear. A home.

"Hey, Dale," Earl said, waving him over and pushing out a stool with his foot.

Dale stepped over just as a woman closed a small refrig- erator behind the counter and began pouring cream into the line of orders.

"This here is Kandy," Earl said. "Kandy, you've heard me mention Dale."

The woman momentarily stopped what she was doing and faced Dale, holding out a hand. She was tall, thick. Her ebony features were striking, showing signs of age, lost beauty, and a hard life. Her eyes were a unique shade of pale blue, and the grip she used to take Dale's hand said she worked hard and took what was hers.

"Pleasure to meet you," Dale said, respectfully.

"Thanks for coming by. I just need a minute to catch these orders up. In the meantime, can I get you two something? Earl, your usual?"

Earl shifted uncomfortably and half-glanced at Dale. "No, I'll take a coffee. Black."

Dale raised an eyebrow at his friend. "For me, too," Dale said.

Kandy turned away and returned to work, her hands moving fast and purposeful.

When Dale was confident Kandy was out of earshot, he leaned over to Earl. "So, I got to ask."

"Don't. Just don't."

"Come on, I must know."

"Let it go, Dale."

"For as long as I've known you, baring the occasional shot of tequila, I've only ever seen you drink three things; black coffee, beer, and more beer. So please, pretty please, tell me what your usual drink is in this place."

Earl signed. "So, what did you think of her?"

"She seems nice. And you're changing the subject."

"Just nice?"

Dale smiled. "More than nice, Earl. Genuine, sturdy, no nonsense or bullshit about her. I liked her straight off. Now back to—"

"I really like them eyes," Earl said. "A man could get lost in those eyes."

"Sounds like a man already has; now are you gonna spill or—"

"I'm back," Kandy said. She held two black coffees and

ushered them over to a table near a window. As she sat down, she hollered over her shoulder to the two twenty-something baristas behind the counter, "I'm taking five."

Dale and Earl sat after Kandy did and warmed their hands around the coffee. Dale took a sip. The liquid was thick, black, and hotter than hell. Perfect.

"Thank you so much for coming by," she began. "I wanted to ask if you could pop in on Karl while you're up there."

"Who is Karl?" Dale said.

"Kandy's son," Earl said. "Goes to Fresno State, plays football, doesn't have a full scholarship but close enough. Wants to major in Education, become a teacher like his daddy was."

Kandy touched Earl's hand. "Earl is such a good listener."

Earl turned three-and-a-half shades of red.

"Yeah, he's special that way." Dale took another sip. "So is Karl sick or in some trouble."

"Don't know," Kandy said. "I just... I just have a really bad feeling."

Dale took another sip, not yet convinced this was worth their time.

Earl must have sensed this. "Anything besides a feeling?" Earl asked.

Kandy nodded. "My boy calls me every day, several times on the weekend. It was part of the deal we made so I'd let him move so far away."

"Fresno is only four hours by car," Dale said.

Kandy's brow hardened. "That's four hours further than I like."

"Yes, ma'am." Dale took another sip.

Kandy sighed. "I know what I sound like. And what you must be thinking."

"Don't worry none bout that," Earl said. "Just say what you think is going on."

"Karl started seeing this girl. A white girl. No offense."

Dale chuckled.

"Met her in some nightclub in the Tower District. Lot of the college kids hang out down there. I walked through on a visit a few months back. Not my kind of place. But this girl, the one he's seeing, plays in some band. Karl sent me some of their songs." Kandy made an expression like she'd just tasted milk that had gone bad. "Amazing what these kids listen to nowadays."

Earl grinned. "Yes, sir, I've heard cows dying in labor that was more pleasant t'listen to."

Dale set his coffee down, still not convinced. "Well, Kandy, my condolences on your son's misplaced affections toward a musician. That usually never goes well for nobody. Is there any other reason for your concern?"

Kandy took a deep breath. "A week ago, Karl said she'd been bitting on him."

That got Dale's attention. He sat up straight, and so did Earl. "Did he mean in a love bite kind of way?"

"That's what I thought at first. The old fashion hickey. Girl marking her territory. Hell, I've marked up a man or two."

"But you don't think that no more?" Earl said.

Kandy shook her head; her eyes were moist.

Dale leaned forward. "What changed your mind?"

"I ain't heard from my boy in three days."

"Shit," Earl said.

Shit was right, Dale thought. Everything he'd heard so far said that Karl was a momma's boy. Not the cutesy, nauseating kind that you might find in an affluent middle-class neighborhood filled with nuclear families and helicopter parents. But the kind that grows when a mother and child have no one else but each other. The kind in which *protect, take care of,* and *nurture* are more than just words.

"He don't answer my texts. He don't return my calls. I even called his RA at the dorm. He said Karl was in his room but was too busy to come to the phone. The RA let it slip that my son was entertaining a lady."

"Well," Earl said, "if this is his first girlfriend, he might just be—"

"No, sir," Kandy interrupted. "Girls been hanging on him since he was fourteen. He looks and walks like his daddy, and that man was Denzel Washington-fine. I accepted it early on that my son was going to be familiar with the ladies way before he should be. That's why we talk about everything, and I mean everything. I bought him his first Trojans and told him what to do with them. This isn't a case of first time getting some. None of that virgin bullshit. Something's wrong. I know it. I feel it in my bones."

Dale took a long pull on his coffee. "Well, I don't argue with bones."

Kandy narrowed her eyes. "Are you making jokes?"

"No, ma'am," Dale said. "First off, Earl's the funny one. Secondly, I'm dead serious when I say I believe your bones. I learned a long time ago that bones do not lie."

A wave of relief swept over Kandy's face. She grabbed Earl's hand. "Thank you. Thank you both."

"It'll be our pleasure to check in on your boy," Dale said.

"And as much as I'd like to sit here and watch you work all day," Earl said, "we need to get on the road. Can we get a pot of this to go?"

Kandy slapped Earl's hand. "Sure thing." She jumped up and headed back to the counter.

"Did you know anything about what was going on before we got here?" Dale asked.

Earl shook his head. "Ain't been in here for five or so days. Was spending time with you on our little Mexican field trip."

Dale grimaced. "Yeah, let's not do that again real soon. But it was an education."

Earl scoffed. "The only thing I learned was that I do not

want to see you in shorts ever again."

Dale raised his mug. "Right back atcha."

Earl lowered his voice. "So, what do you think?"

Dale scanned the room. "Not here. It's getting crowded, and I hate whispering. Makes me feel like a little girl keeping secrets. Besides... We got four hours of freeway ahead of us. Plenty of time to reckon all this."

By the time Kandy returned with a to-go pot, Dale had finished his coffee. She gave them the campus dorm information, thanked them profusely, and said she'd be up in Fresno herself in two days, whether she could get the time off or not.

Dale got the sense that Earl wanted to say goodbye to Kandy without him standing there, so he picked up their coffee, put his hat on, and tipped the brim at Kandy. "It was a pleasure meeting you. Earl, I'll see you in the truck."

Earl's and Kandy's voices faded behind him as Dale headed for the door. He couldn't make out the words, but he could tell that the tone had changed. It was the tone folks use when they wish to be heard and understood by only one other person in the entire world.

When Earl finally joined Dale in the cab, he didn't immediately buckle up. He just sat there with a stupid middle school grin on his face. Dale let it go, put the truck in gear, and headed north.

Almost an hour passed before they brought up the subject. "So, what are your thoughts on Karl?" Dale said.

Earl rubbed his chin. "I know we're thinking the same thing, but there hasn't been one of them this side of Salt Lake since Dubya was in office."

"Yep. California and the four corners have been clean for a while, but if Karl's girlfriend is in a band..."

"Bands tend to travel, go on tour and such." Earl finished Dale's thought. "Ah, shit. I thought we'd seen the last of those blood-sucking sonsabitches."

"On the upside, least we know what we're dealing with." Dale glanced over at his friend, hoping to see the same exhilaration he himself was starting to feel at the prospect of putting down some good, old-fashion nightwalkers. But it wasn't there. In its place was concern. And a little dread.

"You ever met this boy...Karl?" Dale said.

Earl shook his head. "Was looking forward to it. But not like this. Sure as hell not looking forward to tellin' his mamma that Karl is in a bad way, iffen that's how things are when we find him."

"I'm sure he's fine. Heck, we might have this whole thing wrong. I'm not always right," Dale said.

"You're preaching to the choir on that front, Good Buddy."

"Hey, I said I'm not always right," Dale snapped. "But I'm not often wrong."

Earl folded his arms. "Mexico. Bermuda shorts. No suntan lotion. Need I say more?"

"Yeah, I's wrong on that in a big way. I healed up nice, though."

Earl suddenly found his smile, pointing at a sign. "Hey, the Dirty Crank is coming up in a few exits. Nice place. Lots of memories there."

Dale remembered the roadhouse that mostly catered to outlaw bikers very differently.

"You member that time when we hung out with them gang fellas... What was their organization called?" Earl said.

"Satan's Soldiers."

"Yeah, them fellas. We played darts or some such."

"You didn't play darts. They threw darts *at* you."

"Well, they were just funnin'."

"One of them tried to knife you in the back."

"Yeah," Earl smiled. "Good times."

Although aggravating, Dale did envy Earl's ability to only

recall events in a way that seemed like everything was all one big, fun adventure. Fact was, those bikers had been picking on Earl like schoolyard bullies drawn to what they thought was a defenseless fat kid. Dale had been content to let Earl handle it until one of the shitheads pulled a blade. Dale put the knife wielder and three of his friends in the hospital that night while Earl enjoyed tossing two others through a window. A shot putter in high school, Earl always had a knack for distance throwing.

"Ah, we had a good tussle with them fellas," Earl said. "'Member?"

"I remember needing stitches."

"We outta stop by sometime, relive some good times."

Earl's delusionary event recall was one of the things that made Dale believe that his friend was a good person. A decent person. Far better than Dale was. A three-hundred-pound redneck boy scout if ever there was one. It was also that same part of Earl that allowed women to take advantage of the big oaf. Like Kandy could be doing. Dale had no problem protecting his friend from knives and other implements of pain, but when it came to matters of the heart, Dale was helpless against a woman begging favors. He just hoped that when this was at an end, no matter how it goes down, good or bad, Kandy with a K would still give Earl the time of day.

"Man, I could use a good tussle 'bout now," Earl said. "You think maybe if things are okay with Karl we could pop on by and say hey to some of them fellers?"

"No," Dale snapped. "I do not enjoy the violence in our lifestyle."

Earl shot Dale a snarky gaze.

"Okay, I do not enjoy it as much as you do. And I have zero interest in seeing the inside of that shithole."

"Fine. Time for my beauty sleep, anyhow." Earl rolled over. "Wake me when we hit Fresno."

"Hey, before you nod off, why don't you tell me what your usual drink is at Kandy's."

"Can't hear ya. Sleeping."

"Earl."

"Sawing some logs over here."

"Earl."

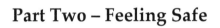

Part Two – Feeling Safe

Dale let Earl pretend sleep for the next half hour, then let him real sleep the rest of the way. When he drove onto campus, he found a spot toward the rear of the first parking lot he came across. It was late on a Friday afternoon, and the lot wasn't that full. Although Kandy had given them info on the dorm room, Dale wasn't sure where the dorms were on the moderately large Cal State campus. He just put it in "Park" and hoped for the best. Even if they were on the wrong side of campus, it wasn't like the two of them couldn't use some exercise.

"Hey, Sleepin' Ugly. Wake the hell up."

Earl rolled from one side to the other, face puffy. "We there?"

Dale opened his door. "Yes, so rise and shine."

Earl opened his door and slid out of his seat. "Think we should bring some toys?"

Dale walked around and met Earl on his side of the cab. "It's at least two hours till sunset. We should be all right."

"That sounds like some famous last words," Earl said as the two moved through the lot.

"You have your personal odor. That's weapon enough to take on man or beast. If we need more than that, we'll improvise."

"Just feel a little naked is all," Earl said. "Not sure what we might be walking into."

"Hell, Earl, if we only went places where we knew what we were getting into, we'd never go nowhere."

Students heading through the parking lot and staring at their smartphones passed by, none of them looking up at the two large men. Dale and Earl looked as out of place as sushi on a Denny's menu, but still, they garnered little notice. After more than a dozen had passed, Earl said, "How in the heck do you think they keep from bumping into things?"

"There's probably an app for it," Dale said. They had reached the sidewalk, and Dale realized they didn't know which way to go. He tried to get the attention of a student in a hoodie playing a video game by waving a hand. The young man passed them by without looking up. He tried again at two young women walking with each other, each focused on texting. He even tried a polite. "Excuse me." No luck.

Earl chuckled. "You couldn't get their attention if you were Elvis."

"Pretty sure they don't know who that is, but by all means, show me how it's done," Dale said.

"You just need to know how to talk to this generation." Earl took a few steps, placing himself in the path of a young woman. She had a thickly knitted beanie that ran down the sides of her head and covered each ear. Perfect headwear if it had been 40 degrees cooler. Earl waited until she was five feet away, then he held up a hand in a friendly manner. "Hey, there, young lady."

The young woman immediately stopped, looked up from her iPad with wide brown eyes. Her expression looked as if she had just woken from a nightmare and realized, with terrifying suddenness, that whatever was tormenting her in the dream had followed her into the real world.

"My friend and I are visiting, and we're wondering if you could—"

"I do not feel safe!" the woman shouted, unblinking, eyes

locked on Earl.

"Beg pardon?"

She held out her hands as if she was preparing to repel a boulder. "I do not feel safe. Please let me pass."

"All right." Earl stepped back next to Dale. "I was just hoping you could tell us—"

"I have the right to feel safe." She moved by Earl and walked away quickly, looking back over her shoulder. When she was twenty feet away, she refocused her attention toward her iPad.

"What the hell was that all about?" Earl said. "I got the words serial-killin' rapist written on me somewhere?"

"Wouldn't say it's spelled out or anything," Dale said. "If it makes you feel any better, you always make me feel safe."

"I do appreciate the sweet talk, but that does not get us any closer to where we need to be." Earl took a step, looking as if he was about to give it another try with a young man on a skateboard whose jeans were so tight just looking at him made Dale's BVDs ride up an inch.

Dale grabbed Earl's shoulder. "As entertaining as it is watching you bring the generations together, I think I know how to get there."

Earl furrowed his brow. "Got some sort of enhanced powers of navigation I was unaware of?"

"No, I just thought we'd glance at that campus directory over there." Dale pointed up the sidewalk.

"That works," Earl said with some relief.

After scanning the directory, Dale was pleased that his choice of parking lots was not the closest to the dorms, but it wasn't the farthest either. They moved purposely through campus, doing their best to keep clear of students—neither of them wishing to be shouted at again—and soon arrived at the freshman dormitory. They approached a double door with a security card scanner on one side. Kandy had mentioned that they'd need to sign and get buzzed in if it was after nightfall. During the day they shouldn't have a problem, but Dale felt the need to check in so that they didn't spook anybody.

Earl stood by the double door while Dale moved to the security window. He tapped on the glass. "Hey, there."

A thin, pale, barely college age boy with purple hair looked up from an iPad, pulled out his earbuds, slid the window open, and said, "'Sup."

Dale did his best to ignore the wave of male body spray that rolled out. "I'm here to see Karl. Can I head on in? I already got his room number and everything."

"You got a last name?"

Kandy hadn't mentioned it, but he was sure Earl knew it. Dale glanced over at Earl, who had pulled a flyer from the wall and was staring at it, his lips moving. Dale didn't like to bother his friend when he was reading.

When Dale didn't answer, the kid behind the window continued. "We have three Carls. Well, one prefers to be called Carlos now, oh, and one is really a Carla, but is changing it to Carl... Is your Carl trans?"

"What?"

The boy rolled his eyes. "You know, going through gender reassignment?"

"I s'pec' not." Dale sighed, starting to wonder if checking in had been a mistake.

"Well, the only other Carl here, don't know him, plays sports or something," he said as if the word *sports* tasted bitter. "And spells his name with a K."

"Yep, that's him," Dale said impatiently. "So, we'll just pop on up. You want me to sign something." Dale brought his hand up, gesturing for the clipboard laying on the kid's countertop desk, then glanced over at Earl just in time to see him open the dormitory door for two approaching young ladies. His friend held the door open and smiled as the two entered. The two women never looked up from their phones or gave Earl a return smile for his courtesy.

When Dale looked back, he'd expected to find that the kid had slid the clipboard with the sign-in sheet through the security window. But it wasn't. In fact, it was further away, and the kid's hands were covering it as if it were Top Secret intel.

"Are you family?'

"What?" Dale said.

"Karl with a K, are you his family?"

"No, a friend of the family. See his mom asked us—"

"If you're not family, I'll have to call up and check if he knows you."

"See, he don't answer his phone, that's—"

"Hey, Dale," Earl shouted, as he held the door open for another female student. "What's the holdup?"

"I'm working on it, Earl," Dale shouted back, then narrowed his eyes at the boy. "See, he don't answer his phone, not even when his mom calls. That's part of the reason we're here. So, we're just gonna go check on him real quick like. We'll be out of your purple hair in no time."

The boy shook his head, returning Dale's stare. "If you're not family, I cannot let you in."

Dale took in a long deep breath as he looked down at his boots, the same boots he was mentally kicking himself with for allowing his polite nature to get the better of his instincts. Why he had to relearn that same damn lesson over and over was beyond him. He exhaled, hard, looked back up through the glass, and said. "Look here, Sparky."

"My name is Theo."

"Of course it is," Dale said. "Why don't you take a look at my friend over there."

The young man leaned forward, taking in Earl's size.

Dale took a little step back. "Now take a gander at me." Even though Dale's was beefy, it was easy to see that there was more muscle in one of Dale's arms than the kid had in his entire body. "And now, just for shits and giggles, take a look at yourself. What are ya? Ninety pounds of cotton candy and body spray?"

Dale was a little surprised that the kid actually did. When the young man looked back up, Dale continued. "It's pretty clear that the door my friend is holding open at the moment is not locked." Dale looked over and shouted, "Earl hold onto that door."

"Yes, sir."

"So, when you say you can't let us in, you lookin' like you look and us lookin' like we look, I'm just curious, how exactly are *you* going to make that happen?" Dale narrowed his eyes. "I'll give you a sec to do the math on that one."

The boy seemed stunned, clearly in a situation he had heard was possible but couldn't remember what they said to do during his five-minute orientation. "I can't... You need..." He suddenly looked at his clipboard as if it had the answer written on it somewhere. His eyes came back up, clueless. "I'll have to..."

"All right, muffin top, you seem a bit flustered, so let me help you out," Dale's tone remained stern. "Option one, you could call campus security, but by the time they skateboard on over, my friend and I will be long gone. Now what I recommend is option two."

"Which is?"

"You relax, go back to whatever you were doing on that device, and pretend that I'm smart enough not to have walked over here to talk to you in the first place. Get my meaning, Sparky?"

"It's Theo," the boy said, and then slowly put his earbuds back in and reached for his iPad.

"Of course it is," Dale said as he turned away.

"What the hell took so long?" Earl said.

Dale moved through the open door. "Ah, for some reason I feel the need to relearn the same lesson every so often."

"Which one is that," Earl said as they moved toward an elevator.

"It's better to apologize than to ask permission."

"Yep, that is a good one. There should be bumper stickers."

Elevator doors opened, and a small crowd of coeds shambled out like freshly risen zombies, all being pulled forward by whatever device they held.

Dale and Earl nodded hellos that went unanswered, then they stepped inside. Earl pressed the button for the second floor. As the door closed, Earl held up the flyer he'd been reading earlier. "Listen here," Earl said, then cleared his throat. "You have the right to feel safe. Do you feel threatened by those that don't seem to respect your culture, background, and/or life experiences? Do you feel triggered by hostile points of view that are out of place on a campus of higher learning? You have the right to feel safe. Join C-U-S every Tuesday and Thursday in the quad for a rally and safety workshop."

Dale raised an eyebrow. "C-U-S?"

"Says here, Cultural Unity and Safety." Earl looked up. "What're your thoughts on that?"

Dale sighed. "I'm trying not to have any." The elevator door mercifully opened, and they stepped out. "What's the room number?"

"Two thirty-seven."

Dale scanned around, looking for signs indicating which room numbers went which way, but the only sign they could see was on a door labeling a study room. The door was ajar, and Dale could see figures moving inside. He looked over at Earl. "Right or left?"

"Uh... Why don't we ask these folks in here?" Earl stepped to the study room.

"Earl, don't..."

Earl stuck his big head inside the study room, started to say something, but was interrupted by a scream. Earl then quickly stepped back and closed the door. He looked a little pale. "Them two are not studying. I ain't done a lot of studying in my day, but I'm pretty sure that ain't it."

Dale sighed. "Would you please stop scaring the natives." He gestured to the right. "Let's try our luck this way."

"Suits me," Earl said, taking the lead.

The hallways were wide, but not wide enough for the two to walk side by side, so Dale fell in behind his friend and listened as Earl read the room numbers out loud. The corridors were mostly empty, and there was a general calm in the air. Maybe it was the soft-colored paint on the cinderblock walls or the retro mini lounge areas they passed every time they took a corner, but there was a sense throughout that everything was okay, copasetic, groovy, no reason to fret. Which is why Dale suddenly became alarmed when they finally found Karl's room.

It was as if the area around Karl's room was in a different building entirely. The air felt heavy and thick. Dale could feel it settling on his bare arms, and he wanted to wipe it clean. And the smell... Musty. Dank. A sick room that hadn't been aired out even though the patient had died weeks ago.

Earl faced the door, grimacing. "What is that smell?"

"Dirty, wet dog."

Earl nodded, then ran his fingers over the door. There were scratches on the wood as if someone had taken a knife to it. Earl traced one of the gouges with a finger and glanced over at Dale. "You still think leaving our toys in the truck was a good idea?"

Dale lowered his voice. "I didn't say it was a *good* idea. If Karl's girl is what we s'pect her to be, and she is in there right now, we should be able to handle the situation. We can improvise."

"If your overconfidence gets me up and killed, you'll not be getting a Christmas card from me this year."

"Noted," Dale said.

A soft moan drifted out from under the door.

"Signs of life," Earl said, "or thereabouts."

Another moan followed, so close the first one hadn't yet faded. Dale couldn't tell if they came from a male or female, which didn't bother him, but what did make his skin crawl was that he couldn't tell if the sounds were of pleasure or pain.

"Longer I stand here, the more questions I have," Earl said. He took a breath, then knocked on the door.

A moan answered, long, not caring who was listening.

Then Dale knocked, harder. The door shook.

"Hey, Karl, open up," Earl shouted. "Your mom sent us to check on you."

They could hear movement inside, shuffling, then something fell, a lamp possibly, crashing to the ground. Then Dale swore he heard a growl, deep, animal-like. It suddenly faded and became a whimpering moan like before.

"I'm tired of the view from out here," Earl said, and without taking a breath, he put his shoulder and considerable weight into the door. The door popped like a champagne cork, and Earl stumbled inside.

Dale reached out and grabbed his friend before he went too far in to the dark room. A ragged curtain covered the room's only window. Only a few beams of light escaped the curtain, casting a soft glow. There was a single bed on either side of the narrow room. The one to the left was empty, but the one on the opposite side writhed with movement. Legs and arms hung off the side of the worn mattress, and a thin, wet sheet draped over what looked like two intertwined bodies.

Dale searched for a light switch but ended up knocking a pizza box and some dishes off a shelf. The box bounced on the floor and mixed well with the other garbage and debris covering the dorm room carpet. Soda cans, partially full containers of Chinese food, and that was just the stuff he could see. Earl stepped across the room, garbage crunching under his boot heels, and flung the curtain open. Light filled half the room but didn't directly fall on the occupied bed, leaving the forms unlit.

"Karl," Earl said. "Is that you?"

The young man sat up as a female form slid to one side, long, disobedient hair covering her nakedness. Karl attempted speech but clearly wasn't awake enough for that. An unruly parade of syllables fell out of his mouth until his ears must have registered that he wasn't saying anything. He put both hands over his face, feeling around as if he was trying to find something familiar.

Earl started to move toward the bed but stopped abruptly as the woman pushed herself up. Her bare legs swung out, feet touching down on the garbage-covered carpet. Dale tensed and reached for a bookend on the shelf. If was heavy and felt like a statue of some kind. Not killing bloodsuckers heavy, but heavy enough to get one's attention.

She rose from the bed, nude and unashamed. Her skin glistened with sweat. Long strands of black hair clung to her cheeks, neck, shoulders, and chest. She made no effort to pull the hair away, get the unruly velvety strands under control, just let them lay wherever her recent activity had placed them.

Earl stepped back until he stood next to Dale, and even though he didn't need Earl to stand next to him, Dale felt much better when he did. He glanced down at the floor and took notice of how close the sunbeams were to her feet. Dale gestured to what he hoped was a bathroom off to the left of the dorm room. "Miss, why don't you go freshen up. Give us a minute here with Karl."

"And maybe put some clothes on," Earl added. "We can see all the way to Christmas."

Her head tilted slightly; one yellow-tinted, feral eye became visible through untamed hair. She seemed to scan Dale up and down, a half smile snaking its way up one hair-covered cheek. The young woman lingered for a few moments, not in any hurry to cover up or follow their suggestions. She raised her arms up, stretching, hands curling into fists. Dale was surprised to see thick patches of underarm hair glistening with sweat. He peered a little south, taking in the unmanicured landscaping covering the inside of her thighs. The black pubic hair continued up past her navel and petered out over her stomach.

She must have caught where Dale was looking because her smile twisted a little. She pursed her lips and sent him an air kiss. The invisible kiss hit him with a chill, and he gripped the bookend a little tighter.

She moved toward the bathroom, taking a route that didn't come into direct contact with the sunlight. When the door shut, Earl looked at Dale. "Ain't seen hairy pits like that since my parents did the naked peyote dance back on the reservation. Thought kids today were shaving off all their body hair."

"They are," Dale said.

"Why you suppose they do that?"

"Make room for more tattoos and piercings, I guess," Dale said. "You keep an eye on her, and I'll have a word with sleeping beauty over here." Dale knelt down next to the bed, getting eye level with a very out-of-it Karl. He peered into his unfocused, pale blue, dilated eyes. "Karl, you in there?"

His lips moved, but nothing useful came out, then the boy nodded.

"You hung over, been drinking?"

He shook his head.

"How about drugs? I'm not the law or nothing, so be honest with me."

He started to shake his head again, but then said, "No. No drugs. I'd get kicked off the team."

"All right, then. Are you sick?"

"Hey, Dale," Earl said from the other side of the room.

"Just a second, Earl."

"No, I'm not sick...just... Where is Lana?"

"Your lady friend is powdering her nose."

"What?" Karl said, his speech getting stronger.

Dale was about to explain but stopped as he noticed the marks on Karl's skin. Scratches, deep, some looking infected and in need of stitches, wrapped around his chest, over his shoulders, and disappeared down his back. Dale tried to follow them but then noticed the other marks on his neck.

"Hey, Dale!" There was alarm in Earl's voice, but Dale was too transfixed by the gnawed skin, torn and scraped along Karl's jugular to stop his inspection.

"Just a sec, Earl." Dale put his hand under Karl's jaw and guided his head over to some light for a better look. The skin appeared to have been gnawed on, a dog's chew toy. Was this the work of an inexperienced bloodsucker? Orphaned after being sired, no master to show it how to use its fangs. It was a theory, but Dale wasn't sold on it yet. Something was not right.

"Dale!" Earl shouted.

"What!" Dale returned the shout and got to his feet. It was then that he heard it. Coming from the bathroom, the animal-like moaning they'd heard earlier.

Dale joined Earl at the bathroom door. Earl had put his boot up against the door to keep it from flying open. They stood quietly for a moment as items crashed to the ground inside. The moans came again. Then there was a scream. A scream derived from pain, but one that also seemed to delight in its anguish.

"Oh, no. Not again." Karl said, drawing his knees to his chest. "She's coming. She's coming."

"Whose coming, kid?" Dale said.

"She'll be mad," Karl added. "So mad."

"Karl," Earl said. "Who is coming?"

Karl said nothing, just pointed to the bathroom door.

There was a loud scraping sound, claws on glass.

Dale stepped away from the door and put his hand on the handle.

Earl met Dale's eyes. "Are you sure that's a good idea?"

"How many bloodsuckers you put down from the other side of a door?"

"Uh...zero." Earl sighed, then stepped away from the door, hands held up in surrender.

"On three," Dale said.

Earl nodded unenthusiastically.

Dale counted down, and when he reached one, he yanked the door open.

The two large men stood shoulder to shoulder, staring into the dimly lit bathroom. The woman stood in the middle of the room, broken glass under her bare feet. Her pubic hair, which was thick before, was now an overgrowth of blackness covering her legs, reaching toward her breasts and intertwining with the distending hair from her armpits. It was then that Dale realized that the hair from her scalp he had earlier thought clung to her face with sweat was, in fact, growing from her face, black, thick, and outlining a protruding, vicious snout.

The creature growled.

"Ah, crap on a cracker," Earl said as the woman reared back with clawed hands. Before she lunged, Dale swung the door shut, and the two men put their weight against the thin wood.

"That is not a bloodsucker," Earl announced.

"Yeah, I got the status update, Earl."

The werewolf, heavy and strong, hit the inside of the door. Claws scraped the wood.

"Not again," Karl mumbled. "Keep her off me. Please."

A howl erupted from the bathroom, long and loud. It echoed against the porcelain and tile like a blast from a foghorn.

"Oh, no, we don't need to bring any toys," Earl said.

"Not now, Earl."

"We'll just improvise, he says."

"Could you bust my balls later?"

"Oh, count on it," Earl said.

A thunderous roar boomed from inside, then a hair-covered hand exploded through the top of the door just above Earl's head. Its claws arched down toward Earl's face, but before they thrust into his forehead, Earl reached up with both hands and caught the creature by the wrist and twisted hard to the right.

Earl's wide eyes met Dale's, and Dale could see that his friend was struggling to hold onto the creature. His friend had the tiger by the tail and could not let go.

"Dale!"

"What!"

"Dale!"

"What!"

"I...do not feel safe!"

Part Three – Bears, Gorillas, and Puppy Juice

The hairy wrist writhed in Earl's grasp, and Earl's fingers were slipping.

"Can you pull it out more," Dale shouted.

"Pull it out more? That doesn't seem to be the best of ideas."

"Trust me."

Earl grunted, put a boot up against the door, and pushed off. The creature's forearm began to emerge, and Earl strained against the thing's rage. When Dale saw a hairy elbow, he reached up with both hands and grabbed the forearm.

"Toward me on three," Dale said. "One, two..."

Both men forced the creature's trapped arm in Dale's direction. There was a snap of bone, immediately followed by a howl that felt as if it could blow the door off its hinges. They released the limb and stepped back. The broken appendage dangled like a damaged pendulum twisting off its designed route. Its owner growled and slowly withdrew its arm. Protruding bone hung it up on the jagged wood outlining the hole in the door. But with a violent, and clearly painful, tug the busted appendage disappeared back into the bathroom, wooden shards tumbling to the trash-covered floor in its wake.

"Well, that was all kinds of fun," Earl said. "Hell, I've had an easier time holdin' onto a greased pig. What now, fearless leader?"

Before Dale could respond, a low growl filled the room.

One that didn't come from the bathroom. Dale spun around and met Karl's eyes. The boy's pupils had darkened, and his chest was heaving. A well-toned athlete, Karl's developed pectorals and abs pulsed as if each muscle was taking a breath. Karl's mouth hung open, caught between a gasp and a scream. He held up a hand, and Dale watched as the boy's fingernail thickened into claws.

Earl took two quick steps toward Karl and raised a massive fist. "Sorry 'bout this, kid." Earl clocked the young man on the side of the head. Karl spun toward the wall, spun back, then slumped onto the bed. Earl knelt down and touched Karl's forehead. "He's out. Breathing steady, looking more human every second."

"How'd you know that'd work?" Dale said.

Earl shrugged. "Never know 'til ya try."

"Freeze assholes!" came a shout from behind.

Dale looked over at the campus security guard standing in the doorway with a drawn service revolver. If Barney Fife had a portly, crimson-haired nephew with Coke bottle glasses, Dale would have sworn he was staring at him. A familiar pair of skinny jeans stood behind the guard.

"That's him, officer," Theo said, pointing at Dale. "He didn't sign in and made disparaging remarks about my manhood."

The campus security guard moved the gun back and forth between Dale and Earl, with at least a pot of coffee's worth of bulging eyes. He finally stopped and held the gun on Earl. "Did you... Did you just hit him?"

"Well, yeah, but there's a really good reason."

"I know this looks bad," Dale said. "But we do got reason."

A roar came from the bathroom, and Dale was shocked that, just for a moment, he'd almost forgotten about the demon-bitch sprouting hair in the bathroom. Dale thrust his body up against the door just as it started to come open. Earl was next to him in a second, and they were back to where they'd been just a minute ago, except this time there was a gun pointed at them.

"What was that?" Barney Fife's nephew said, aiming the pistol at the Dale and Earl.

"You remember that good reason we mentioned a sec ago?" Earl said.

"Yeah."

Howls of rage exploded from the other side of the bathroom door.

"We got it trapped in the bathroom," Earl said.

Dale could feel his boot heels sliding backward. "Shit! Put your back into it, old man."

The faded Berber carpet offered little opportunity to dig in, and Dale could feel this going south, fast. *If this thing gets out and starts tearing up a dormitory full of kids...*

"What the hell is that?" the guard said, stepping into the room, Theo in tow, gun still aimed at Dale and Earl.

The door strained, the sound of cracking wood echoed in Dale's ear, and his boots slid back. The door inched open. A snout and hellish teeth trust forward. The mouth opened wide, and Dale got a whiff of its breath, foul, coppery, in dire need of a Tic Tac. He flipped over to put his back flush against the door. The security guard aimed his gun at the emerging set of teeth and looked as if he was preparing to fire.

"No!" Dale said. "You'll just make it mad."

The guard started to lower the gun a little when it suddenly went off. Dale felt the bullet's impact vibrate through him as it ripped through the door. Miraculously, it missed both large men by inches, piercing the door at the point where Dale and Earl's shoulders were touching.

Dale and Earl glared at Barney Fife's nephew, who immediately said, "I'm sorry, I'm sorry, I'm sorry."

"Put that away and come help us," Earl growled between tight lips.

KEVIN DAVID ANDERSON

He holstered his weapon and joined them at the door. Dale was pleased that, with his help, the backward slide of the situation had stopped. They still had a very upset werewolf's head pushing its way out, but for the moment they were holding.

"What can I do, what can I do?" Theo said, waving his arms and bouncing up and down like a kid on a pogo stick.

Dale got an idea. Not a good one, but worth a try. "All right, Sparky, come on over here," Dale said between clenched teeth, just audible over the growls rapidly growing to a fever pitch.

"It's Theo," he said, bouncing over to the door.

"I need you to get something out of my pocket." Dale thrust his left hip out while trying to keep a grip on the door.

Theo seemed to understand and dug his skinny fingers into Dale's pocket. "What am I looking for?"

"A ring."

Theo withdrew his hand; a few candy wrappers fell out, but clasped in his narrow digits was a ring. A man's wedding ring.

"Hey, is that..." Earl said.

Dale snatched it from Theo, held it in front of the creature's face, its teeth snapping, and waited for it to open wide. When it seemed that the mouth was as open as it was gonna get, Dale tossed the silver ring deep down its throat.

The beast gagged. Its snout lunged upward furiously, then withdrew. Under the weight of the three men, the door slammed shut, shaking the wall. Dale put his ear up against the door. He heard grotesque hacking and long, painful gags. Finally, after a minute, there was a thud. Dale imagined the thing on the floor, his silver ring becoming the worse kind of ulcer a werewolf can have.

Earl and the security guard slid to the floor. Exhausted, Dale joined them.

"Was that a bear?" the security guard said.

"Oh my god, oh my god." Theo was bouncing again.

128

"Uh...well," Earl stammered

The security guard shook his head. "Because it did not look like a bear."

"Well, it all depends," Dale said.

The security guard turned to Dale. "On what?"

"Oh my god." Theo now bounced in a circle.

"Will you be writing a report on this?"

"Kind of have to," he said. "I fired a gun inside a student dorm. Hell, I've never even drawn my weapon before."

"In that case," Earl said. "It was a bear."

The security guard stared forward blankly. "What the hell is a bear doing in the dormitory? I mean, how would it even get inside?"

"All fascinating questions," Earl said, leaning forward and meeting Dale's gaze. "I got one for you, old buddy. What the hell are you doing with that ring? You done told me you tossed it in Lake Okeechobee."

Dale cast his gaze on the bouncing Theo and let out such a long sigh that when he finished he felt completely deflated. "Not now, Earl. We got more pressing concerns at the moment."

Earl held up a finger. "To be continued."

"We got it trapped for now," Dale said. "But we need to start thinking about how to get it out of here."

"Oh my—" Theo said. "Wait. What do you mean trapped?"

Dale was thankful Theo had stopped bouncing for a second. It was very distracting. He thrust his thumb over his shoulder. "It's trapped in the bathroom." But even as Dale said it, there was a sinking feeling in his stomach.

Theo tilted his head. "What about the other door?"

Dale and Earl spoke at the same time. "What other door?"

"Oh my god, don't you know? The dorm rooms all share a bathroom," Theo said. "There's another room on the other side of the bathroom."

The two truckers hopped up so fast they almost stepped

on the security guard. Dale pulled the door open. The musty odor of a dozen wet dogs hit them like a puff of cigar smoke. Blood, vomit, and hair products saturated the tile floor. Broken glass and shattered toiletries were scattered everywhere. But what wasn't there was the dying remains of a she-wolf. The door leading to the other dorm room was open.

Dale rushed into the connecting dorm room. There was an oversized computer monitor in one corner, some kind of space video game running. Two students with their backs to the bathroom, both wearing headsets, clicked away, firing at whatever virtual invaders were attacking Earth.

Dale and Earl stepped into the room as unobserved by its occupants as the werewolf had been just a few moments ago. The door to the hall stood ajar, and Dale could see a blood trail. Dale, Earl, and the security guard followed the blood, with Theo a few feet behind. They moved down the hall and through a small lounge area with students sprawled on fluffy chairs and couches. Dale stopped momentarily to see if any of the half-dozen students looked as if they'd just seen a monster, but none did. While one student slept, the rest continued to gaze into their phones and devices. *Click, click, click. Scroll, swipe, scroll.*

Dale looked back at Earl, who shrugged.

"Oh my god," Theo said in a hushed voice.

"Theo, buddy," Earl said. "You need to calm down."

Theo nodded very enthusiastically but continued to silently mouth the words, *Oh my god.*

They continued down the hall, following the blood. It dripped for another thirty feet; then it was gone.

"Shit," Dale said. They scanned the hall, looked for open doors. Nothing. Dale was about to double back when a door at the far end of the hall flew open, and a young man tumbled out. He hit the wall, then bounced back and fell on the floor, his phone, in pieces, sprinkled onto the carpet.

He was sitting up by the time they reached him, and without being asked what happened, he pointed at the door he'd just come through, and said. "Man, there's a really big dog on the stairs."

Dale didn't wait to see if he was okay. He spun on his heel, hearing pieces of smartphone crack under his boots. He flew into the stairwell, Earl right behind him. Dale hesitated, wondering if he should go up or down. If the thing was smart, it would go down, hit the lobby, and escape out the front. But it had to know they were following, and it might be trying to lose them.

"Which way?" Earl said, leaning toward the stairs heading down.

Before Dale answered, there was a scream from above, followed by fast descending footsteps. Within a few seconds, a young woman came running down the stairs holding an iPad over her head like a shield, her heels clicking on the cement steps. "I do not feel safe, I do not feel safe," she screamed as she passed them, continuing down, never slowing .

"So, up then," Earl said.

Dale ascended, taking two steps at a time. When he turned the corner, he could see Earl was behind him but not closely. Dale didn't wait, climbing even faster. Soon there was a door. Large red letters read ROOF ACCESS. The metal handle had been torn away. Dale stepped out onto the roof, small pebbles crunching underfoot. Less than twenty yards away, the creature, limping in pain, one arm cradled in the other, reached the roof's edge. It jumped up on the ledge.

"Hey," Dale yelled.

The creature looked back. Its eyes glinted with a human expression, anger and wrath. It growled at Dale and raised a hairy middle finger. Then it whirled around and leaped.

Someone came up behind Dale, and he turned, expecting to see Earl. But it was the security guard who stood next to

him. They both walked slowly, in silence, to where the creature had jumped and peered over the edge. There were two
large trees below, both about a floor away from reaching the
roof. A few broken branches lay on the grass. Leaves were
still drifting to the grass below, twisting in the breeze. But
there was nothing else.

"That was not a bear," the security guard said.

"Nope."

"Bears don't give people the bird."

"Not generally, no."

There was a distant clicking sound from below, high heels
on cement. They peered across the dorm's front lawn and
watched the woman who had passed them on the stairs run
down the sidewalk screaming, "There's a gorilla on the stairs.
Big ass gorilla!"

"Shit," the security guard said. "So, not a bear. Not a dog,
definitely not a gorilla." He looked at Dale. "What then?"

Dale raised an eyebrow. "I think you have a pretty good
idea of what you saw."

"What I saw doesn't exist. Not really, and not here."

"What's so special about this place."

"It's not special, but there aren't things like that here. Tran-
sylvania, or Paris, or New York, maybe. But Fresno?"

Sounding winded, Earl finally arrived. "What'd I miss?"

The security guard met Earl's exhausted gaze. "There're
werewolves in Fresno. Apparently."

Earl slapped a heavy hand on the guard's shoulder. "Oh,
good. Everybody is all caught up, then."

"Jeez, Earl, you have got to get in shape," Dale said. "I've
been up here a day and a half waitin' on ya."

Earl took a deep breath. "I'm in shape. It's more love machine than Stairmaster. Where'd she git to?"

Dale pointed down to the grass. "Skedaddled."

Earl looked over the edge. "Well, shit on a shingle. We're

not gonna get our run in on time this week, are we?"

"It does not appear so," Dale said, looking back as Theo stepped out onto the roof and jogged over.

"Oh my god, is it here? Is it here?" Theo's eyes were wide; his hands were shaking.

Dale got the impression that if this kid didn't get a grip soon, he'd explode. "Hey, I want to thank you, Sparky, for helping me out back there. We were in a tight spot, and you didn't lose your cool."

The enthusiasm faded a bit from Theo's face, just enough to convey that he was not excited about his new nickname.

"Trust me," Earl said, "that's high praise coming from him."

"Okay," Theo said. "Thanks, I guess."

A siren sounded below. Two campus security cars moved toward the dorm.

"Oh yeah, I called for backup," the security guard said.

"Sparky, can you do me one more solid?" Dale said.

Theo nodded enthusiastically.

"Hop back down to Karl's room and sit with him. Don't let him leave. Can you do that?"

Theo clearly realized that he was taking instruction from someone he didn't know and briefly looked at the security guard, seemingly asking if he should comply.

The security guard nodded. "That's a good idea. Make sure he's all right."

When Theo was out of earshot, the security guard said, "Does Karl have something to do with that thing?"

"She's his girlfriend," Earl said.

"Lana?" the security guard said. "That was Lana?"

"You know her?" Earl said.

"Well, yeah, she's the lead singer in a band that headlines over in the Tower District. Doesn't talk very much. They're playing at the Blue Oyster Club. Tonight, I think."

Dale felt it was awfully convenient for him to know all

this. He turned to the security guard and noticed his name tag. "Steve, how exactly did you come by this info?"

He stuck his thumbs in his gun belt. "Hey, I'm a hip guy. I go clubbing. I know bands and music and cool stuff."

"Steve, I got Karl to save, werewolves to kill, I don't have time for bullshit," Dale said.

"Fine," Steve said. "The coaching staff, with alumni funds, pay us under the table to keep an eye on their players. Check out who they're seeing, hanging out with. Keep an eye out for drugs and whatnot."

"You spy on the players," Earl said.

"No...not really. Fresno is very passionate about their Bulldogs. College sports is serious business here. Especially football. They're just looking out for the players, the University, the whole program. You know... Go, Dawgs."

"We're not judging," Dale said. "And it seems we can put your info to use. Can you help us?"

Steve nodded. "Karl is a good guy, and in a few years, he's gonna be a great player. What can I say, I'm a fan. How can I help?"

"First off, I wouldn't tell your friends down there nothing about wolf people. Less they know about what you've seen... They'll likely think you're nuttier than squirrel shit. You'll end up on desk duty, and that doesn't help me none."

"I was already thinking that," Steve said. "What else?"

Dale looked over the edge just as the campus security cars skidded to a halt downstairs. The woman from the stairwell ran straight at them, arms raised. "While she tells them about the gorilla, do you think you could sneak Karl and us outta here. We need to get him some puppy juice."

"Puppy juice? What's that?"

"It's the one thing that'll keep him from becoming like his girlfriend."

"Medicine," Steve said.

Dale nodded. "There are a couple of other things we're gonna need. Do you have access to the athletic department?"

"I got keys to everything."

"Perfect. Here's what..." Dale caught sight of Earl's arm. "Hey, Earl. That bitch scratch you?"

Earl held up his forearm in the sunlight. Long, deep scratches glistened, blood trickled down his elbow. "Goddammit. If I turn into one of them, I'm gonna—"

"It'll be okay, big guy."

"That's easy for you to say. You don't have wolverina virus running through your veins."

"The only thing that's changed is that we need a bit more puppy juice than we did a few seconds ago."

"I swear, Dale. I'm gonna spay and neuter that bitch."

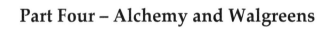

Part Four – Alchemy and Walgreens

Steve managed to get Dale, Earl, and Karl off campus without a fuss. They made plans to meet up later in the Tower District, where Dale hoped to put an end to Ms. Lana and whatever hold she had on Karl.

After making a few purchases at a pawn shop, they got something for Karl to eat: burger, fries, shake, and onion rings. Karl seemed a good sort. Every bit his mother's son. Polite, well-spoken, and seemed to respect his elders. He reminded Dale of his own boy. Not as old, but equally soft spoken and had a kindness about him.

"And what are we doing here?" Earl said.

Dale rounded the parking lot of a shopping center and headed toward the back. He parked the truck, and before the air brakes had stopped hissing, he said, "You and Karl unhook the trailers, and I'll meet you back here in ten."

"Where you off to?"

"Just a little recon. See you in a few." Dale jumped out and slammed the door. A few phone calls had helped him narrow things down to this location, but it was his knowledge of who they were seeking that guided his next few moves. He scanned the parking lot, and it didn't take long to find a ride that fit the bill. He thought for a moment that it was too obvious, then he remembered that the person he was looking for wasn't wise, just knowledgeable. And there was a difference.

After completing his task, he headed back to the truck,

pleased to see that Karl and Earl had set the trailers up on stilts, wheels were locked, and they were sitting back in the cab. Dale jumped on in, reached for a rag from under his seat, and whipped the black grease from his fingers.

"Should I even ask?" Earl said.

"You could, but time's a-wastin'," Dale said and turned to the rear compartment. "Hey, Karl, I need you to stay here. Earl and I will be right back."

Karl popped an onion ring in his mouth and nodded.

Earl looked out into the parking lot. "We're gonna find him here?"

Dale nodded. "Let me do the talking."

Earl pointed at the nearest retail store, The Liquor Barn. "In there?"

"No, over there." Dale pointed at the drug store across the way.

"Walgreens. You're telling me there is an alchemist at the Walgreens?"

"Everybody has got to make a living, Earl. He's a pharmacist."

"What's an alchemist?" Karl said, still chewing.

Earl turned around, "It's kind of a chemist that uses a science not many folks take stock in anymore."

Karl picked up another onion ring and raised an eyebrow. "What?"

"Just Google it," Dale said, stepping out of the cab. "Come on, Earl. It's getting dark."

"I'm prettier in the dark," Earl said. "Sit tight, Karl. We'll be right back."

The two large men headed across the parking lot side by side. Cars immediately stopped when they stepped in their path, not because it was the law in California, but more likely the drivers dreaded the beating they might receive if they hit either of them, not to mention the damage to their cars.

"An alchemist at the Walgreens? In full view of every-body?" Earl said.

"They're not as flamboyant as they used to be," Dale said. "Besides, this isn't a full-fledged alchemist. Just an apprentice. In hiding."

"Where's the master?"

"Dead."

"Old age?"

"Nope. Killed by his own apprentice."

"Well, that's just disrespectful," Earl said. "Long story?"

"Very."

"Ain't they all."

As they approached the entrance, four large men, each big-ger than the next, moved through the automatic doors. Cases of domestic beer were under their beefy arms. Dale shot them a glare, hard, stone, ice. The men moved fast, quick-stepped it over to four motorcycles illegally parked in handi-capped stalls, and wasted no time in firing them up.

"Hey, looky there," Earl said. "It's some of them Satan fellas we had a tussle with a while back. Think they 'member us?"

Speeding away, one of the four men turned back and held up a middle finger. "Fuck you, assholes!"

Earl smiled. "Yeah, they 'member us just fine."

"That's the second time I've been flipped off today," Dale said, stepping through the automatic doors. "I'm beginning to think that Fresno is not that friendly."

"It's not Fresno, it's you," Earl said. "Hell, first time I met you, I wanted to flip you off."

"You did flip me off."

"Oh, yeah," Earl said as they moved through the candy aisle. "You just don't put out that friendly vibe, ya know?"

"I have you for that," Dale said, grabbing a Heath bar.

"My natural joviality in no way counteracts your sourpussness."

Dale moved toward the pharmacy, scanning the faces behind the counter.

"I mean, besides me, how many friends do you really have?"

"I have lots of friends," Dale said.

"Occupational acquaintances, underworld associates, and people that are sociable with you 'cause they're afraid not to be don't count."

Dale scowled at Earl, then turned his attention back to the people in white coats behind the counter. His eyes locked on his target. "Hey, Patel," Dale said in a tone that could be heard throughout Walgreens.

A young olive-skinned man looked up from his labors. His eyes went white, and his dark skin tone lightened by at least three shades. He dropped a tray full of pills and darted to the back. A rear door was flung open, and he was gone.

"Ya see, right there," Earl said, gesturing to the back door now slowly closing. "Case in point. I take it you've met."

"We've had dealings," Dale said, digging out his wallet.

"No shit."

Dale tossed a dollar on the counter, then held up the Heath Bar to the remaining yet stunned pharmacists. "You all have a nice day," Dale said, and headed back toward the entrance. "See, I can be friendly."

Earl rolled his eyes. "Should we move a little faster?"

"No," Dale said. "I know where he's going."

They stepped back into the parking lot and headed for a shaded corner. Under an elm tree was a black Mercedes Benz Sprinter, long, extended cargo van, new, flashy. Behind the wheel, Shabdkosh Patel, former alchemist apprentice and a man on The Council's Most Watched list, desperately tried to start the van. He yelled something inaudible, then put his forehead on the steering wheel.

Dale strolled up to the driver's side and knocked on the glass.

The apprentice sighed, then rolled the window down. He looked at Dale and said, "Disconnected my battery cable?"

"Yep," Dale said.

"Please, Mister Dale, I had no idea it would go down like that. All the planets were in line, and nothing indicated—"

"Shabdkosh," Dale barked. "Shut it a minute. I ain't here to revisit ancient history, and as much as I want to wring your neck, I got bigger problems than you."

Shabdkosh looked a little relieved. "Okay, so, you need something from me?"

Dale nodded, then grabbed Earl's wrist and held up his friend's forearm so Shabdkosh could look.

The apprentice's eyes became thoughtful taking in the long scratches that now had tiny black hairs protruding from the wound. He stepped from the van. "When did it happen?"

"Few hours back," Earl said. "Itches like—"

"We got another case back in my cab," Dale said. "A young man, been chewed on for a while."

Removing a pair of reading glasses from an inside pocket of his pharmacist coat, Shabdkosh more closely examined Earl's arm. "And does the other one have this same growth?" He touched one of the hairs with his index finger.

"Not that I could see," Dale said.

He removed his glasses. "That is good. For him, not you, Sir," Shabdkosh said to Earl. "Your body seems to be accepting the infection very rapidly. Metastasizing at an accelerated rate."

"None of that sounds good," Earl said.

Shabdkosh pointed to an area that had not been scratched just below Earl's elbow.   "See here...more growth."

"It's my Native American heritage," Earl said. "My people have always been touched by the ways of the skinwalker and shapeshifter."

"You were adopted," Dale scoffed.

"So, you're here for puppy juice," Shabdkosh said.

Dale nodded. "How long?"

"An hour or so, if you have what I need."

"We picked up silver at a pawn shop. A lot. It's in the cab."

"We are going to need quite a lot." Shabdkosh took a step back and looked Earl up and down. "How much do you weigh?"

Earl sucked in his gut. "I fluctuate. Two-eighty-five to two-ninety..."

Shabdkosh didn't seem convinced.

"Dammit, Earl, he's not fitting ya for a prom dress," Dale said. "This is your life we're talking about. Tell the man how much you weigh."

"Fine. Three forty," Earl said. "Three fifty after a nice lunch."

"Jesus," Dale said. "I am definitely getting you a tread-mill for Christmas."

"Don't you dare!"

"Gentlemen!" Shabdakosh chimed in. "How much does the other one weigh?"

"Two hundred," Dale said. "Maybe two ten. I'll go fetch him and the silver. Why don't you get started."

"How's he gonna do that?" Earl said. "Don't he need to go to a lab or something?"

Dale put his hand on the van. "What do you think this is?" He turned to Shabdakosh. "A Mercedes? Really? Not very stealthy for a man who doesn't want to be found."

Shabdakosh. "I like a bit of style. So shoot me."

"Maybe later," Dale said. "Get started."

Shabdakosh slid open the side door to the van and stepped inside. Dale turned to go, but Shabdakosh poked his head out and said, "Mister Dale, if I do this for you, are we good, you and me."

Dale narrowed his eyes. "We're miles away from good,

Shabdakosh. If you even—"

"Dale," Earl snapped, cutting him off. Earl faced Dale and smiled wide. "Smile. Friendly. Be nice."

Dale took a deep breath. He looked at Shabdakosh. Forced a tight-lipped smile. "Do this for me, and I will definitely not kill you today."

Shabdakosh nodded. "That works for me," Shabdakosh said, then disappeared into his lab.

Earl put his hand on Dale's shoulders. "Ya see, you're smiling, making friends. Not killing folks. Turning over a new leaf. Keep this up, and by this time next month, I could probably throw you a party and have people actually show up."

"Just watch him," Dale said. "Stay close."

"Roger that."

"I'll get Karl and the silver, be back in ten."

"Hey, you gonna eat that?" Earl said, pointing at the Heath Bar in Dale's hand.

"How much do you weigh?" Dale said.

"Okay, that is just mean."

Dale turned and walked away.

"See if I throw you a party now."

The parking lot lights were flittering to life as the sun fell behind the surrounding hills. Lycanthropes didn't necessarily have any advantage at night other than the ones most predators enjoyed under cover of darkness, but as the sun sunk, so did this feeling in his stomach. It burned, made him angry, very angry. And he knew why.

That fang-sportin' bitch had hurt his friend. His only friend. Best friend. She was gonna die with his boot on her face, bleeding and screaming. *Jeez*, Dale caught himself. *That was some dark shit. Maybe Earl is onto something. Maybe I need to lighten up. Smile more.*

He reached the cab and pulled the door open. The feeling in his stomach instantly got worse. The cab was empty. No onion rings. No Karl.

"Goddammit!" He slammed the door. He had grossly underestimated the hold Fangzilla had on the poor kid.

Back to the darkness. Bitch is gonna die. Bleeding. Screaming.

Part Five – Side Effects and Cookies

"Is it going to hurt?" Earl said, eyes locked on the large-gauge needle.

Shabdakosk nodded. "Oh, yes. Quite a lot, really."

"And how many of these shots do I need?"

"Three over the next twenty-four hours." Shabdakosh moved the needle toward Earl's arm. "Starting with this one."

"Wait, wait." Earl covered his forearm. "Are there any side effects?"

"Many. Blurred vision, nausea, vomiting, slurred speech, painful urination, bleeding, paralysis, loss of consciousness, possible coma, and intestinal bloating."

"Christ, that sounds like a party I don't want to go to. What're the positive effects, then?"

Dale put a hand on Earl's shoulder. "We don't have ta shave your entire body every other day."

"Oh, yeah." Earl uncovered his arm.

"On the positive side, there is temporary immunity," Shabdakosh added. "For the next seventy-two hours, give or take an hour, you cannot be re-infected by the Lycan virus."

"How's mine coming?" Dale asked.

Shabdakosh looked over at a digital timer counting down. "Just a few more minutes."

"You getting some immunity shots, too?" Earl said.

"Not shots. I can take mine orally."

"So, I get three painful shots, and you get to take a pill."

"Mister Earl, your situations are very different," Shabda-kosh said. "He has not been infected, but as for you..." Shab-dakosh gestured to Earl's scratched arm. So much thick black hair was protruding from the wound that the original scratches were no longer visible. Long strands were also emerging from his bicep, his shoulder, and up and down the backside of his arm.

"Jesus, Earl. Take the damn shot already."

"Fine," Earl said, laying his forearm out flat on the table. "What about Karl? You got puppy juice ready for him."

Shabdakosh prepped Earl's shot, clearing out any air bubbles. "All ready. A little different than yours. Not as many side effects. Two shots. A heavy dose, then a follow-up booster. He is young, in good shape, and his infection, from what Mister Dale described, is unlike yours."

"How so?"

"Your young friend Karl was a planned infection. An attempt at breeding. Yours was not."

"What's the difference?" Earl said.

"Well, how can I explain," Shabdakosh said. "Imagine a young couple planning to have a child. They prepare a home, a room, get their finances in order, take parenting classes. Ideally, it's a slow process, much of it occurring even before fertilization."

"Okay."

"That was Karl. You, Mister Earl, were an accident."

Dale grinned. "A sloppy, drunken, one-night stand. Didn't even get her name."

"Shut it," Earl snapped at Dale. "Accident or not, isn't the result the same?"

Shabdakosh nodded. "Yes, but we aren't concerned with the result; this infection is not going full term. The puppy juice, as you like to call it, is the abortion, and the mixture of the antidote is different based on the intent of the infection."

"I still don't understand."

"Just take your morning after shot like a man," Dale said.

"You know what, partner? I have ju—"

Shabdakosh quickly stuck the needle deep into Earl's vein. A hail of obscenities shot from Earl's mouth. Some made sense. Many did not. When the needle was empty, Shabdakosh withdrew it, sliding his chair away from the table.

Earl scowled at the alchemist apprentice. Dale felt the sudden need to protect the young man as Earl started to rise. He put a hand on Earl's shoulder and gently pushed him back in his seat. "How are you doing, old friend?"

"I'm just ducky," Earl snapped.

The timer went off behind them. Shabdakosh stood, turned it off, then moved into a small kitchenette inside his lab. He opened an oven door and pulled forward a rack with four chocolate chip cookies. "All ready, Mister Dale."

"Are you shittin' me?" Earl said. "Your medicine is cookies?"

"Well, Shabdakosh usually puts it in brownies, but I don't care for brownies. Too rich," Dale said.

Earl covered his forearm with a hairy hand. "I all kinds of hate you right now."

* * *

Shabdakosh prepared Karl's shots for travel while Dale walked Earl to their truck. Still reeling from his first shot, walking in a straight line was a task for Earl, and even though Dale believed he had a firm grip on his friend, they almost went down twice, like two unattractive barflies stepping out of a pub at half past closing.

"I need to rest," Earl said, still a hundred yards from the truck. He bent over and put his hands on his knees. He looked like a man in need of a good, deep, god-fearing puke.

Dale put a hand on his back. "What's going on?"

"Dizziness, nausea, my feet are like jello. Feels like there're a million bugs crawling around on my scalp, and just to make things extra special, every so often I get the sensation that I've peed myself." Earl looked up at Dale. "I haven't, have I?"

Dale shook his head. "But I'll keep you posted."

"You do that." Earl stood, and they got moving again. "That's all I need. You know how hard it's gonna be to find adult diapers in my size?"

Dale smiled, glad that his friend's sense of humor was trying to come back. It had been absent in the hour since Sabdakosh stuck him, and it was encouraging that Earl could walk, or at least stagger now. But Earl would have to be able to do much more than that if he was going to be of any use. At the moment, he was three hundred-and-fifty pounds of dead weight, and Dale debated whether or not to set him up in a motel and go take on the pack by himself.

They reached the truck, and Dale opened the cab.

Earl gazed up into the compartment. "Who the hell put my seat all the way up there?"

"Are you gonna make it, partner," Dale said. "There is no shame in taking the night off."

"No, Sir," Earl said. "I got a date with one hairy bitch, and we are definitely gonna dance."

Dale slapped Earl on the back. "Then cowboy up."

Earl grabbed the door, put his foot on the runner, and pulled himself inside. It was a slow process, but after a half minute, Earl was in the seat. "I think you should drive."

"Good call," Dale said.

Earl suddenly shut his eyes, shook his head, then blinked several times.

"You good?"

"Everything just went purple." Earl continued blinking, then gazed down at Dale. "Jeez, you look like a Teletubby. And not any of the cute ones."

"Mister Dale," Shabdakosh said as he approached.

Dale turned and lowered his voice. "Is Earl gonna be all right?"

Shabdakosh's face didn't exude confidence. "I've given him the biggest dose possible. An amount that would kill most men. If he survives the next few hours—"

"If?"

"When he gets through the next few hours and receives his second shot, he will be through the worst of it. Until then, no meat."

"What do you mean, no meat?"

"I recommend he stay away from meat for the next two days. Flesh of any kind will only reinvigorate the virus."

Dale smiled. "That's gonna be fun."

Shabdakosh gave Dale the rest of the shots, Karl's in a red velvet bag and Earl's in a gray, and explained how to use them. At Dale's request, Shabdakosh formulated Karl's first shot to not only begin the reversal of the Lycan virus, but knock him out as well. Dale tossed them in the cab and checked on Earl. His friend was swatting at the space in front of him as if chasing a large butterfly that only he could see.

Obviously reading concern on Dale's face, Shabdakosh said, "The side effects should dissipate in the next few hours."

Dale ran a hand over his face, then glared at the alchemist apprentice. "If he dies, I will find you."

Shabdakosh took a step back. "I have done everything you asked and more. Are we quite through, Mister Dale?"

"After what you've done?" Dale pointed a finger like a gun. "I'll let you know when—"

"Hey, Tinky-Winky!" Earl shouted.

Dale turned. "What!"

Earl mouthed the words, *Be nice.*

Dale took a deep breath and turned back to Shabdakosh. "I do appreciate what you've done for my friend. As he is fond of pointing out, he's the only one I got."

Shabdakosh nodded. "Sometimes one is enough."

Dale thought he saw loneliness in the young apprentice's eyes. On the run, terrified of being discovered wasn't the kind of lifestyle that allowed many friendship opportunities. Dale put a hand on his shoulder, gently turned him, and started walking back toward Walgreens. "I probably shouldn't tell you this, but The Council knows where you are?"

Shabdakosh eyes went wide, looking ten times more terrified than when he first saw Dale in the pharmacy. "Are you sure?"

Dale nodded. "How do you think I found you? They owe me a few favors. Seems they've had eyes on you for a while."

"Shit," Shabdakosh mumbled. "Why haven't they..."

"Come to collect ya? I've no idea. I gave up trying to understand them years ago. But the long and short of it is, you need to move on."

"Damn." Shabdakosh looked at the Walgreens. "I really liked that job. They have benefits."

"Anything else I need to know about Earl's care over the next few days?"

Shabdosh shook his head. "There is one thing. I debated if I should tell you because I don't know what it means."

"Do tell."

"The hair samples I examined from your friend's arm were certainly Lycan in nature, had all the shapeshifter markers, but they were different."

"Different, how?"

"As I said, I'm not sure, but I want to say the markers are inversed. Almost as if they run contrary to how they should. I've found nothing like it in the records."

Dale shook his head. "Will it affect your cure?"

"My formulation is based on the hair samples, so I was able to constitute the antidote based on the abnormalities. It will work."

Dale tried to gauge Shabdosh's confidence in his own words. He figured it was about fifty-fifty. The young apprentice had done his level best, or at least truly believed he had.

"Fair enough."

Dale started to say goodbye as Shabdakosh pulled a card from his pocket and held it out. "Mister Dale, should you ever want to find me."

Dale took the card. It was blank. On both sides.

"It'll take a day or so for the message to get to me, but I will get it."

Dale didn't have the energy to ask how the card worked, so he pocketed it and shook Shabdakosh's hand.

"I hope I never see you again, Mister Dale."

"Right back atcha, kid."

* * *

Dale turned off of Van Ness Avenue onto Olive Street, the main commercial drag of the Tower District. He looked at his watch. 10:30 p.m.

"We're early."

"Maybe we could cruise around, find them biker fellas. I could use a little warm-up before the main event," Earl said.

"I'm not in the mood to get into a fight just for fun."

"You never are." Earl folded his arms. "It's that glass jaw of yours."

"What?" Dale said, looking for a place to park. "I can take a punch."

"No, Sir. 'Member that guy in Detroit? Put you down with one little love tap."

"What guy?"

"You know, that half-mechanical fella."

"That was a cyborg. An eight-foot-tall, experimental, clinically insane cyborg. And he near killed the both of us."

"Excuses, excuses. You got a sissy jaw," Earl said.

Dale downshifted and turned into a parking lot. He searched for a dark corner, but the trendy neighborhood was well lit with neon and strings of white lights sewn into the trees and over the outdoor cafes. The marquee of the Tower Theater with its neon highlights was the district's center-piece, a beacon chasing away the darkness and illuminating the crowds of college-age people moving up and down the side-walks. Along a cinderblock wall, tree branches from residential properties hung over the parking lot like a canopy. Dale slipped the truck underneath, tucked away, like a car in a garage.

"Hey, that looks like Steve," Earl said.

Dale engaged the brakes and looked across the lot. Two figures walked toward the cab. "Is that kid with him?"

Earl nodded. "Yep." He opened his door as they approached. "Howdy."

"Hey, guys," Steve said. "I brought dinner."

"Thank you, Jesus," Earl said.

Dale jumped down, then walked around and looked at Theo. "Sparky, you don't have to be here. In fact, I'd much appreciate it if you weren't."

"My name is Theo, and I can help."

"How so?"

"The club, The Blue Oyster, I know it really well. I know the owner, one of the bartenders, even some of the band man-agers. I know where the exits are; there are only two, by the way. Front and back."

Dale thought for a moment. His first impression of this kid was the typical, apathetic, disinterested in anything not deemed hip, and as uninvolved with his surroundings as every-one else in his generation. But maybe... "Why do you want to help? You hardly know Karl."

"True, but I have some Bulldog pride. I like the sports

and basketball."

"Karl plays football," Earl said.

"What's the difference?" Theo said. "Look... Those things came onto my campus, my home, and messed with a class-mate, and..."

"And?" Dale said.

"This is the most exciting thing that has ever happened to me. Ever. Please let me help."

Dale looked at Steve, who had ditched his campus police uniform for street clothes, jeans, Fresno State t-shirt, canvas jacket. Steve met his look with a shrug. Dale peered up at Earl, who was eyeing the bag of food in Steve's hand. "What do you think, old man?"

"I think the kid knows the lay of the land far to well to be sent home. We should use him. At the very least, scout the inside for us."

"Oh," Theo interjected. "I started that already. Karl is at the bar. Some of his sports friends are at a table just behind him."

"Teammates?"

"I assume. They're students, and hella big."

"We'll have to deal with them first. Don't want them get-ting in the way of us taking Karl out of there." Dale ran a hand over his face, sighing deeply. "All right, Sparky, you do what I say, when I say. No deviations. Savvy?"

"Yes, of course."

Earl tapped Theo on the shoulder. "Pay him no mind. What he's saying is thank you for the assistance, it's much ap-preciated, just be mindful, and don't get yourself killed."

"Appreciated, mindful, don't get killed. Got it." Theo nod-ded. "What do we do now?"

"Eat," Earl said, holding his hand out toward Steve.

Steve reached into his bag, sorted through the contents for a moment, then pulled out a sub sandwich and handed it up to Earl. "This one's for you."

"I am hungrier than Oprah on a diet." Earl unwrapped a meatless hoagie. "Now hold on here. Something is missing here."

"That's what I was told to get you, a veggie sandwich."

"And who in the hell told you that?"

"Me," Dale said. "Doctors orders. You're on a veggie diet for a few days."

"Oh, hell no." Earl tossed the sandwich on the dashboard. "I'll starve."

Dale smiled. "I worry about a lot of things, but you starving ain't one of them."

Steve passed out the rest, then said, "I'm gonna get my car and bring it over. See you in a few."

As Steve left, Dale met Theo's eyes. "So, Karl's teammates, how many?"

Theo took a bite of his vegan wrap. "Three." He swallowed. "And Karl, I don't want to say he's drunk or anything, but he seems really out of it, ya know. When his friends talked to him, he just kind of sat there and mumbled."

Dale knew that Karl was very much in a newborn state, a trance-like condition that meant he would never be far from the pack—or Lana. At least as long as she was alive, a condition Dale was itching to remedy.

"You know when his girlfriend's band goes on."

"Yeah, the Lon Chaney Juniors go on at eleven."

"The who?" Earl said.

"Her band, Lon Chaney Juniors. They're from Austin, I think. Named after some old-timey dead actor guy."

"Jeez," Earl said. "Wonder how we missed that?"

"Maybe you didn't ask Miz Kandy enough questions," Dale said.

"Hold on, partner." Earl climbed down from the cab, shaky. "You were there, too. You could have asked more questions."

"I mean before that," Dale snapped.

"Before what?" Earl took an unsteady step toward Dale.

Dale regretted his last comment, immediately and deeply. Ever since they left the coffee shop in southern California, he'd wanted to ask Earl if his head was on straight with this woman. He'd watched silently over the years as his friend would get turned around, upside down, and backward over members of the opposite sex, never getting a fair shake in any relationship. But these were not the kinds of things they talked about. Beyond fighting the ever-growing darkness in the world, their conversations revolved around beer, chili, combustion engines, and then back to beer again. But Earl's heart was bigger than his brain, and even his stomach, which is saying something, and Dale couldn't help but wonder if Ms. Kandy, Kandy with a K, was the real deal.

"You doing all this for the right reasons?" Dale said.

"Bitch scratched me. She gonna pay."

"Yes, but before that. You know."

"No, I don't."

Dale sighed. "I just hope that if we're alive when this is over that Miz Kandy appreciates all you've done, that's all."

Earl looked a little perturbed. "No matter how this all shakes out, she ain't gonna know nothing close to the truth about what's about to happen. So that don't matter. I don't do dumb shit like this all for the appreciation of a lady. I'm not a fool."

"Then why do you do it?"

"Man, you're stupid," Earl said. "I do it because it's what you do. And you can't find anyone else as dumb as you to do it with."

"Well, that's...okay, then!"

"All right!"

For several beats, silence consumed the parking lot like nerve gas. As the two men stared at one another, two crickets chirped in the background, but even they fell quiet after a few awkward seconds.

Finally, clearly uncomfortable, Theo said, "Should you guys hug or something?"

"Shut up!" both men shouted at Theo as Steve walked up.

"What'd I miss?"

"They were gonna hug," Theo said.

"Were not," Earl said.

"Not even," Dale added.

"We just agreed that he's stupid and I'm dumb," Earl said.

"Well," Steve said, confusion dripping all over his face. "Glad that's all cleared up. Can we go kill werewolves now?"

Part Six – Nachos and Sensitive Nipples

Happy to see that Steve had brought everything and then some, Dale told everyone the plan. There weren't any questions. It was pretty simple.

Earl reached into the trunk of Steve's car and pulled out one of the Fresno State practice helmets. "Man, I haven't worn one of these since high school football."

"Oh, yeah?" Steve said. "What position?"

"Offensive line."

"I figured that, but what position?"

"That was his position," Dale said, looking at Theo and Steve. "Now, are you two clear on what to do?"

"Wait for you guys to get his teammates outside, then we stick Karl," Theo said, holding up Karl's first injection."

Dale folded his arms. "As he starts to doze, he'll look drunk. You guys help him to the restroom—"

"Slip him out the back, we got it," Steve said. "What I want to know is how are you two going to get a first-string center and two offensive tackles to follow you outside so Theo and I can sneak Karl out?"

Earl grinned. "It's the old Rope-a-Dope move followed by a Sleepin' Beauty."

Steve shook his head. "I have no idea what that means."

"Never mind about that," Dale said and looked at his watch. "The Cheney's should be on stage by now, so we need to get on with it. You two go get in your positions."

Theo and Steve exchanged glances, then Steve said, "Go, dogs."

"Go, Dawgs," Earl echoed.

They strolled off toward the club, and Dale couldn't tell which one said it, but one of them whispered, "They're so weird."

Earl stuck fingers in his mouth and seemed to be exploring his gums. "My teeth feel soft."

"The side effects should be on the thin side by now." Dale opened the truck's cab and pulled out some rags that he dampened a few minutes ago.

"They are. Just a few odd sensations left." He ran a hand over his chest. "My nipples are sensitive."

Dale sighed. "Not necessary to share everything. Here." He handed the rags to Earl, who started wrapping them around his fists. He then stuffed one in his back pocket, eyeing his friend, who did not seem to be focused. "Look, Earl, you good to do this? I don't want to get my clock cleaned by some college footballers 'cause my partner was preoccupied with his nipples."

Earl's eyes turned steely. "I'm fine. And leave my nipples out of this."

"You brought 'em up." Dale turned and headed to the club.

"Just never felt like this before," Earl said, falling in line behind Dale. "Can't a man acknowledge a new sensation without judgment?"

Dale looked back. "No."

"Fine," Earl snapped as they reached the entrance.

God-awful thumping sounds escaped through the navy blue door. Before Dale could open it, it swung outward, and a thin male stumbled out, his thick wool beanie pulled down over his eyes, and his long scarf scrapped the ground. He exhaled, and a cloud of strawberry-smelling smoke filled Dale's nose. He moved past, taking another hit off his vape pen. Dale caught the door and stepped in. A few clouds hovered in the dim light, each one smelling of a different kind of berry.

"Nightclubs sure do smell pretty nowadays," Earl said.

Dale winced as they moved toward the thumping beat. "Music is still awful, though."

They reached the end of the entrance corridor and stood on the edge of the main room. Not as big as Dale had expected. A rectangularly shaped den with twenty or so very trendy looking tables and uncomfortable chairs. Less than half the seats were filled, some patrons looking at the stage, some not. A dozen young adults stood in front of the band, dancing, or flailing, or something or other. To either side, there were monitors showing images of wildlife predators taking down prey in all its gory details. Through the flashing lights and images, Dale tried to focus on the band members, but it was difficult to see through the dancers. The only thing he could determine was that Lana was not on stage.

Dale wasn't interested in the she-wolf at the moment. He wanted to locate Karl and, more important, Karl's teammates.

"Can I help you gentlemen with something?" said a voice at Dale's right.

Dale glanced over at a man who wore a baby blue tight-fitting tank top, the name of the club stenciled over his slightly puffed-out left pectoral. His arms were well toned but not like a nightclub bouncer would need, more like a yoga instructor.

Dale's first instinct was to say, *Go fuck yourself*, but then he felt Earl's hand on his shoulder, and his friend whispered, "Smile."

Forcing his lips to curl upward on either side of his face, Dale said, "We're fine."

Blue tank top moved away, but Dale could feel the man's eyes on him. Deciding not to give a jackalope's fart, he turned back to Earl. He was going to tell him to wait by the door but stopped short as he noticed Earl looking down at his chest, his fingertips making circles around his right nipple.

Dale slapped Earl's hand. "Stop that."

Earl folded his arms.

"Do you think you could stop touching yourself long enough to do this?"

"I'll do my part. You worry 'bout yours."

Dale had never felt this uncertain about Earl. Whenever they went into the fire, Earl was always in step with him, so much so it was as if they were one. But right now, Dale was feeling way out of sync with his only friend. At another time, in another setting, it was something they could discuss over beer and a macho helping of heartburn-inducing nachos. But at the moment, they were standing in a den of beasts and nachos were not on the menu.

"You say something about nachos?" Earl said.

"What? No."

"I swear you just said something about— Hey, that must be Karl's teammates." Earl pointed to a table that could barely contain the three massive young men. They each had a fore-arm on the table, which left room for little else.

"Stay here," Dale said. "I'll send them your way. Be ready."

"I'm ready," Earl said. "Think they serve nachos here?"

"Earl!"

"Sorry. I'm ready."

He didn't feel good about it, but he left Earl by the door, hoping he could stop focusing on nipples and nachos long enough to watch his back. Dale zigzagged between the tables, prepared to say "Excuse me" as he moved, but no one looked at him long enough for him to extend the gesture. Eyes were either focused on the unpleasant sounds extending outward from the stage or into a glowing handheld device.

As he approached a sizable portion of Fresno State's offen-sive line, he looked past them and glimpsed Karl huddled at the bar, his eyes locked on the stage. Steve and Theo were inching up on him, one at each side, getting into position. Karl didn't seem to notice, and if he did, Dale got the sense he wouldn't care. The young man seemed to be in another world, one run by a pack, and Dale got pissed off all over again for not noticing before how much hold the she-bitch had on him. He clenched a fist.

"Gentlemen," Dale said in a voice that even the beasts on stage could hear.

Three very beefy, pale, and round-eyed faces turned his way.

Dale pointed at Earl. "See that fella over there?"

There were two nods and one grunt.

Moving his focus from face to face, Dale said, "See now, he told me that your momma gives his cousin hand jobs while your sister blows his dad once on Tuesdays and twice on Sundays."

The three stared back at Dale as if he'd just asked them to solve a Chinese algebra problem.

After an excruciatingly long moment, the one in the middle tilted his head like a lost dog and said, "I don't have a sister."

"My cousin's back in Louisiana."

"His dad is overseas."

"I think you have the wrong table, sir."

Dale rolled his eyes. *Football players...* "Let me give this another go. That guy over there said the Bulldogs SUCK!"

The three behemoths got to their feet as if their chairs were on fire. They stepped past Dale in single file, looking like a mountain range on the move.

"Earl!" Dale shouted.

Earl stopped playing with his nipples long enough to look up and take in the avalanche coming his way. Faster than most would ever give Earl credit for, he spun around and headed for the parking lot.

Before he pursued, Dale looked at the bar and saw Steve

stick Karl in the neck. The freshman running back appeared angry and animated for a second, then began to slump. With no more time to see how that part of the plan was gonna play out, Dale turned away and headed for the door.

He just caught sight of the Fresno State linemen turning the outside corner of the nightclub, heading straight for the back parking lot. He hoped Earl was keeping at least a truck length ahead of them. In his strange, un-Earl-like state, his friend wasn't in the right place to take all three.

Luckily, the three players continued to walk single file as they marched toward the spot Dale suggested Earl lead them to. But as they approached the spot, they abruptly slowed, like a herd of buffalo nearing a canyon wall. Dale stepped to the side and peered around them, checking to see if Earl was still in front. He wasn't.

Damnit.

A fast scan revealed no sign of Earl, and Dale was forced to momentarily wonder if he could subdue all three. *Maybe,* he thought, but it would take luck, timing, and the reflexes of a much younger Dale.

Crap on a cracker.

Dale reached back and pulled out the rag from his ass pocket, but before he could do anything with it, Earl stepped out from behind a box truck and wrapped his hands around the football player in the caboose position. His left arm enveloped the player's chest while his right clamped hard over his face. The Bulldog bucked, and Earl's feet came off the ground for a second, but only a second, as the chloroform did its work. Earl staggered with the player, who tried one last time to reach around and grab his attacker. In another second, it was over, and Earl lay the big boy down on the asphalt, gently, but not silently.

His teammates turned around, catching sight of Earl setting their fellow bulldog's noggin on the ground. Their pale complexions turned red, hot, pissed. The two charged Earl like boulders in a rock slide. Earl brought his hands up, but not into fists. He held them out defensively, preparing to take the full force of their rage with the pleading palms of his hands. The first to reach Earl knocked his hands away like any good offensive linemen, then pushed him back against the nightclub wall. The impact was thunderous, and Dale imagined it could be felt on the inside.

As the second player neared, Dale realized that neither of the football players had noticed him. He stepped quickly, came up behind the one raising a fist to bring down on Earl's face, and slapped a cloth-covered hand over his mouth and nose. Dale hadn't really gotten a good hold of him before he'd done that, and it proved to be an instant mistake. The player spun back to face Dale, and their bellies smacked into one another. Dale managed to reposition the rag under the player's nose, but not before a fist hit him in the solar plexus. Dale clenched his teeth and absorbed the impact like a defenseless punching bag. Dale could see another blow coming, and he shifted to try and take the punch in another spot. No such luck. The player's fist plowed into Dale, but at least it wasn't nearly as powerful as the first. The chloroform was taking its sweet time, but the big man was feeling the effects. Another punch was thrown, but the player's knees buckled at the same time. He went limp. Dale lunged forward to catch him, curling his arms under his armpits as he fell. Just when Dale thought the kid was out of fight, he lurched from the neck up. Dale took the headbutt square on the forehead.

Sonofabitch.

Dale stepped back, watched the kid tumble to the asphalt, and blinked away the white stars floating in his vision. Indigestion, triggered by the blows to the belly, burned up his esophagus as if he'd eaten two roadside chili dogs with all the fixings doctors recommend not eating.

Earl somehow managed to subdue the remaining Bulldog and stepped over to Dale. He grinned. "You okay."

Dale steadied himself and glowered at Earl.

"It's that glass jaw, isn't it?"

"I took one to the forehead—and what the hell happened to plan A?"

"Plan A? Which one was that again."

"You lead them out back, keep their eyes on you, I sneak up from behind, take them down one at a time, quiet, stealthy."

"Oh yeah, I member that one now. That was a good one. We oughta do that next time."

Dale half sighed, half belched. "Old man, are you in there? Cuz I really need you now. We're 'bout t'pull into the station, and there ain't no time to change the destination."

Earl's voice deepened. "I'm fine. Just felt like a little warm-up tussle before the main event."

"Well, you really ought to let your partner know when you change things up."

"Of course, you're right," Earl said, glancing down at his pecs.

Red taillights illuminated their feet as Theo backed up his Prius. He parked it just a few feet away, and Dale could see Karl in the back, head resting on the window. Steve and Theo got out and met them at the first fallen Bulldog. In teams of two, they worked on getting the football players inside Theo's hybrid. At times, it was like trying to pull off a reverse C-section, but after a good ten minutes and Steve flashing his campus security badge twice—none looked at it too hard—to discourage passersby from getting involved, the deed was done. It wasn't pretty, and it was hard to tell where one lineman ended and another began.

"You two okay to get them into their rooms," Dale said.

"Yeah," Steve said. "I have a few off-duties, also on the alumni payroll, that are gonna meet us at the dorm. We should be okay."

"Alumni payroll," Theo said. "Why would the alumni—"

Dale saw a flash of panic on Steve's face. "Hey, there," Dale said, stepping forward and placing a distracting hand on Theo's shoulder. "I want to thank you for tonight. And apologies for anything I said that might have offended."

"Pretty much everything you say is offensive to somebody. But I don't care. This has been the most exciting thing that has ever happened to me. Are you sure you don't need more help? I could stay."

Dale shook his head. "This next part is gonna involve a lot of pain. Mostly Earl and mine, so best you and Steve not be here."

"Hey, guys," Steve said. "There are about twenty people in there. How are you gonna keep them out of harm's way?"

"I, uh, sort of did something about that," Theo interjected.

"What did you do?" Dale said.

"I kind of mentioned to someone inside that they should be ready to clear the place out fast because there might be a fight."

"Ah, Theo," Earl said.

"But that's it, I didn't mention the band or werewolves, nothing like that."

"Who did you tell?" Dale said.

"Puja, he's one of the owners. Wears a blue tank top, smells of ocean breeze body spray. I've known him for, like, ever. Almost nine months. He's completely trustworthy."

Dale shifted his gaze to Steve. "Is that true?"

Steve nodded. "Yes. He does smell like an ocean breeze."

Dale sighed. "Is he trustworthy?"

"Well," Steve said, "he is a Bulldog fan."

"That'll have ta do," Earl said. "Go, Dawgs."

"Oh, and she's here. Lana," Steve said. "I saw her step on

stage as we were taking Karl out the back."

"Good to know she showed," Earl said, glancing down. The hair on his arm had receded, but black stubble, three-days' beard growth, still plagued his forearm, around the elbow, and disappeared up his biceps. "I hate gettin' stood up."

After a quick goodbye, Theo and Steve headed back to campus in the filled-to-capacity Prius. If it had been an elevator, the cable would have snapped before they got out of the parking lot. Steve had given Dale the keys to his Camry, and the two road-weary truckers moved across the parking lot. Dale was feeling iffy about the rest of their plan, the iffiest part being his partner. He wondered what was going through his friend's head. He didn't have to wonder long.

"What do you think men have nipples for anyway?"

"Will you shut up about your nipples," Dale snapped.

"You do not have to bark at me. Save that tone for folks you don't like. Which seems to be everybody."

As they arrived at Steve's car, Dale took a deep breath and prepared a thoughtful response. "You're right. As for why men have nipples, it is a fascinating topic, one we should discuss at length at a different time and place, preferably over beers. Many, many beers."

"And nachos."

"Yes, I imagine nachos will be involved."

"I accept your apology, and don't think I missed the sarcasm neither."

I didn't apologize, but moving on. "Let's suit up."

Dale popped open the trunk, reached in, and handed Earl some shoulder pads.

"Why do we need all this," Earl said. "Thought we had immunity for a few hours?"

"We do," Dale said. "Immunity from being re-infected by a werewolf, not from being torn apart by one."

"Ah, excellent point."

"Ya, well, I get some wood on the ball every once in a while." Dale pulled out a bat, then slipped on a donut weight. He had pre-bent the silver steak knives he'd picked up at the pawn shop and wedged the handles between the weight and the bat. They stuck out from the wood at odd angels, creating a formidable mace, something Snake Plissken might fashion on the fly.

They squeezed their heads into practice helmets covered with stick marks, which wrapped around both sides, a variety of paint colors from other helmets decorating the front. Combining football, baseball, and even hockey equipment, Dale and Earl assembled athletic body armor that made them look like very confused sports enthusiasts. Because of the small crowd in the club, they'd decided to forgo bringing any firearms. It wouldn't do to help people by killing them with a stray bullet. After tucking away some of their more-conventional, silver-plated throwing blades, silver-spiked knuckle-busters, and the bowie knife Earl insisted on calling *Betsy*, Dale grabbed Earl's facemask. "Ready?"

"These pads are chaffing my—"

"Earl. Iffen you say nipples one more time. I swear t'God."

"Nevermind." Earl slung a hockey stick over his shoulder with one hand and patted his sheathed knife with the other. "Let's do this."

They headed to the back entrance, the one Theo and Steve had escaped from with Karl. They filed into a hallway with Dale on point. Closing the door behind them, Earl flipped the deadbolt. Even over the thumping music, Dale heard the bolt slide into place with a *thunk*.

Dale tapped the bathroom doors with the bat, signaling for Earl to make sure they were clear. Earl stepped inside each one to make sure nothing was going to spring out behind them. He returned to the hallway, threw Dale a nod, then the two moved forward into the nightclub.

They stepped into the main room. The air seemed thicker than before. Obviously, a smoke machine had been used in their absence, part of the stage show, but that wasn't it. The room now seemed heavy, foul, unclean, very much like Karl's dorm room.

Even though the two men were behemoths and looked as if they had just stepped off a *Mad Max* movie set, they garnered little notice. The dancers continued to gyrate, those at tables continued to stare at their handheld devices or the monitors around the stage. The bartender was busy asking female patrons what they wanted and ignoring males impatiently tapping credit cards on the bar. The only one who seemed to notice them was Blue Tank Top.

Dale expected him to come over, pull out a phone, and call the police, something. But he didn't. What he did do took Dale by surprise. Without any preamble, he leaned over to the table nearest him and whispered something to the couple sitting at it. The couple stood up fast and headed for the exit. Blue Tank Top repeated the process at the next table, then the next. Dale grinned at Earl. *Theo.*

With the place emptying out from the rear forward, Dale turned his focus to the stage. There were six figures arranged on the raised platform, two guitars, a bass, one keyboard, drums, and a she-bitch standing in front of it all. Her arm, the one they'd snapped a few hours back, didn't have any kind of a brace on it. She looked very much like she did when she sauntered out of Karl's bed, ungodly hairy, unkempt, and moving as if she didn't give a damn. Her wardrobe was straight out of Stevie Nick's playbook, and her hair found exotic ways to be visible, snaking out where the fabric parted and dangling like rainforest vines.

The rest of the Lon Cheney Juniors, four males and one female, pounded away on their instruments to the unsettling sounds of Lana's tortured vocals—a mishmash of words, no more than two or three at a time, and sounds, grunts, howls. It was like listening to one of Doctor Moreau's experiments trying to sing.

Dale moved to the edge of the dance floor. Dancers began to notice him and immediately left, where Blue Tank Top would then step in and show them the door. With only a few patrons left, Dale nodded to Earl, signaling that it was time for him to cover the front door. Dale then looked back at the stage, taking in the rest of the band. Only three others seemed to be as hairy as Lana; both guitarists and the female keyboard player had huge mutton chops and lion-like manes that ran down their backs and over their faces in places. But the drummer and the bass player were looking extremely human; one was even bald, a man in his early fifties.

Were there humans playing with these monsters? Time to find out. Dale picked up a chair and hurled in on stage. The music stopped. Beady sets of Lycan eyes turned toward Dale.

"Well, how do!" Dale shouted. "My names Dale, and that over there is my good friend, Earl. Say hi, Earl."

"Howdy," Earl said with a wave of his hockey stick.

"Now that introductions are out of the way," Dale continued, "I'd like to say that we are here to break up the band."

"That's right," Earl added. "We are your Yoko Ono!"

Dale looked over at Earl, eyebrows raised.

"Yeah, I'm sorry, Dale. That sounded way more intimidating in my head."

"Where...is...my...pet?" came a gravelly voice that seemed to have to fight to piece together each syllable.

"Well, slap my ass and call me Sally. It speaks, which is amazing, cuz you sure as hell can't sing," Earl said.

"Karl ain't yours no more," Dale said, locking eyes with Lana. "But you don't have to worry about that or anything else because you and yours ain't leaving this room."

Lana growled as her teeth grew and her claws descended from elongated fingertips.

Dale swung the bat in a half circle and slapped it into his free hand. "Now before we get started, is there anyone human up there? Best speak up now or die with the pack?"

The balding drummer stood up fast, with a hand raised. "Me!"

"Me, too!" The bass player dropped his instrument.

"Now, why in the world would you two... Don't you know what they are?" Earl said.

They both nodded.

"We just taught 'em to play, man, and helped them pretend to be human," said the bass player. "That's it."

"That's right," the drummer said. "We had nothing to do with any killings or eating people, man. Nothing at all."

"Well, ain't you two a couple of real saints," Earl said. "How about we put that on your tombstones. Didn't have nothing t'do with eating people."

"I got a family," the drummer said. "I just needed these gigs. Do you know how expensive braces are?"

Dale pointed the bat at the trembling bass player. "How 'bout you? You got a family?"

He shook his head. "But I really want one. You know, someday. Not soon, though, cuz I'm just doing me right now..."

Dale had a trailer full of loathing for the dark things that prayed on mankind in the night. He'd seen mothers torn to pieces while still holding their children, screaming, and those shrill sounds of terror were never far from his mind. But he had a special kind of disgust for humans that helped make it possible. Humans that sold out their own kind to creatures that thought of us as cattle.

But those assholes were not the mission. Saving Karl was.

"Get gone," Dale said. "Now."

There was a slight hesitation as the two musicians looked

at one another and then to the transforming figures on stage. During all the chit-chat, the werewolves had turned into their half-animal/half-human form, growling, and the two men seemed to be wondering if their non-human bandmates were going to let them leave. They could easily open them up or snap their necks as the men began to sidestep by, but they didn't. The beasts just met their eyes as they passed, almost like dogs watching their owners leave for the day.

When they stepped down onto the dance floor, they headed straight for the door, neither looking back. The bartender and Blue Tank Top—the only other humans still in the club—stood at the entrance to the tiny hallway that led to the front door.

Dale nodded at them and said, "Lock the door on your way out."

The sound of the front door shutting filtered onto the dance floor, weaving its way through the smoke drifting across the stage and mixed nicely with the tearing of clothes as the werewolves' human costumes fell away.

"And then there were four," Earl said. "Which ones you want?"

"I'll take the two ugly ones," Dale said.

"You gonna have to be a little more specific."

Lana stepped forward, claws raised, and through pointy teeth forced a single human word. "Die..."

"Well, that's enough chit-chat." Dale raised the bat and rushed the stage. The other female Lycan leaped. Dale tried to deflect the attack with the handle of the bat, but he didn't shift in time. Teeth sunk into one of the hockey gloves, and he felt the pressure on his hand as the creature bit deep. Just as the fangs penetrated the glove, one of Earl's throwing knives thumped into the creature's neck. The werewolf dropped at Dale's feet, hairy, clawed hands grasping at the knife handle. Dale wasted no time; he swung the bat down and buried two of the six-inch silver knife blades into the werewolf's skull, one through an eye socket, the other through the temple.

The beast writhed, legs kicking out, knocking over chairs. Dale put a boot on the thing's neck and pulled the bat free, making sure that the blades did more damage coming out than going in. He was going to bring the bat down again but saw two of the creatures bound in Earl's direction.

Earl hooked one around the belly with the hockey stick and used its own momentum to hurl it across the room. It flew as if it were part bird, crashing snout first into the bar. Liquor bottles crashed to the floor in a storm of broken glass and colorful liquids. The other werewolf hit Earl hard, and they went down in a tangle of hairy limbs, athletic equipment, and a cloud of Earl-spawned obscenities.

Dale had to make a quick decision. The werewolf that hit the bar was dazed, and he needed to capitalize on that, immediately. But that meant turning his back on Lana, still on the stage, and leaving Earl to wrestle on the dance floor. And Earl wasn't at his best on a dance floor—dancing or fighting on his back. Dale had to trust that his friend could handle it. He'd been in worse spots. They both had.

Pushing down with practiced force, Dale thrust his boot hard, hearing and feeling two cracks of bone. The beast at his feet stopped moving, and Dale moved toward the bar. The creature Earl had flung into the bar had just reached its feet when Dale hit it. It was a full helmet-to-helmet spearing tackle, the kind that now gets players thrown out of the game, fined, and suspended. Dale didn't know if it was the situation or the football equipment he was wearing that inspired his attack, but he instantly regretted it. There was a pop in his shoulder, searing pain in his neck, and worst of all, he'd dropped his bat. *Shit.*

Dale threw off his hockey gloves and brought up his fists, a silver-spiked knucklebuster on each. The werewolf, holding its side, cradling broken ribs, leaned against the bar. Dale smashed his right fist into the creature's head, aiming for an eye socket. Blood and hair flew as its head snapped to one side. Before Dale could follow with another blow, the beast lashed its clawed hand open-palmed at Dale's face. Dale bobbed to the side and almost avoided the attack, but its elongated fingers unintentionally clasped Dale's facemask. It immediately tightened its grip and pulled Dale in, a fish in a net.

The smell of whiskey, beer, and fruity-flavored margarita mix filled the shrinking space between them as Dale used his left fist to work on the creature's broken ribs. A clawed hand slashed across Dale's midsection, slicing through the baseball catcher chest guard, the tips of its claws grazing his flesh. Dale knew another slash at his midsection would cause the hoagie he'd had for dinner to spill out onto the barroom floor. He needed distance, now. Flipping off the chin strap, Dale thrust himself backward and violently pulled his head free of the helmet, leaving some skin and some precious follicles from his deteriorating hairline.

He nearly fell but steadied himself on the bar. He got a forearm up just in time to block the helmet swinging wildly at his head. It bounced off his arm just as Dale reached over the bar and grabbed the blender's pitcher, thick, heavy glass, and hurled it at the beast. It hit the creature directly on the snout. Dale heard teeth and bone crack as the heavy glass hit the floor. Dale took a second, stood up, and admired his handy work. That's when Lana hit him.

He took the blow on the side. Same side as his bad shoulder. Lana drove him up onto the bar, and he tumbled over it with all the grace a two-hundred-and-fifty-pound man clad in a mishmash of sports equipment could afford. He broke the fall with his face and good shoulder, now rapidly becoming his worse shoulder, and rolled up onto one knee faster than a jackrabbit with his tail on fire. He was immediately thankful that he hadn't stood up all the way, as Lana took a swipe at his head. He hunkered out of the way, but she nicked his ear, slicing through cartilage.

The bar creaked under the stress of Lana climbing on top, sounds that told Dale he had less than a second to find something useful. One hand searched the bar's interior while the other grasped at the ground pushing through wet, broken glass that cut into his fingers, and then... *Well, shit. Even a blind hog finds an acorn every once in a while.* Dale didn't question his luck; he just grasped the handle of his bat, brought it up as he stood, and used it to block Lana's next strike. She lashed out again, one foot on the bar, the other scratching the wood at its base. Dale blocked it as well, and this time he made sure her hand contacted a blade. It wasn't a perfect counter, but one of the silver knives extending from the bat slid across her wrist.

She howled as she fell off the bar, landing back on the outside. She slapped her hands down on the bar, met Dale's gaze, and roared. It was a predator's gesture of dominance, an attempt at intimidation. Dale was far from intimidated and only saw opportunity. He pushed forward through the rank breath soured by rage, and with a swift motion, he brought the bat down on Lana's hand, impaling the claws to the bar.

Her free hand immediately lashed forward at Dale's neck. He retreated out of the way but saw that the other werewolf, broken snout, cracked ribs, and bleeding from one eye, was coming over the bar. Dale had nowhere to move. Each direction had claws.

He looked over at Earl on the dance floor, who was on his back, a werewolf sitting on his belly, claws raised. Two of Earl's knives were buried it its shoulder, but it didn't seem to be slowing it down.

"Earl, would you stop playing with that one," Dale yelled. "I got a situation over here."

"I'm tusselin' as fast as I can," Earl yelled as the beast

swung at his head. Earl caught the hand, his fingers intertwined with hairy claws. It looked for a second like they were about to play a round of mercy, then the beast thrust its open mouth forward and bit into the football helmet's facemask and started thrashing like a shark tearing away a hunk of meat.

Dale was wondering if there was any way he could get over there to help when he caught sight of Betsy in Earl's free hand. Earl thrust the enormous bowie knife up with lightning speed. The beast stiffened, then trembled slightly as Earl forced the blade upward, entering under the jaw, traveling through the brain, and ascending through the top of the skull. The pointy half of Betsy stuck up out of the beast's broken skull like a unicorn's horn...although nowhere near as magical looking.

The werewolf with the broken snout landed on Dale's side of the bar, growling; glass cracked under its weight. Dale stepped back and felt Lana's free claw rake down his back. Not deep, but enough to leave scars. He moved forward again, getting out of reach, then grabbed a wine bottle off the self, a cheap chardonnay. He hurled it at the thing's chest. It thumped hard but didn't break until it hit the floor. It staggered the beast for a second, so Dale reached for another bottle, a George Dickel's No. 12, Tennessee Whiskey, 90% proof. He put that back reverently, then reached for another chardonnay.

The wine bottle crashed into the creature's head with a *thunk*. It brought a hairy hand to its head as it wobbled like the town drunk come Sunday morning. Dale glanced back at Earl to see how close his friend was to taking one of these things off his hands, but Earl was still on his back. His friend had pushed the dead beast off him but was now rocking back and forth like a turtle on its back. An enormous, overweight, covered-in-sports-equipment, very out-of-shape turtle.

"Earl!"

"I'm coming, goddammit," he shouted as he rolled, grunted, and rolled some more.

Lana had turned her attention to the knife pinning her to the bar and was pulling at the bat with her free hand. Somehow, she had pulled the weight loose from the bat, and the bent knives tumbled free onto the bar. Dale reached for the Louisville Slugger as she ripped the knife pinning her free with a howl. Before Dale could get a grip, Lana hurled the bat across the room.

Shit.

Lana jumped onto the bar, landing on all fours. Dale could feel the other one behind him. He was stuck between a rock and a bigger, meaner, uglier rock. And both rocks had claws. Dale eyed the silver knives on the bar but didn't think he could get to one before Lana was on him, so he reached for a bottle.

A chair shattered against the bar right next to where Lana crouched. All eyes, werewolf and human alike, turned toward Earl.

"Now, Dale, you ain't been flirtin' with my date, have you?" Earl stood on the edge of the dance floor.

"I'm ashamed to admit it. You know how I go for the exotic types."

Earl hurled another chair, this time at Lana's head. The beast moved, and the chair sailed over her and took out a set of trendy cocktail glasses. "I hope you've given your heart to Jesus, you egg-sucking bitch, 'cause your ass is mine."

Dale snatched two of the bent knives and held one in each hand. "I believe my friend asked you to dance."

She snapped at Dale, biting the air, saliva dripping on the bar, then turned back to Earl and launched. Lana bounded from one table to the next, then rose into the air and dived at Earl. Dale really wanted to watch and see how that would turn out, but he had his own hairy problem to deal with.

He whirled around to face the other werewolf. It rose up high, and with a bent and damaged snout, it bared its teeth.

182

And that's when Dale saw something in its eyes. Maybe this was the first time the creature had ever stood toe to toe with a human not paralyzed by shock and fear, or maybe this was the moment that occurs in most fights. The moment when one party realizes that things have gone south in a big way, and it was time to think of self-preservation, survival. Dale could see it in the thing's blood-soaked eyes. It was gonna bolt.

As if it hadn't sustained any wounds, the beast leaped over the bar, landing on a table, and lunged for the front entrance. *Damnit.*

Dale pushed himself over the bar as his new injuries combined with the thousands of miles already on his body all screamed in opposition. He landed not at all cat-like on the other side. The beast had tried to frog hop from table to table, as Lana had, but the second one gave way, and it fell to the floor, giving Dale just enough time to catch it. Dale tackled it from the back as it tried to get up, and it landed face first on the floor. It howled as Dale sat on its back, pinning it with all his weight. The beast whimpered under the sound of more of its ribs cracking, and it clawed toward the door only a few yards from freedom.

Dale didn't like having to put down a wounded animal, but since he was the one who had wounded it in the first place, he decided he was okay with it. He thrust the silver blades deep into the back of its skull and sat on it 'til it lay still.

Rolling off the thing, Dale took a deep breath and started the slow process of standing up. As he rose, he saw Earl make a deadly slash with Betsy. Stepping closer, Dale had to admire his friend's moves, thinking that for the first time since he'd known him he didn't look completely awkward on a dance floor. Although not graceful, and bleeding from both arms and his side, Earl was in his element, and Lana was in her final moments.

Obviously, with severed tendons, Lana dragged one leg,

and her right arm hung useless. Earl slammed her to the ground and grabbed hold of her scalp. The beast roared one final time as Earl stuck Betsy all the way through her neck, twisted, then sliced forward, her esophagus and other neck pipes exposed in a gaping wound. Earl snapped what was still clinging to her body and freed Lana's head. The husk fell forward with a splat.

Dale made his way through toppled tables and chairs.

"Enjoy the show?" Earl said, watching Dale approach.

"What can I say. I like watching you dance." Dale held out his hand. "Can I borrow that."

Earl flipped the knife around and handed over Betsy, handle out.

Dale flipped over Lana's dead, hairy, deformed body with his boot. He quickly slashed the belly and opened the cavity with the efficiency of a coroner. Finding the stomach, he opened it up and reached in, digging through the contents. It took a few seconds, but he found what he was looking for.

Standing back up, he slipped on his wedding ring. Normally, it was a little tight, but with the amount of crimson lubrication on Dale's hand, it slid into place nicely.

Earl glared at him.

"What?"

"You do know we're going to have words about this."

Dale sighed. "I figured, but later. We need to get gone."

In a few minutes, the four dead werewolves were going to revert to their natural born state, and to the outside world, it'd look like they'd just killed four people. Naked people, but still four people, and normal, nice, polite, non-werewolf-killin' society tended to frown on that.

"Agreed," Earl said. "I do not look good in an orange onesie."

Grabbing what equipment they brought, they moved to the rear exit. Before they got to the door, Dale noticed that, besides a large hockey stick, Earl held a plate of nachos in his right hand.

"Put the nachos down."

"They'll just go to waste."

"Earl!"

"I'm starving."

"Do they got meat on em?"

"No. Maybe. A little."

"Drop em'," Dale said, reaching the back door.

"I didn't have none."

Dale pushed the door open, looking back. "Is that nacho cheese on your lip?"

"Freeze assholes!" screamed one of the many police officers standing just outside the rear door, aiming their service revolvers at Dale. Patrol cars filled the back parking lot.

Earl dropped his nachos.

Part Seven – When Assholes Freeze, and
Emoticons

"Are your handcuffs chaffing you?"

"No, Earl, mine are downright comfortable. I'm thinking about getting a pair."

"Wow, you're just all kinds of sarcastic-grumpy tonight." Earl squatted on the curb, his knees up against his belly.

"I'm just trying to come up with something to reckon all this to the law. I don't want to call in any more favors. I'm runnin' low as it is."

"Hey, what do you think Blue Tank Top is over there saying to the cops?" Earl said.

The owner, Theo's friend, was speaking with the arresting officers using lots of hand gestures.

"Don't know, but he sure is expressive."

After a minute, the officers waved at two other cops, who bent down and helped Dale and Earl to their feet. Once up, they escorted them across the parking lot and to the nightclub's back entrance, where Theo's friend was giving his report.

"I'm sorry, fellas," said the Fresno Police officer who, only twenty minutes ago, held them at gunpoint. He undid the cuffs. "We got a call saying that two guys came in and attacked the band."

"Yes, but I told them what really happened," the owner, Puja, said, smiling with perfect white teeth.

"Ya did?" Earl scratched his head.

"Step this way," said the officer, gesturing inside the club.

Dale and Earl followed him inside with Puja one step behind.

Closing his eyes as they walked, Dale tried to come up with something that would explain why they just executed four people.

"I guess a big thank you is in order," the officer said.

Dale opened his eyes and looked down, expecting to see four naked, blood-covered, and very dead bodies littering the club. But instead...

"How they got in here is a mystery, but if you two hadn't put them down, don't know what could have happened."

Wolves. Four bloody wolves lay dead on the floor. And not half-human/half-canine, just average wolves.

"I was pretty sure these things were extinct in North America," the officer said.

"These ones sure are," Earl said, chuckling.

Looking at Earl, the cop didn't seem to get the joke.

"I mean, yeah," Earl said. "Me, too."

"We've had some people go missing in the last few weeks, kids mostly. One was the police chief's nephew."

"Sorry to hear that," Dale said.

The cop gestured toward the dance floor. "We found some jewelry and human remains in the one you opened up over there."

"And if it wasn't for these two gentlemen," Puja put a hand on Dale's shoulder, "we could have had another tragedy right here tonight."

"Yeah," the officer said, looking at Dale and Earl with a suspicious eye, the kind all good cops have. "Well, I got to go tell the chief what's happened here. I'm not looking forward to that. You two probably ought to get to the hospital. Your bleeding all over the floor."

"Will do, Sir," Earl said.

The officer stepped away, taking out his smartphone.

Dale and Earl looked at Puja, both trying to express gratitude without jumping up and down like school kids who just found out it's a snow day.

"I don't know what to say," Dale said.

Puja looked over at the cops, seemingly making sure they were out of earshot. He lowered his voice. "I was sick to death of those goddamn reverse werewolves squatting in my club. Not good for business when the band feeds on your patrons."

* * *

"A reverse werewolf," Earl said. "Wolves that turn into people. You ever heard of such a thing?"

Dale shook his head. "I'm definitely looking into it when I get the chance. Damn, we're so late. Still gotta pick up my cab, then drop this shit off."

"It's all right. I don't like San Francisco anyhow. Smells funny." Earl tossed their log book on the dash. "That sure was awful nice of Steve and Theo to pick us up at the E.R. Didn't want to slip out of town without saying bye," Earl said, looking at his stitches. "Hey, how many did you get?"

"Seventy-six, I think," Dale said.

"Ha! Eighty-four. I win."

"It's not really the kind of contest you want to win, Earl." Dale downshifted as they approached the Bay Area port.

"Don't care, I win. When we stop for coffee, you're buying."

"Ah, that reminds me. Are you gonna tell me what your usual drink is at Kandy's coffee shop, or am I gonna have to ask Miz Kandy herself."

"I'll make a deal with you, Romeo. I'll tell you about the drink if you tell me why you lied to your best friend about your wedding ring?"

"Mostly, to avoid this conversation."

"You can't possibly still have feelings for that woman. She's shot at you. Tried to stab you. Twice. Hell, she set your truck on fire."

"I don't expect you to understand foreplay. Our relationship is complicated."

"You call her Bitchzilla."

"And I do so with deep affection. She is the mother of my son."

"Dale, if you're gonna keep filling my tank with shit like that, we're gonna need to pull over."

Dale was quiet for a moment as he looked at the silver ring on his wedding finger. It didn't shine like the day he bought it. The sparkle was gone, and the engraving had faded. He removed it from his finger and stuck it in his vest pocket.

"I honestly don't know why I kept it, Earl. Maybe if I had any idea, I could move forward. Start something new. But maybe I just don't want to."

"It's much easier to gut monsters than to start all over again. Startin' from scratch is like changing churches. The end game is the same, but the rules are always a bit different."

"Amen brother," Dale said. "Speaking of new beginnings, it's your turn."

"My turn?"

"Your usual. What is it?"

Earl let out a long sigh, like someone who'd just realized they left their wallet at home after driving all the way to work. "Before I tell you, I would like a little credit for stepping outside the everyday habit we all get into of doing the same old things over and over."

"Oh, quit stalling. What the hell is it?"

"Fine," Earl barked. "It is a non-fat soy chai latté, and I find them delightful."

Dale sat for a moment trying to picture Earl drinking what... whatever the hell that was.

"What, no comment?" Earl said.

Dale shook his head slowly. "I'm speechless."

"Well, hell, if I'd have known it would have rendered ya speechless, I'd have started drinking them years ago."

Earl's phone chirped, indicating a new text. He pulled the smartphone from his pocket. "It's from Kandy. She says, heard from Karl today. He is doing fine. Thank you so much. I owe you big time, dot, dot, dot, heart emoticon. Oh yeah. What do you think it means?"

"I think it means she is grateful," Dale said.

"Well, I got that. I mean the heart emoticon. Women don't just go throwing no heart emoticons round to anybody."

Dale rolled his eyes. "I don't know. Why don't I find you a group of fourteen-year-old girls and you all can order up some of them chai lattes and talk about it."

"Oh!" Earl threw his hands in the air. "There it is. Judgment. You're just jealous that I got a sweetie, and you're a lonely, old sourpuss."

"Can it, Earl."

"Jelly, jelly."

"Swear to God, I will turn into oncoming traffic."

"You so jelly."

Serendipity

The tiny head covered in dirty blonde curls rolled across the wooden basement floor, leaving a trail of crimson. The small body it had once been attached to stood motionless, fangless, for what seemed an eternity.

Dale closed his eyes and rubbed his brow hard, but not hard enough to wash the scene from his mind's eye. It had been days since he'd been in that basement making heads roll, but the images were not fading. Not this time.

Now, hundreds of miles away, Dale opened his eyes, still not believing where he stood. *Why the hell did Earl want to meet here?* He scanned the street. What he saw made Dale wish he had a cigarette. He didn't smoke. Not in years. He just had the desire to blow smoke in people's faces. Not regular folk, just the uptight, narcissistic, well-t'do high society types that passed him on the street. Each one gave Dale that what-are-you-doing-here glare, followed by a curse dismissal and an upthrust chin. But what did he expect, standing on the sidewalk in Brentwood, an upscale neighborhood in Los Angeles filled with trendy shops, chic eateries, and exotic cafés? And not a decent cheeseburger for miles.

It was the kind of place that put Dale in a mood. If he hadn't already been in one.

Earl best have a good reason for dragging me out here on a Saturday.

He had been leaning on the wall outside a boutique that

sold...well, Dale didn't know what they sold, but one of the women who worked there, with hair of an unidentifiable color and enough makeup to shroud her true complexion in mystery, asked him not to stand in front of their window. She even offered him five whole American dollars to move.

Ten feet east of his previous position, and five dollars richer, Dale folded his arms and tried to disappear within the shadow of an overhang. His face sported what Earl called Dale's sourpuss expression, weathered, worn, tired, and yes, moody. Dale didn't feel up to whatever the hell Earl had in mind, but he had been unable to come up with a good excuse. Besides, he hadn't seen his friend in a week, and he hoped that when they finished with whatever they were doing here, they'd find a suitable watering hole and get a beer. Or two.

He didn't know how much he should tell Earl about his long, tense, exhausting trip. He didn't like including him when The Counsel was involved. He preferred to keep his friend as far away from those assholes as possible. But going down south alone was getting more and more dangerous, where it seemed to be all fang and no religion. At least not any religion Jesus would own up to. With Counsel resources, Dale had spent the last few days cleaning out a nest east of Shreveport. Dark, nasty, fouler than a room full of afterbirth. But that wasn't the worst of it. Not by a long shot.

They were kids. Goddamn kids.

Dale had always believed that the bloodsuckers didn't sire kids. Or maybe Dale just wanted to believe it. Wanted to believe that there was some honor amongst monsters. Some rules that they played by. But not anymore. Not after what he'd seen. Not after what he had to do.

Earl not being there was the right move. His stomach was large, but it wasn't made of the stuff required to do what needed to be done. The Native American tribe that adopted and raised Earl had given him the name Wide Shadow. It wasn't a light-headed comment on his weight but rather an endorsement of what the tribal elders had noticed about his character. Earl had the propensity to protect anyone smaller than himself, anyone that fell inside his shadow. Even at age eleven, Earl protected kids, standing up to bullies, even adults. He'd never stand by while a kid was being hurt, and he definitely didn't have what it took to take the head of a child, even if it just looked like a child. It would break him.

But Dale could handle it. At least, that is what he told himself. He closed his eyes again. The image of two young boys floating above the floorboards, there long toenails scraping the wood as they charged him, clawed hands outstretched. In his unescapable memory, he lifted the machete and...

Screeching tires ripped Dale from the past. A cherry red Mercedes Benz backed into a handicap spot at the curb. Dale glanced at the license. No handicap sticker.

A twentysomething male dressed like James Spader from *Pretty in Pink* threw open the door. He stood up, perfectly abled in his patent leather loafers, and undid the snaps on his driving gloves. He paused dramatically, as if someone was taking his picture.

"Hey," Dale said. "You know you're in a handicapped spot."

The young man, all of one hundred-and-sixty pounds, said, "It's fine. I'm not staying long." He removed his gloves.

"My mom lost both her legs overseas to a landmine."

Confusion swept over the man's face. "I beg your pardon?"

"Serving her country. Our country," Dale said. "And she never could understand why an able-bodied person like yourself would take a space that she so desperately needed."

The man smiled and stepped up onto the sidewalk. "Well, that is a sad story. But don't worry. There're no disabled veterans in Brentwood, for God's sake." The man casually chucked Dale on the shoulder. "They only have these spaces because of some silly law, I'm sure. It's an inconvenience, really."

An image of his fist connecting just under the man's jaw flashed through Dale's mind. A fountain of teeth and blood flew upward. The young man fell back, coming down on the trunk of his cherry red Benz, then his limp, bloodied body slid to the asphalt. Dale unclenched his jaw and grinned.

"Now, you have yourself a great day," the man said, and gave Dale a double finger-gun salute.

Dale took a deep breath and let it out slowly. Very slowly. Lately, he'd been trying really hard to stay relaxed. Trying to maintain his calm. Focus on his blood pressure. Not kill every asshole he meets. It was a work in progress. An uphill battle sometimes, but he was working on it. Earl was convinced that if Dale could learn to relax more, it might make him a better person. The only problem with that reasoning is that Dale didn't want to be a better person. Not in the least. The reasoning from his doctor during his last physical, however, did make an impression.

"Lower your blood pressure or you will have a stroke before you're fifty," he'd said after looking at Dale's blood work-up.

Dale felt healthier and meaner than ever. But the blood pressure and cholesterol medicine he'd just been put on told a different story.

"Hey, Walking Ugly!" Earl said from a few yards away.

Dale grinned at the sight of his friend. Earl dressed nicer than usual. No ball cap. His jeans didn't appear to have any holes and the shirt... Wow! The shirt... It had a collar, the buttons were buttoned, correctly, and it looked to have been ironed. Not recently, but sometime in the past year.

"Why you dressed for Sunday service?"

"I'm not." Earl gave Dale a quick once over, who wore his usual, jeans, t-shirt, and a leather vest. "My God, you look like ten miles of bad road. You even own a mirror? I told you to dress nice."

"Thought you were joking."

"Why would I joke about that?" Earl said. "Hell, Dale, I have broken appliances on my porch that listen better than you."

"We ain't seen each other in a week. Is it necessary to begin with insults?"

"Ain't necessary. It's just enjoyable is all," Earl said, then held his arms wide. "Would ya rather have a welcome back hug?"

"Hell, no." Dale chuckled and stepped away from the wall. "It's good to see you, Old Man."

Earl smiled. "Back atcha, Ugly."

"So why the hell are we in this seven-figure income bracket of a neighborhood?"

"It's a little surprise." Earl reached for the door just to the right of Dale, opened it, and gestured inside. "Age before beauty."

"You're older than me."

"Yeah, but I'm prettier."

Cautious and more than a little curious, Dale peeked inside. He gazed into a large lobby, with padded, high-backed chairs along the wall. They reminded Dale of barber chairs but much less utilitarian. A marble table stood in the middle with a centerpiece feature that was part gazebo, part rain forest, and part Egyptian obelisk. Water drizzled down the bronze sides, splashing onto exotic ferns before disappearing beneath an elaborate base.

Dale looked back at Earl with a raised eyebrow.

"Go on in," Earl said.

Dale didn't move.

"What's wrong," Earl said. "Ya scared?"

Dale looked back at Earl. "Think you can manipulate me that easy?"

"Heck, no, I got all kinds of respect for ya." Earl held the door a little wider. "*Baawk, baawk.*"

"You're juvenile." Dale glowered, then added, "And no-body really likes you."

Earl chuckled. "Everybody likes me." Then, not gently, Earl pushed Dale forward.

Dale's boots echoed on the polished marble tile as he fol-lowed Earl toward an elegantly polished concrete desk deco-rated in what the artist thought was Native American petro-glyphs. Most of them were, but as they neared the desk, Dale noted that the artist had mixed traditions, united markings from different regions and even continents.

On the wall behind the desk was a marquee with two-foot-tall capital letters that read, SERENDIPITY.

Before Dale could ask where the hell they were, a thin young man dressed in earth tones, wearing something that wasn't shorts or pants, and not really a skirt, but something that sort of encompassed all three of those garments, appeared next to them.

"Greetings, my new friends," the young man said. "Wel-come to Serendipity. My name is *Airb*. How may I serve you today?"

Earl stepped forward. "I called the other day about the certificate I won."

A smile so big it almost touched both of his ears grew aggressively on Airb's face. "Yes, of course. You must be Earl. I recognize that burly voice." He reached out as if to touch Earl's shoulder, but it fell short, and he just swished his hand through the air, like someone about to do a magic trick. Then he turned to Dale. "Oh, this must be the friend you mentioned." Airb looked Dale up and down. "Yes, I see what you mean, Earl." He waved his hands in front of Dale. "There is a lot of *teen-sion* here."

"You don't know the half of it, Herb," Earl said.

"Again, my name is *Airb*." He reached over and grabbed

several pieces of tan paper and held them out. "Why don't you look over these menus and decide what we will be doing today. I can personally recommend the Pacific Ocean Seaweed full body polish. It's an exfoliation experience that fights aging and dehydration while smoothing out those..." He zigzagged his finger, like Zorro, in front of Dale's face. "...uneven textures."

Dale didn't understand a thing Herb, or *Airb,* had just said. Hoping to reduce his confusion, he looked down at the menu printed on papyrus. The word Serendipity ran across the top, and just underneath, it said, *A Day Spa from the Ancients in the Modern World.*

Dale looked up at Earl. "No."

Earl nodded. "Yes."

"No," Dale insisted. "Sometimes I think your brain is rattlin' around up there like a BB in a boxcar."

Earl smiled at Airb. "Ah, Herb."

"It is pronounced, *Airb.*"

"Yeah, sorry. Can you maybe give me just a minute with my friend?"

Airb waved his hands. "Of course, that would be no problem whatsoever. Tell you what, while you decide what you want, I'll order up a couple of lemongrass mojitos. They are to die for."

"Sounds delightful," Earl said.

As Airb whooshed away, Dale said, "In the parade of bad ideas, this has to be your Grand Marshall. What're you thinking?"

"I'm thinking that a month ago my best friend came to me after seeing his doctor and asked me to help find some relaxing activities because if he didn't reduce his blood pressure, his head was gonna pop off."

"I meant like getting a beer, going fishing, deer hunting, human trafficker killin'. Y'know, fun stuff."

"Just give this place a try. A day spa is one of the most relaxing, rejuvenating, life-reaffirming experiences you can give yourself."

"Whose tree-hugging ass did you pull that from?"

"It's on the brochure."

Dale rolled his eyes.

"Look, while you were off the radar last week, Kandy and I went to a fundraiser for the Humane Society. We did the silent auction thing and won a couples' session at this place. Last day it's good is today, and Kandy had already made plans to go see her boy. So instead of letting this go to waste, I thought we'd do you and your blood pressure a favor and give it a go."

"Humane Society, huh?"

"Yeah, Kandy has a thing for dogs. She's always rescuing strays."

"Explains her interest in you."

"Hilarious," Earl said. "It's all paid for. It ain't gonna cost you nothin', which is right in your price range, you colossal cheapskate."

"I'm not cheap."

Earl scoffed. "You pinch pennies so tight you can hear honest Abe screaming from the grave."

Dale tried not to, but he chuckled.

"What do you say?" Earl said. "A couple of stress-free hours. No hitting or killing anything. No unnecessary brooding. An entire afternoon dedicated to relaxing. Call it a mini vacation from being you."

"I can't put my finger on it, but there's an insult in there somewhere."

"Yeah, probably." Earl put a hand on Dale's shoulder. "Come on, man, for your health."

Dale took a deep breath. He'd never say it out loud, but from the moment he'd stepped inside Serendipity, a wave of calm had been washing over him. Maybe it was the decor, something about the water rolling down the strange rainforest obelisk feature, or maybe there was something in the oxygenated air that beckoned him, but whatever it was, it had a soothing effect. But it wasn't the calming atmosphere trying to convince him to stay. That came from a darker place.

"If I stay, I don't want there to be a lot of strangers' hands on me," Dale said.

Earl nodded. "I am aware of your touching policy. I'll ask Herb to recommend activities that're low on the human contact side. Although it might do you some good to be slightly more touchable than a cactus covered in porcupines. But you do you. Does that mean we're staying?"

Dale looked past Earl as a tall man entered the lobby from the street. The angles on his square jaw were only sharper on his tight haircut. A navy-blue blazer not only covered a muscular body, but did a piss poor job of concealing the fact that he was armed.

"Yeah," Dale said, giving in to the familiar sensation, the one that always reached out from the dark. Sometimes coming to him in a dream, but more and more in the wake of day, an unmistakable feeling that he had arrived at a place he needed to be. "We're staying."

"Wow," Earl said. "Thought that be a lot harder."

"What can I say. You're as persuasive as future father-in-law with a shotgun."

Earl raised an eyebrow. "There's an insult in there somewhere."

"Probably."

Earl clapped his hands together. "Okay, you go pop a squat, and I'll go talk to Herb."

As Earl stepped over to the desk, Dale moved toward the chairs along the wall, keeping a vigilant eye on the man now moving about the perimeter of the lobby. He knew what the man was doing, had seen it many times before. This is what private security doing advance recon, securing the area for some muckety-muck, probably already en route, looked like. Dale had dealt with the type before, from those long-disbanded Blackwater assholes in the gulf to the much more dangerous Locknar in Eastern Europe. Never hard to spot, they were always more bravado than stealth.

Dale glanced over at Earl, who was talking to Airb like they were old pals. Dale was a bit jealous of Earl's ability to make friends with people he had nothing in common with. He took a deep breath, tried to remember why they were here. *Relax,* he told himself as he eyed the shoulder holster just visible under the man's jacket. Looked like a Glock 17, possibly fourth generation. Before he could stop himself, Dale ran the stats through his mind's eye. Semi-automatic, standard mag holds seventeen nine-millimeter, most likely non-standard with at least one back-up, could hold up to twenty-two, polymer frame, metal barrel and slide, fixed polymer combat-style sights... Dale closed his eyes and took a deep breath. *Relax, ya jackass,* he scolded himself. *Jesus, I'm wound tighter than a two-dollar watch.*

"Well, we're all set," Earl said, strolling back. "We're gonna start off with a sauna, then get a hot rock massage, and follow it up with a healing session of Reiki." Earl sat down. "It's all easy on the touchin' and is supposed to tune up our chakras. Not entirely sure what that is, but it does sound relaxing."

Dale leaned back, folded his arms. "I'm sure it will be," he said, maintaining a steady glare at the security pro canvassing the lobby.

"Serendipity?" Earl said, still holding the menu. "What is that exactly."

Dale rubbed his chin. "They're like happy accidents. Sort of when things happen by chance or without intention and they end up being uplifting or beneficial in some way."

"Kind of like karma?"

Dale shook his head. "No. Same ballpark. Different game."

Earl snapped his fingers. "Like last year. You broke down in Barstow, 'member? I came to get ya, and we bumped into that shithead who'd been hunting the working ladies at the chew n' chokes. 'Member?"

"Yeah, but what..."

"After we put him down, I found that unopened case of Kentucky straight bourbon in his cab. Now that was some Serendipity."

Dale chuckled. "No, that's just stealing from a dead ass-hole."

Earl folded his arms. "Well, I was certainly uplifted."

The security man exchanged a few words with Airb at his desk. Airb nodded several times, and Dale got the sense that their host felt unnerved. Airb reached under his desk, fiddled with something, then picked up his iPad and held it defensively against his chest. If Dale had to make a guess, he'd say that Airb had just switched off the security cameras.

The man with the square jaw turned away from Airb suddenly and moved toward the front door. He paused slightly, looking over in Dale and Earl's direction. Dale knew they were being sized up. Dale and Earl looked about as out of place as a couple of debutants in a trailer park, and Dale could sense the man calculating, processing the risk factor the two rednecks posed. He gave the square-jawed man his best go-fuck-yourself glare over a contradictory have-a-nice-day smile.

In the blink of an eye, Square-jaw decided that the two large yokels were not a threat and continued to the door.

"Hey, looky here." Earl pointed to the papyrus menu. "Says they have a lava rock you can rub on your elbows to make them smooth."

"Why would grown men need smooth elbows?"

"Don't know, just sounds nice," Earl said. "You know, it

ain't necessary for you to toss dog crap on everything."

"Sorry, force of habit."

"Like most of your habits, it ain't doing your blood pressure no favors," Earl said. "Speaking of bad habits, you speak to your ex-wife?"

Dale sighed. "Not in a spell. I'm trying to lower my blood pressure, not have an aneurysm."

"You need to find a less-irritable woman. Swear that ex of yours could start an argument in an empty house."

"I find her eccentricities charming."

"Eccen..." Earl shook his head. "The cheese done slid off that woman's cracker a long time ago."

"Can we steer clear of my love life?"

"Fine," Earl said. "You want to tell me what you were up to last week?"

The question brought an image to Dale's mind—a pile of severed heads, the heads of children, burnt to a crisp and smoldering in a church basement. "Not especially."

"Was it Counsel business?"

"Leave it be, Earl."

"Fine, keep your damn secrets," Earl said, sounding a little hurt. "There is something I'd like to talk to you about anyhow, if you have a minute."

"My ass and ears ain't goin' nowheres."

"Gentlemen," Airb said, strolling over. "I think we are ready for you now."

Dale took a deep breath as he stood.

Airb's face lit up. "Oh, Dale. Your vest is brilliant. Tell me the designer."

"Ah, Harley Davidson."

"I am not familiar with Mister Davidson's work, but I will Google him immediately."

Dale smiled. "Hey, Airb. You expecting some big shot company or something?"

The light seemed to fade from Airb's face. "Yes. State Senator Kavanaugh will be stopping by for a few hours." Airb turned and gestured for them to follow. He moved back to the front desk, where two lemongrass mojitos were waiting. He scooped them up and handed them to Dale and Earl. "You will love these. Organic and gluten-free."

Dale nodded. "Always a concern of mine."

Earl shot Dale a disapproving glare that very clearly said, *Be nice.*

"Anything to worry about," Dale said.

"Absolutely not, gentlemen."

"It's just you seemed a little anxious when his security man was here. You okay?" Dale brought the mint-flavored straw to his mouth but couldn't convince himself to take a sip.

Airb brought his hands together in front of himself, almost in prayer. "Thank you for asking. I am well." He lowered his voice. "Senator Kavanaugh is not my favorite client."

"Oh."

Airb leaned closer. "He is a little handsy with the staff. There have been complaints."

"Well," Earl said. "Just bounce his prissy, ass-grabbin' butt outta here next time."

Airb took a deep breath. "Wish that I could. Seriously. His family owns this building, and most of the block really. He's our landlord."

"Sorry to hear that. Must put a lot of pressure on you," Dale said.

"It is manageable," Airb said. "But this will not dampen your day. I promise you, Dale, when you leave Serendipity, you will be more relaxed than you have ever been before. How are the mojitos?"

"I can honestly say, it's like nothing I've ever tasted," Earl said.

"Excellent." Airb spun on a heel and glided toward a

rounded staircase. His strides were elegant, each step more graceful than the last. He approached the stairs, and his garment swayed in dramatic, choreographed motions, giving him the allure of a glamorous starlet from the 1940s. Even the light seemed to hit him in the most flattering way. He gestured up the stairs. "Gentlemen, walk this way."

Dale and Earl couldn't walk that way to save their lives. But they could follow, and that's what they did. Up the stairs and onto the second floor, which was decorated as serenely as the lobby. Artificial, but realistic, candlelight illuminated vegetation that seemed to be rooted in the walls. Artwork depicting natural settings felt very staged, but to Dale's mind relaxing.

Airb gestured to another small waiting area. "Hanna will be with you in a moment. Please enjoy the mojitos, and I will see you after, looking very relaxed, I'm sure."

Dale and Earl took seats. An all-female staff, as many as eight, wearing soft pink polo shirts with the Serenity logo on the pocket moved about their business. When one would pass by, they'd throw Dale and Earl a smile, and with each one, Dale felt a little more at ease.

Earl took a sip of his mojito and said, "Are you gonna try that, or are ya just gonna move it from hand to hand like a hot potato?"

Dale would kill for a beer right now. Didn't even have to be a good one. He brought the straw up to his lips and took a whiff. "Smells like it was poured into this glass via someone's unwashed ass crack."

Earl sighed and removed the straw from his mouth. "Well, that paints a picture. Thanks for that." He set his drink down on a table, where it would remain. "Kavanaugh," Earl said. "I don't follow politics much. But I've heard of him. Can't member what for though."

Dale folded his arms. "You might be remembering the

abductions."

"Could ya tickle my memory a bit?"

"'Bout five or six years ago, two of Kavanaugh's kids, the youngest, I think, a girl and a boy, both not quite ten, got snatched from their private school."

"Oh yeah." Earl's expression dulled as the dark details were clearly flooding back. "Yeah, that was awful. Never found them kids, did they?"

Dale shook his head. "FBI played it like a kidnapping. A wealthy family held for ransom. They went by the numbers, but they'd of had more luck finding a chicken with teeth than finding those kids."

"Jesus, I hate it when the dark touches the little ones," Earl said.

"I know you do," Dale said. "Kavanaugh got elected to the State Legislature the next year."

"He lost his kids, then went on the campaign trail?"

"We all grieve in our own way, I guess. Think he's the minority leader in the State Senate now, or some such..."

"Anyhows," Earl said. "I wanted to talk to you about something. Been thinking about this for a while now."

Before Earl could get any more out, Airb came back up the stairs with a man of Asian descent right on his heels. The man was well dressed, jacket, no tie, and an unusually robust black mustache. As they arrived on the second floor, his brown eyes moved from side to side, scanning the area. Dale figured that the honorable State Senator had arrived and the well-dressed mustache was securing the floor.

The security man followed Airb down the hall and into a room to the right. Before they came back out, Kavanaugh's entourage moved up the stairs. A man who Dale recognized, Kavanaugh, lead the small pack. Not a good-looking man, receding hairline, combover hair to hide the receding hairline, pointy cheekbones, and a lipless smile that only a mother would kiss, voluntarily. Following close behind Kavanaugh were a few more members of the security detail. The square-jawed one Dale had seen earlier and a tall, thin man. At least a foot taller than the others, the thin one had deceptively broad shoulders and wore his suit loosely, casting the illusion that he was thicker than he really was.

The last one up the stairs was bald, had scarcely noticeable white eyebrows, and black eyes. Dale thought they might have been colored contacts, but he couldn't imagine anyone choosing to have black pupils. Of course, he couldn't imagine why grown men wore man-buns, shaved their pubic hair, or bleached their assholes, so clearly the world wasn't restricted to the limited confines of his imagination.

When Kavanaugh stepped up onto the floor, he glanced at Dale and Earl, and for a split second, Dale thought the man might come over and offer to shake their hands, some sort of politician's reflex, campaigning autopilot that steered him toward potential new votes. But in the blink of an eye, Kavanaugh dismissed the two large bumkins as nobodies, not worth a moment of his time, and he turned to move down the hallway.

Earl leaned over to Dale. "Well, he's got all the warmth of a penguin's nut sack."

Dale smiled.

In the hall, an employee carrying a stack of towels tried not to make eye contact with the Senator, clearly wanting to avoid notice. She failed.

"Hey, sweety," Kavanaugh said to the employee, who abruptly stopped. He moved close to her. "Will you be taking care of me today?"

"Ah, no, I'm off in a few minutes." She continued walking.

"That's too bad," Kavanaugh said as he turned to watch her walk away, his lipless grin curling up his right cheek. When he finished staring at her ass, he happened to look Dale's way.

Dale locked gazes with the man and gave him a hard stare. The one he reserved for those who were approaching the line.

Kavanaugh's worm-like grin squirmed up the other side of his face as if to say, *What are you gonna do about it?*

"Steady," Earl whispered. "Today is about relaxation."

"I'm as chill as an igloo," Dale said.

Kavanaugh turned away and moved down the hall, where Airb stood in a doorway. Dale tried but couldn't take his eyes off him. There was something wrong with the man, or more to the point, the weight of him. Dale couldn't quite put his finger on it, but it was as if his shadow didn't fit the man's body. The darkness that trailed him was more than just his shadow.

The Senator gave Airb a little shove before stepping into his room. Dale watched until he was out of sight, and then felt the hair on the back of his neck stand up as Kavanaugh's shadow took an unnaturally long time to follow—a snake's tail lingering behind.

Raised voices grabbed Dale's attention. On the other side of the floor, several of the staff were arguing. Dale couldn't discern the details, but he could guess. None of the employees smiled anymore when they passed by. Their strides were stiff, uncomfortable. Dale glanced at Earl to see if he'd noted the change in tension since Kavanaugh's arrival and was surprised to see a stupid grin on his face.

When Dale realized that Earl was looking at Kavanaugh's security detail, all lingering in the hall deciding what positions to take, he deduced the source of Earl's amusement. "You're given 'em nicknames, ain't ya?"

Earl chuckled. "How'd you know?"

"Your juvenile amusements have been well established," Dale said. "Whatcha got so far?"

"See the one with the square haircut and right angles for a jaw? That there is Blockhead. Reminds me of the bad guys in Gumby."

Dale chuckled. "Very nice."

"The follicly-challenged one is Q-ball."

"Naturally."

"The tall one is Beanstalk."

"Classy, I like it."

"And the Asian fella is Jackie Chan."

"No, no," Dale said.

"Why not."

"Well, for one, that's not a nickname, it's just appropriation of someone else's name. And two, it's sort of racist."

"Oh, damn, you right." Earl brought a hand to his chin. "How about Won Ton."

"No."

"Egg Roll?"

"No," Dale repeated. "Get off Chinese food."

"How about... Sushi?"

"Earl..."

"It's not Chinese," Earl countered, then rubbed his belly. "Damn, now I'm hungry."

"Jesus." Dale shook his head.

"Okay, you think of one."

The security men broke apart in the hall, and the one still needing a nickname headed their way. Dale was impressed at the size of the man's facial hair, thick, well groomed, and reminded him of something you'd see in a stag film from a different era. Dale learned over toward Earl and whispered, "How 'bout Pornstache."

Earl let loose with laughter, then tried to swallow it as Pornstache approached. The Asian man took a position at the top of the stairs, and Dale tried to identify the weapon inside his jacket. Before he could, a petite gal with a warm smile said, "Morning gentleman. My name is Hanna, and I'll be taking care of you." Her shoulder-length, peach-colored hair twirled a bit as she held out a hand gesturing to the hall. "Would you follow me."

They stood, and as they moved toward the hall, Dale glanced over at Pornstache one last time, trying to get a look at his weapon. The slight bulge in his jacket didn't seem to fit any handgun outline Dale sorted through in his mind. Then he thought, *It couldn't be....no, it could be. Nunchucks. Who the hell carries nunchucks?*

"So, y'all..." Hanna said over her shoulder while leading them down the hall. "Uh, you two gentlemen are gonna start with the sauna." She stopped at a door, opened it, and gestured inside. "This will be your treatment room."

As Dale stepped in, he noted that their room was next to Kavanaugh's. The one Earl had dubbed Blockhead stood outside the door.

"There're some towels inside," Hanna said. "I'll give you gentlemen a few minutes to disrobe and put those on."

Earl paused in the doorway and lowered his voice. "Do we leave our skivvies on?"

Hanna lowered her voice. "However your most comfortable, Sir."

"I'm most comfortable in a bar, preferably with poor lighting and pool table in the back," Dale said.

"Dale," Earl snapped and pushed him inside. "You'll have to excuse my friend. First time at a spa."

Hanna smiled and kept her hushed tone. "It'll be our little secret."

Earl shuffled inside and picked up a towel. It fell open, soft, thick, but a tad on the small side. "Er," Earl said and patted his belly. "I'm gonna need to Velcro four or five of these together."

Hanna smiled, stepped to an all-white wardrobe, and opened the double doors. "We got you, sug...Sir." She gestured inside and added, "Bigger towels and robes are in here."

Dale raised an eyebrow suspiciously at Hanna, sensing she had a secret.

Earl stepped to the wardrobe and reached for the largest robe. "So what's it going to be, keepin' them BVDs, or are you doing the full monty?"

* * *

The smell of rich cedar in the sauna brought Dale back to when he was a boy, no more than twelve, hunting in the Smokey Mountains in Tennessee with just a bolt action .22 and a terrible tracking hound named Buck for company. That dog couldn't find a dead skunk if he'd been standing on it, but there never was a finer friend. Or more loyal. Not 'til Earl, anyway.

For the moment, Dale had forgotten the horrors of last week, and just about everything else that was itching him in hard to reach places. His muscles and joints were feeling the kind of relaxation only a bottle of top-shelf whiskey could bring. He had the urge to tell Earl right then and there what a great idea this was. But heaping praise and gratitude upon one another wasn't really the cornerstone of their relationship. Besides, Earl was breathing kind of funny.

"You all right?" Dale said. "You sound like a Peterbilt going uphill."

"Leave, my..." Earl took a deep breath. "...truck alone. Jesus, its hotter than two rats fucking in a wool sock in here."

Dale ran a towel over his head. "Why don't you step out. Ain't no shame in it."

"I'm no candy-ass. I can hang as long as you can," Earl said. "How long we been in here? Half hour?"

Dale smiled. "About ten minutes."

"Oh, Jesus, I'm gonna die."

"Just step out, Old Man," Dale said. "I'll catch up with ya."

"Fine," Earl said, slowly getting to his feet. He wobbled a bit, a mountain off balance, and braced himself on the wall. "I'll be right outside."

As Earl moved to the door, it opened abruptly. The security man, Q-Ball, stuck his hairless head inside. Dale felt his black eyes looking them over. He also felt his calm wither.

"Excuse me," Earl said, hoisting up his towel.

Q-Ball stood in the doorway, blocking Earl's exit. Earl looked back at Dale with a shrug, then back at Q-Ball. The security man slowly stepped from the doorway to let Earl pass. The pace at which he did this sent the very clear message, *I'm getting out of the way because I want to, not because you want me to.*

Jesus, Dale thought, gazing upward. *Just one asshole-free day. Is that too much to ask?*

After Earl stepped out, Q-Ball reappeared. "How about you?"

"How about me what?" Dale said.

"You gonna be much longer?"

"I'll be as long as I need to be," Dale said, stretching back onto the hot strips of cedar.

Q-Ball's eyes narrowed. "Maybe there is some other activity you could try now."

Dale had a *Go-fuck-yourself and the blind, deaf, dumb mule you rode in on* all loaded in the chamber and ready to fire, but before he did, the Senator stepped into the sauna.

"That's all right," he said, putting a hand on Q-Ball's shoulder.

He stepped inside and took a seat. Dale expected him to remove his robe, but it remained on as he leaned back onto a cedar bench. Dale hadn't spent a whole lot of time in saunas, but he was pretty sure that wearing a robe inside was odd. He did feel the need to inquire, but that would break the unwritten rule most men followed—no eye contact or meaningless chit-chat with strangers in elevators, public restrooms, and any place other males were in various stages of undress.

Instead, Dale leaned back and breathed in the warm, wet air, trying to relax, or at least look relaxed in the presence of someone he'd much rather put through a window. Sweat trickled down his face, and he kept his eyes shut. Silent minutes passed, and without Earl's constant talking and belabored breathing, his mind started to wonder. It didn't take long for it to wander to a church basement a few miles outside of Shreveport, and the images, never far from Dale's memory, began to rotate like a slide show. Two kids, a boy and a girl, dirty blond hair, clawing their way up a basement wall, dried blood under their nails. They hissed through tiny fangs just big enough to see in their young mouths. He swung his weapon.

Dale's eyes opened, and he sat up fast. Sweat stung the corners of his eyes, and he breathed deep. The hot air didn't feel good anymore. He glanced over at the Senator, who merely raised an eyebrow. Dale wiped the sweat from his head and tossed the towel on the bench. He sensed it landed kind of funny and he turned to look to make sure he hit the bench.

A chill moved over him. The towel had landed across the toes of a child.

Its feet were dirty and bare, standing on the very bench he was sitting. Dale turned slowly, looking up. The child, gaunt, skin pale, clothes threadbare, peered down. Dried blood covered the lower half of its face, and as its lips parted, small ivory fangs emerged.

"Hot enough for you," Kavanaugh said.

His voice made Dale jump, as he had forgotten the man was even there. He turned to the Senator, whose lipless grin looked like two dead worms smashed together.

"You don't look so good?" Kavanaugh said.

Dale turned back to where the child stood, but now found his towel laying on the bench touching only hot cedar. He reached over, grabbed it, and wiped his face.

Jesus, I'm losing my goddamn mind. In the past few days, his nightmares had become daymares, images flashing in his mind almost every time he closed his eyes. Now it seemed he no longer needed to shut his eyes. The ghosts from last week were just going to materialize whenever they goddamn pleased.

Dale stood and stepped to the exit. He pulled the door open and paused in the doorway, glancing back. The dead fanged child was back, sitting next to Kavanaugh. The grains in the cedar were just visible through its translucent form, now leaning its head on Kavanaugh. At the Senator's feet was another child, maybe female. It was hard to tell. It curled into a ball, knees to chest, clothes torn to shreds, head nearly bald, save for several hellish, greasy, and twisted strands. Burnt scalp peeled away from bone, some of it touching Kavanaugh's toes. The man, still in his robe, didn't seem to notice.

"Can you shut the door?" Kavanaugh said. "You're letting all the darkness out."

"What?" Dale said.

"The heat," Kavanaugh repeated, pointing at the door. "You're letting all the heat out."

"Yeah, right, sorry." Dale stumbled back and let go of the door, letting it shut slowly. "Fuck me," he mouthed softly.

Earl, extra-large robe cinched up, stood by a water cooler holding a full glass. "Hey, Dale, looky here," Earl said. "They got water with pieces of fruit in it. I don't know if it's on purpose, but it sure do taste..."

Dale turned to face Earl.

"What's wrong?" Earl said, taking a step toward Dale. "You look like a spider's ghost just crawled up your ass."

Dale wanted very much to come clean and say, *I'm seeing things, and hearing things, and oh yeah... The revenants of the thirteen vampire kids I chopped up and set on fire might have followed me back from Louisiana. Either that or I'm nuttier than a porta potty at a peanut festival.* Dale wiped his face with the towel, suddenly remembered what it had been touching a few moments ago, and tossed it to the floor.

"Hey, there's a towel bin right there." Earl pointed. "Just 'cause you're a redneck don't mean you gots to act like one."

Dale grabbed his robe off a hook. "You see anything odd since we been here?" He tightened up his rob and walked past Earl.

"How odd?" Earl said. "Like a chicken soup sandwich odd, or you and me at a day spa odd?"

Dale grimaced. "Let's just get this done," he said, moving past Earl.

Earl stepped in line behind him. "That is not a very relaxing mindset you got there."

When they got back to the room, they laid face down on the tables and waited for Hanna to start the next phase of their day spa treatments. Earl had left the door open, and Dale had a nice view into the hall as Kavanaugh passed by, heading back to his room, robe cinched up to the neck. And right behind him, weighing down the man's shadow, were the two children from the sauna. The clarity of the forms didn't fill out as before, but where there were dark, child-size silhouettes, Dale's recall filled in the details. *Why is this happening?* Dale had been haunted before, but not like this. Not so vividly.

"Is it usual for a State Congressmen, or what did you call him?" Earl said, pulling Dale from his thoughts.

"What?"

"Kavanaugh, what did you say he was?"

"Uh... Minority Senate Leader."

"Yeah, one of them. Is it normal for one of them to have one, two, three, four, bodyguards?"

Dale had wondered that, too, but with the images of dead kids using his head as their own personal amusement park, he hadn't put very much thought into it. "Can't say," Dale said.

"Maybe what happened to his family created some justifiable paranoia."

"Yeah, I guess a loss like that can do things to ya."

There was a knock at the door, and without waiting for a response, Hanna stepped in. "Are we all ready?"

"Ready as I'm gonna get," Dale said.

Hanna stepped over to Earl's table first, and Dale tilted his head to watch. She removed a towel from a medium-size tray, revealing a pile of glistening stones piled inside a granite bowl. Using a pair of tongs, Hanna retrieved a rock from the bowl and began placing them on Earl's back. Every time a stone touched Earl's skin, he made a yummy sound like the one he makes when biting into a chili dog.

"I'm happier than a dead pig in the sunshine. Dale, you're gonna love this."

Dale remained skeptical.

Before Hanna placed the final rock on Earl, he asked her a question. "You're not from here, are you?"

She paused and stiffened, and her voice became measured. "Yes, I am. I live just over the hill in Encino."

"Yeah, but that is not where your parents and kin are," Earl said.

"Don't put the girl on the spot," Dale said, having suspected the same thing.

"I'm guessing Alabama," Earl said.

Hanna slumped. "Close. Smyrna, Georgia. Please don't tell nobody."

"Your secret is safe with us," Earl said.

"Thank you," she said, her voice sounding natural. "First month out here, I couldn't get a job to save my life. You interview with a southern acescent and everyone thinks you're stupid and were raised in a trailer park."

As Earl and Hanna continued chit-chatting, Dale heard voices through the wall, slightly raised, but nothing alarming.

Sounded like Kavanaugh was living up to Airb's assessment.

When there was a break in the conversation, which revolved around Hanna trying to follow in Julia Roberts' Hollywood footsteps, also from Smyrna, Georgia, Earl asked, "So does the big shot Senator always travel with bodyguards?"

Hanna stepped over to Dale and placed a warm stone on his shoulder blade. "I don't know about everywhere, but he's always had 'em when he comes here."

"He must be scared of you then," Dale said.

Hanna laughed. "I s'pect not." She placed another stone, and then another.

The hot rocks seemed to melt into Dale's spine. They absorbed his tension like a sponge. Warmth moved down his length, a soothing tropical wave. Parts of his body he didn't even know he'd clenched were unclenching. He felt calm. Calmer than he'd been in years, and it was...well, unsettling.

"So how long have you two been together?" Hanna asked.

Dale groaned.

Earl laughed, then said, "Oh, I don't know. How long would you say it's been, Buttercup?"

"We are *not* together," Dale said, his calm audibly dissipating.

"There is no judgment here at Serendipity."

Earl chuckled enough that a few of his rocks fell out of place. "Naw," he said. "Me and Grumpalufagus over there are not a couple. We're here to work on his blood pressure and a few other of his irritable qualities."

Dale felt Hanna's hand on his back as she placed the last rock. "That is one nice friend you got there."

Dale tried not to smile. "Yeah, he's a peach."

"Now I need to visit some of our other guests." She gestured to a small stereo. "Would you like to listen to some music?"

"Got any Johnny Cash?" Earl said.

Hanna smiled big, showing teeth. "Back at my apartment. But here we have like Yanni, John Tesh, Enya... Honestly, I'd rather listen to fingernails on a chalkboard."

"Silence will be fine," Dale said.

"Good choice. Back in a bit." Hanna stepped out, closing the door behind her.

Earl didn't allow any silence. "So, like I started to say," Earl began. "There is something I've been meaning to ask you for a while now."

Dale took a deep breath and tried not to let Earl's voice disturb his calm. "What?"

"Well, we've been riding the same roads for a while now, and been off-and-on business associates to our mutual benefit, wouldn't you agree?"

"Are you referring to the trucking or the extracurriculars?"

"Well, both. The trucking mostly. The hell-beast wrasselin' is just plain fun."

There was a *thud* next door as if something had been knocked to the floor. A woman's voice, barely audible sounded. "I will...again...stop." Dale could detect irritation in the woman's voice, but not panic. From what he could tell, she was handling her business the best she could in a difficult situation.

"So, what I want to ask you is," Earl said. "How about we make our partnership a little more official?"

"Just cause it's legal now doesn't mean I'm gonna marry you, Sweetie."

"I was under the impression you didn't like jokes of that nature about our relationship."

Dale chuckled. "No, I just don't like it when *you* do it."

"Okay, you jackass," Earl said. "Serious now. I want to formalize this partnership. Create a company, Earl and Dale Trucking. Or E and D Trucking."

"What's wrong with Dale and Earl Trucking?"

"Well, I was just thinking it should be alphabetical."

"Ya idjit, that is—"

Something hit the wall, hard. Dale imagined one of the rolling carts sliding across the floor and smashing into a wall. There were now several women yelling. "I don't care who you are, you keep your hands to yourself."

Dale's calm was departing like Baptists leaving service on Superbowl Sunday.

"I even designed a logo." Earl reached around for his pocket but slapped nothing but towel. "And when I get near my britches, I'll show you."

"I think it's a fine idea," Dale said. "And I will give it some thought under one condition."

"Which is?"

"That if you tell the story of when you asked me to go into business with you, you say we were in a proper bar, had a pitcher of beer, shots of whiskey, and watched football."

"Okay," Earl said. "Who was playing?"

"LSU and Ol' Miss. And it went into overtime."

Earl chuckled. "Fine. You'll think on it."

"I said I would."

A door slammed, shaking the walls, and Dale distinctly heard a woman crying.

"Shit." Dale rolled over and sat up, the rocks sliding off his back. "You hearing this?"

Earl signed. "Yeah." He swiveled his head to look at Dale. "You're gonna go over there and cause a ruckus, aren't you?"

Dale reached for his pants. "You can tell?"

"You've got your ruckus face on. I know all your faces."

Dale stepped into his pants. "That is both sweet and un-settling."

Earl sat up, rocks hitting the floor. "Okay, before you go and destroy a perfectly good day spa, can I just ask you to consider that maybe this place can handle its business. They

don't need a big redneck smashing up the joint to help some
ladies that, in this day and age, probably won't appreciate our
kind of help anyhow."

A shout came from the other side of the wall. And Dale
definitely heard the word, *No!* Sounded like Hanna. "Think
that's our young peach getting squeezed."

"Well, she's a Johnny Cash fan from Georgia. The Senator might've bit off more than he can chew," Earl said.

Dale gave his friend a hard stare. "Earl, what if that was
one of your nieces over there?"

Earl threw his head back. "Oh, goddammit. What did you
have to go and say that for? Now I gots to go over there and
cause a ruckus, too. Shit."

Dale felt the thrill of blood-boiling tension. It coursed
through him like cocaine through an adrenalin junky. "Get
your pants on, Old Man."

It took near ninety seconds for Earl to get dressed, save
for one sock. Holding open his unworn sock, he bent down
and scooped up five of the stones and placed them inside. He
then tied a knot, sealing up the open end.

Dale had retrieved a stone as well. He cradled it in his right
hand. A little thick for skipping, but it felt warm and soothing.
On any given day, Dale's fist could feel like a brick to the face,
but with a large stone nestled under his fingers, it would feel
like a sledgehammer to the skull.

Earl met Dale at the door. He glanced back at the serene
little room they were leaving and sighed. "I really did hope
this would be good for you, Dale."

"I know ya did, Buddy." Dale met his friend's gaze. "And
I do appreciate it. Really. Now, let's go hit something."

A shrill scream boomed from the hallway. Dale pulled
the door open. Hanna, her shirt torn, stepped from the room
next door and dashed down the hall. Scanning the scene, he
noticed that Pornstache stood behind them in the little waiting

room at the top of the stairs, in the rear-guard position, his gaze cast down the staircase. The one Earl called Blockhead stood outside Kavanaugh's door about six feet away. No sign of Q-Ball and Beanstalk, and Dale surmised that they were inside with the honorable Statesman.

"Go deal with Pornstache," Dale said, "then come catch up with me."

"Roger Dodger." Earl stepped into the hall and moved toward the small waiting area. Dale lingered to see how well Earl handled Mr. Nunchucks, but he felt Blockhead's eyes on him, so he turned to face him. Dale used his body to obstruct Blockhead's view into the waiting area, and the two men just eyed one another. Behind Dale, sounds of a scuffle began, the details of which were loud enough to vaguely describe what was happening. A man grunted. A weapon whipped fast through the air, striking flesh. Dale winced a little, thinking he probably should have mentioned the nunchucks to Earl. A good friend surely would have.

There was another, deeper groan, then the sound of someone smashing through a piece of furniture. This got Blockhead's notice, and Dale smiled wide, trying to keep the big man in his place. Dale could see the debate in his eyes—should he help his coworker or should he maintain his post? Dale chose to make the decision for him.

As nonchalantly as a two-hundred-and-fifty-pound redneck in an upscale day spa could, Dale strolled toward the security man outside Kavanaugh's door.

Blockhead narrowed his gaze, understanding Dale's intention. When close enough, he placed a hand on Dale's shoulder. "Why don't you just mind your own business."

Dale smiled wider than he knew was possible. Even showed some teeth. Blockhead had already made two mistakes. The first, putting a hand on Dale. The second, and only slightly more important mistake, had to do with how the man had his weapon holstered, grip laying across his chest. It was clear that the hand on Dale's shoulder was the one he used to draw his weapon. *Big mistake.*

Normally, as a matter of honor and respect for his opponent, Dale waited until his adversary made the first aggressive move. But any man who would stand by as another man mistreated a lady had no honor and certainly didn't deserve Dale's respect.

As quick as lightning to a rod, Dale's left arm shot upward and wrapped up the man's outstretched limb. Dale locked the man's elbow and held his wrist inside his armpit. In a simultaneousness action, Dale brought up his right fist, which cradled the warm stone. Connecting under the jaw, the man's head snapped back like a PEZ dispenser.

Dale pulled Blockhead toward him as he followed through with his blow, trying to avoid the back of the man's head hitting the door. No need to alert Q-ball and Beanstalk about what was happening in the hall.

As Dale pulled him away from the door, still holding his gun hand tightly, he noticed the other hand making an attempt at his sidearm. With Blockhead's oversized physique, the effort was awkward and clearly not gonna work, like a fat man trying to wash his back. But Dale admired the man's die-hard spirit.

To their right was a shelf nook about waist high in the wall displaying a tiny Keebler Elf-sized Zen garden. It was beautiful and serene, and Dale smashed the man's head right into it. Blockhead's mouth hit the edge of the nook with a horrific crack. As the man slid against the wall, legs folding back, Dale noticed several teeth laying on the tiny shelf. He picked up the marble-sized molars and looked at the tiny Zen garden now slightly askew. He straightened it, then took a moment to carefully place the teeth in the sand, making sure to arrange them in a manner that complemented the natural flow of the peaceful pattern. He stepped back and admired his work, feeling very Zen.

Dale bent over the body, part of which was propped up by the wall, making it look like he still had some fight in him. He checked the man's pulse, found it, then pushed the rest of him onto the floor. Retrieving the man's sidearm, Dale removed the ammo and dropped it and the clip in a vase. When he turned back around, Earl was heading his way. In the distance, Dale could see a pair of legs sprawled out on the ground behind him. Earl wiped his lip, smearing blood on his chin.

"Did he get one in?" Dale said.

"He sure as hell did. The dang fool had nunchucks. Who the hell carries nunchucks? The world ain't a Kung Fu movie."

"You shouldn't be so critical," Dale said. "You brought a sock filled with rocks."

Earl smiled, then slapped the weapon he'd learn to make as a kid into his hand. A stone that apparently had been working its way through a hole during the fight slipped out and tumbled to the floor. "Damn, I need new socks."

Dale chuckled. "That's about as hillbilly as it gets."

"Gentlemen, please," Airb said, coming down the hall. "Please, stop."

Dale moved past Airb, heading for Kavanaugh's door. "We just want to have a conversation with the man. Express our opinion on how one should treat a lady, then we'll get out of your hair."

Airb gestured to the bodies on the floor. "Like you did with them?"

"We'll, they were rude," Dale said.

Earl wiped his lip. "Awful rude."

Airb opened his mouth to protest, but a blood-curdling scream boomed from inside the room.

Earl looked at Airb. "What do ya say, Herb?"

Airb looked flustered, then nodded. "Okay. Kick his ass!"

Dale pushed the door wide open. He only had a split second to take in the room. Twice the size of the one he'd been in, it had a tinted window facing the street that was large enough to put a piano through. Q-Ball stood on the far side of the room, close to the window, his right hand held the wrist of a staff member, her shirt violently untucked and a palpable look of terror on her face. Kavanaugh, wearing only a towel, secured her other wrist, and in his free hand, he held a small blade. But it wasn't the dainty knife that struck Dale like a hammer. It was the burned brand mark in the center of Kavanaugh's chest that gave Dale a near-fatal momentary pause.

Beanstalk, a good foot-and-a-half taller than Dale, came at him from the side. Dale saw the muzzle of the Colt Close Quarter Battle Pistol moving toward his head. Dale hunkered low and moved into Beanstalk. Due to the man's stature, it didn't take much effort to come underneath it. Dale grasped his gun hand and redirected the muzzle toward the ceiling just as he fired.

The bullet disappeared into the ceiling.

Dale wanted to relieve the man of the pistol before he got off another shot, but Beanstalk's grip was ironclad. Using both hands, Dale forced the pistol down and toward the window. While punching Dale in the gut, Beanstalk fired two more times, sending both shots through the glass. The window didn't shatter, but a white web of cracks spun from the center outward.

When the first shot rang out, Kavanaugh released the staff member, as did Q-Ball. She ran screaming from the room, and Kavanaugh tried to follow. He dropping his blade onto the massage table and tucked in behind her. Earl moved into his path, and the frail, near-naked man bounced off Earl's belly and landed under the cracked window. And that's when Dale saw them again.

The kids, or revenants of the kids, were in the room as well. They stayed close to Kavanaugh, who didn't seem to notice. As the wheels started to turn in his head, Beanstalk's fist connected with Dale's chest. Even wincing in pain, an image from last week flashed in his mind. The faces of the two kids were screaming at him, fangs bared, as Dale removed their heads. *Why the hell were they haunting him here? And why just the two of them?* He'd put down a dozen of the creatures in that church basement.

Trying to put the pieces together while fighting with a gun-wielding giant was not yielding the desired results. His chest ached, and his back muscles felt as if they were fighting uphill. Dale decided to focus on the physical. He drove the pistol back into the man's lean gut, and if he had a mind to pull the trigger, he'd shoot himself in the stomach. The realization flashed over Beanstalk's face, and Dale took his momentary indecision to pry two of his fingers from the grip. With an upward twist, Dale snapped them like twigs.

Beanstalk dropped the gun and took another swing at Dale's gut but missed. Dale wanted to follow up the finger-snappin' with a headbutt, but he'd need stilts for that. He kicked the pistol under the massage table as Beanstalk went into his jacket with his good hand.

Dale figure it was a knife and probably in no way dainty like the one Kavanaugh brought. Dale reached back to the massage table to grasp the little blade that Kavanaugh had been only moments away from abusing a staff member with. As his finger brushed the handle, he caught sight of Earl, rock in hand, releasing a well-wound-up pitch. The rock hit Q-ball's forehead so hard that he dropped like a battleship anchor.

"Q-ball in the corner pocket," Earl called out.

Beanstalk fumbled in his jacket, making it obvious that the hand he used wasn't his good hand. This gave Dale a second to reach back further and get a hold of Kavanaugh's abandoned weapon. As his fingers enveloped the handle, he knew immediately that something was wrong. Dale held the object in front of his face. *Oh, shit.* Not a knife. Not a dainty knife. Not any kind of a knife.

Kavanaugh had brought a chrome dildo fashioned to look like a knife.

Jesus, what a sleazeball.

Dale turned back to Beanstalk just in time to see that the NBA-sized bodyguard had not brought a dido, but a KA-BAR Marine issue 7-inch, straight-edge blade. It didn't take a weapons expert to conclude that in a knife fight, a KA-BAR beats a dildo every time. He raised his forearm to fend off the attack from up on high. The blade cut deep into the underside of his arm, and Dale felt it hit bone.

Not waiting for Beanstalk to open up his arm with a twist or a downward slash, Dale bulldozed forward and seized the forearm of Beanstalk's knife hand. Holding it firm, he pushed the man back against the wall and lashed out with the only weapon in his hand. He thrust the dildo like a blade into the man's open mouth.

Beanstalk made gurgling, choking sounds as Dale pushed it forward. At some point, a button had been depressed, and a soft hum floated up from the tiny device as it started to vibrate. Dale thrust a knee upward, hard. Unfortunately, his target was too high, and he missed by a foot. Feeling the KA-BAR scraping his ulna, Dale decided it was time to phone a friend.

"Earl!"

Q-ball was trying to get up. Earl kicked him hard in the face, then yelled over his shoulder, "What?"

"Can you give me a hand with Slender Man here?"

Earl turned around. "Who?"

"Earl!"

Earl took two quick steps toward Beanstalk and swung

the sock at his outside knee. There was a sickening crack, and Beanstalk shrieked in pain, then started to fall.

"Timber!" Earl cried.

For good measure, Dale smashed him in the face as he fell. The tree of a man hit the floor hard, his branches spread out like scattered driftwood.

"Hey," Earl said. "Don't go doing that."

"What?"

"Change nicknames in the middle of a fight," Earl said. "It's confusin'."

"Sorry." Dale grabbed the vibrating dildo out of Beanstalk's throat. He didn't want the man to choke while unconscious. Good or bad, no man wants their mamma to know that that's how they went out, choked to death by a novelty dildo.

Kavanaugh suddenly got to his feet and dashed for the door. Earl reached across the table, grabbed what remained of his hair, and yanked him back. He cried out in pain as Earl pulled him over the table. He fell over the other side but remained on his feet.

The two revenants moved toward Kavanaugh, the girl sitting down by his feet. They both looked up at Dale, eyes trying to deliver a message. One he finally received.

"Oh shit," Dale said. "I'm so stupid."

Earl looked confused. "Not that I disagree, but why are ya stupid?"

"They're not haunting me." Dale threw the dildo at Kavanaugh's chest. "They're haunting this pile of shit."

Dale spun on his boot heel in frustration, then reached for a hand towel. He wrapped it around his wounded forearm. Surprisingly, there wasn't much blood, and Dale knew that was a good sign. He bent down and scooped up the KA-BAR from Beanstalk's unconscious grip.

"Not at all sure what my friend is talking about," Earl said, turning on Kavanaugh. "But I'd like to talk to you about how to treat a lady. No means no, asshole. Ain't you got no family learnin'?"

"Forget that," Dale said, pushing Kavanaugh up against the massage table. He took the KA-BAR and put the tip into the brand on his chest. "I want to know about this, and where they are?"

Kavanaugh looked perplexed. "You know what this mark means?" He looked Dale up and down, and even in his less-than-advantageous position, he managed to sound superior. "You?"

"I know all about that ancient glory hole of fangs," Dale said.

Kavanaugh's brow hardened. "Then you know how fucked you are."

"Not as fucked as you, if you don't start talking." Dale pushed the knife in.

Kavanaugh squealed, and a thin stream of blood fell from his chest.

"Whooh." Earl clasped his hand on Dale's knife hand, pulling the blade away from Kavanaugh's flesh. "Look, we came in to protect the ladies and teach these Cretans what happens when you disrespect a woman. Now I think they've—"

Dale wrenched his hand free. "It ain't about that no more."

"Well, enlighten me."

Kavanaugh chortled like a schoolgirl with a secret.

Dale thrust the knife down, stabbing the massage table, missing Kavanaugh by an inch. He then jabbed his index finger at the now bloodied brand. "See that?"

Earl eyed the mark burned deep into Kavanaugh's chest. About the size of a silver dollar, the details on its lower half were obscured by crimson, but above the etching was clear. The top of an Egyptian ankh rising up from something. "It's not to my tastes," Earl said, "But what's it mean?"

"It's The Flesh Talisman. It means he is loyal to them."

"And *they* are loyal to me," Kavanaugh added.

"Loyal t'who...?" Earl said.

"An ancient coterie of bloodsuckers that's known for culti-vating powerful humans." Dale scowled at Kavanaugh. "Or humans seeking power."

"Ancient cota-what..." Earl muttered. "I never heard of 'em."

"Its old news," Dale said. "Ben Franklin and the other founding fathers chased them all back to Europe. Last eyes on 'em had them hunkered down in hidey-holes throughout Mesopotamia."

Earl muttered. "Messama-where."

Kavanaugh's sick, worm-like grin returned. "You've no idea what's coming."

Dale had a pretty good idea. But Earl wasn't grasping the situation. He hadn't had the benefit of Dale's training, the dis-illusionment of knowing and seeing way too much. Dale needed his friend to catch up, or at least get a taste of what they were dealing with.

"You know how a human can earn this mark," Dale said, pointing at The Flesh Talisman.

Earl shrugged.

"It's earned by showing their undying loyalty and commit-ment. A human wanting this mark makes an offering," Dale said. "An offering of children."

Earl's face turned pale; his features dropped like stones.

"And those aspiring to demonstrate their unbound de-votion, attaining the highest level of allegiance... They offer their *own* children."

"He let them feed on his own flesh and blood?" Earl said, his voice stunned.

Dale glared at Kavanaugh and thumped his chest. "They can feed on them, bleed them for fun, or even sicker, they can turn them."

"No," Earl mouthed. "They don't do that."

"Oh, yeah. Ask me how I know," Dale said. "Because they did turn them. Then for whatever reason, they dumped 'em in Louisiana, where they started hunting and turning other kids. Over a dozen by the time I got to them." Dale took a step back. "There was preacher, a good man. He thought they were just sick. So he hid them in his church basement, not knowing what they were. The kids fed on their parents and the entire congregation. They turned a little town into hell on earth." Dale thrust a finger at Kavanaugh's face. "And it's all 'cause of this mangy piece of demon fuck."

Kavanaugh sat up, looking embolden. "Those were my kids to do with what I want." He spit in Dale's face. "You had no business interfering. They were stepping stones to my greater glory."

It took everything Dale had not to gut the man right then and there. But he knew he was worth more alive than dead. Kavanaugh had been sleeping with the enemy. He knew where they were.

Dale wiped the saliva from his cheek, then looked over at his friend to see how he was taking it and immediately knew something was wrong. Earl's pale expression changed to one of pure rage. It was a face he hadn't really seen before. Not like this.

"Earl?"

Before Dale could stop him, Earl's right hand clamped around Kavanaugh's throat. Dale reached for Earl's wrist, but his friend was already on the move. Earl lifted the politician off the floor by the neck and screamed, "Your own children!" He took three fast, leaping steps.

"Earl, no!"

Earl grunted as he shotputted the man through the window. Broken glass crashed all around, nearly drowning out the sounds of Kavanaugh's screams. The screaming stopped suddenly with a loud *thud*, followed by a car alarm.

Dale stepped over to the window. Kavanaugh had sailed clear over the sidewalk and landed, not at all gently, on a familiar cherry red Mercedes. Earl had been an all-state shot-putter in high school, and Dale had always admired the skill he demonstrated when tossing folks.

"Huh," Dale said, staring down.

Earl backed from the window. "Oh, damn, what did I just do?"

"Well, you easily scored a ten for distance, that's for damn sure."

"Gentlemen, where is the Senator?" Airb said, standing in the doorway.

Earl pointed out the window.

Airb sashayed over and peered down. "Oh, my, my, my. Is he dead?"

Dale leaned out the window a bit and took a hard look. "No. He's still breathing."

Kavanaugh moaned and tried to sit up on the car roof that now had a massive dent in the shape of his ass. He slumped back, beginning to sob.

"Jesus, what's wrong with me?" Earl muttered, his hands shaking.

A small crowd began to gather, including the twenty-something James Spader look-alike running up from a nearby shop. He yelled something, then grabbed handfuls of his own hair in frustration.

"Now, that, that right there." Dale chuckled. "That is some real serendipity."

"I don't know what in the hell came over me," Earl said.

Still looking out the window, Dale reached back and put a hand on Earl's shoulder. "Your heart was in the right place. Don't look like Kavanaugh's leg is though. That is definitely broke."

"Jesus, I'm going to jail."

"Don't fret, Earl. It's not the first time you've tossed an asshole out a window."

"I know, but that was my first Senator."

Dale chuckled. "You're moving up in the world. Confronting a higher class of asshole."

Earl turned on Dale. "You're making jokes! I don't think this is funny. This is serious."

"It is serious," Dale said calmly. "But not the kind of serious you're thinking. The law is not what we need to worry about."

"What then?"

Dale tried to think of an answer that would be quick and satisfy, but none came. He turned away from the window, and his eyes fell on the two revenants of Kavanaugh's children. They stood side by side, no longer in tattered clothes, no more burned flesh. They looked like they did the day they disappeared: clean private school uniforms, freshly washed skin, and immaculately arranged hair, the hallmark of a doting mother.

"Hey, Dale," Earl said softly.

"Yeah."

"You see two kids standing there?"

"Yep."

The girl put her hand inside her brother's, and they stared up at Dale. He felt their piercing blue eyes, cold and warm at the same time. It seemed for a moment they might speak, but then they turned and walked from the room, the girl leading the boy as if they were going to school.

"Were they...uh," Earl stammered. "I mean, was that...?"

"Yeah," Dale said. "I think so."

Earl sighed, hands still shaking. "Well, I don't mind saying my butt just puckered right the hell up."

"You need a beer?"

"Like never before."

Dale turned to Airb, who still stared down at the carnage. "Hey, Airb, you got a back exit?"

Airb turned around slowly, his face pale, stunned. "We are not covered for this."

"Trust me, you'll be compensated," Dale said. "Back exit, ya got one?"

"Yes, take the emergency stairs to the right. It takes you to the rear parking."

"Thanks, Airb," Dale said, pushing Earl to the door. "And hey, you and Earl sure were right."

Confusion flashed over Airb's face. "About?"

"Day spas. They're awful relaxing. I ain't felt this good in a long, long time."

Airb raised his hand, looking as if he was going to wave goodbye, but it remained static and seemed as stunned and shellshocked as the rest of his body. "Please give us a favorable review on Yelp."

* * *

Three hours, thirteen stitches, and a fistful of antibiotics later, Dale sat at a table in a dark corner of a poorly lit bar. It was the kind of place where Johnny Cash could be heard singing on the jukebox about walking the line over the soft clack of a pool stick tapping the cue ball. The waitresses didn't mind customers looking with their eyes, but if they looked with their hands, they'd find a beer stein cracked against their skulls and a shotgun escort from the premises. Small objects, bits of glass, teeth, broke under boots stepping on the floor discolored in chaotic Rorschach splotches, stains that were not the products of spilled drinks. To Dale, this was a place of comfort, relaxation, a familiar place. And not a man-bun in sight.

Carrying a full pitcher and two shots of whiskey, Earl joined Dale at the table. He slid his friend one of the shot glasses. In unison, the men raised their whiskey. "To Kavanaugh's little ones," Earl said. "God rest their souls."

"Amen."

The two men drank and returned the empties to the table. The shot of whiskey was calming, but Dale's head still spun, trying to reckon all the events that had to happen to put him where he found himself today. Earl had to fall for an animal-loving woman named Kandy. Kandy with a K. She had to drag him to a silent fundraising auction, where they won a gift certificate to a particular day spa with a specific expiration date, causing Earl to bring Dale instead of Kandy. Dale stopped short of wondering about all the events that led to Kandy being single, a single mom, and unavailable for a free couple's session at Serendipity. But he did resolve that if he ever met the someone in charge of arranging all these circumstances, they were definitely gonna have words.

A TV behind the bar ran continued coverage of the biggest local news story of the day. The TV was muted, but neither of them needed sound to follow the story. They had heard it several times on the radio over the past few hours.

State Senator Frederick H. K. Kavanaugh, while undergoing physical therapy at a spa in Brentwood, was seriously injured when he accidentally fell from a second-story window. A spokesman for Kavanaugh said that, since the tragic loss of his two children, he has been plagued with chronic dizzy spells. This condition was likely the cause of the accident that resulted in a broken femur, pelvis, and multiple contusions. Kavanaugh is in serious but stable condition and is expected to make a full recovery. The outpour of well wishes and support have been overwhelming, and Kavanaugh, or The Honorable HK as he likes to be called, wanted to credit the skilled and rapid response of the city's emergency services, which...

"*Blah, blah*, horseshit." Earl turned away from the TV. "Guess you were right. The law ain't interested in us. A good thing, too. I'm way too pretty to go to jail."

"Knowing what we know," Dale said, "the last place Kavanaugh wants us is in custody."

Earl reached for the pitcher with a shaky hand.

"I got it," Dale said and began to pour. "Are you all right?"

Earl put his hand on his beer mug. "I will be." When Dale finished pouring, Earl took a long, deep drink and swallowed slowly. "I ain't ever lost control like that before. It scared the hell out of me." He took another drink. "It's still scaring me."

Dale didn't know how to respond, so he didn't.

Earl put his empty mug on the table. "Maybe we should head back and try some of that Reiki?"

Dale filled Earl's mug back up. "What the hell for?"

"So, they can tune the chakra that will allow my butt to unpucker."

Dale took a drink. "This ain't the first time you've been violent. I've seen you put down man and beast. Why is this so different?"

"Damn, Dale, you never listen."

"I'm trying, Old Man."

"I wasn't in control. I wasn't behind the wheel. I was nothin' but anger and hate. It was like I was... Well, it was like I was you for a hot minute."

Dale sat back. "There's an insult in there somewhere."

"Probably." Earl took a deep breath. "I imagine there is a lot you gots to tell me now."

"Yeah," Dale said. "There is, iffen you still want to hear it?"

Earl sat still for a beat, then reached into his back pocket. "First things first." Earl tossed down the logo he had sketched for Earl and Dale Trucking. It was round, as was the Anheuser-Busch drink coaster he'd sketched it on.

Dale picked it up. It was crude, not at all professional, but had potential. "You still want to partner up?"

"We've been partners for years. It's just time t'make it legal."

"What about your unpuckered butt?"

"You let me worry about that."

Dale leaned forward and looked Earl dead in the face. "Things are different now. The rules seem to be changing. Maybe there never were any, I don't know. Whatever shred of decency they had, any sense of honor amongst the beasts, it's long gone, and the games anew." Dale tossed the logo on the table. "If you go down this road with me, I can't honestly say where it might lead." He wanted to add, *Or what you might become*, but he kind of felt it was implied.

Earl sat back, brought his mug up, put on his serious face, the one he reserved for deep thinking and watching episodes of *Jeopardy*. After a gulp and a long swallow, Earl's contemplation came to an end. "I can't honestly say I know exactly what you're talking about, but I do know one thing."

"Which is?"

"Whatever is down the road, we're better off driving through it together than we are apart."

Dale raised his mug. "Fair enough."

Earl brought his up as well. "To Earl and Dale Trucking."

Dale scoffed. "I like Dale and Earl Trucking."

"No," Earl said. "It sounds better alphabetical."

"Dale and Earl *is* alphabet—Tell you what. Why don't we settle this like men?"

"Suits me fine," Earl said. "Darts or nine ball?"

"Nine."

The two men tossed back their mugs. They drank long and deep and finished the pitcher before either of them said another word about the future. When Dale sensed the time had come to tell Earl things he needed to know, he ordered another pitcher. It arrived with an inch of froth and a weary smile from the waitress. Dale filled their mugs just as Patsy

Cline's voice floated over from the jukebox. Earl sat quietly and listened while Dale spoke and Ms. Cline sang about the wisdom of walkin' after midnight.

ABOUT THE
AUTHOR

Kevin David Anderson currently lives in Southern California. Before becoming a writer, Anderson earned a B. A. in Mass Communication (TCOM) with a focus on Media Production from CSUF (Fresno State). He worked as a marketing professional for more than a decade, during which he managed award-winning campaigns for both television and radio.

Anderson's debut novel, the geeky, cult zombie classic *Night of the Living Trekkies* is a funny, offbeat zombie novel exploring the pop culture carnage that ensues when the undead crash a Star Trek convention. The Washington Post listed it as one of the top five Zombie novels of 2010.

Night of the Living Trekkies and Anderson's follow up, *Night of the ZomBEEs*, have become required reading in college courses, most notably the class designed for incoming freshman, *How to Survive Your Freshman Year by Studying the Zombie Apocalypse*, at Mansfield University in Pennsylvania.

Anderson's short stories have appeared in almost a hundred publications, from anthologies and magazines to podcasts and radio dramas, in multiple languages and on every continent, excluding Antarctica. Anderson was the first American to be published in the award-winning South African Horror Magazine, *Something Wicked*. Dozens of his stories have been turned into audio productions by voice talents like Jason Hill, Rish Outfield, and Mur Lafferty, on Parsec Award-winning podcasts like Pseudopod, The Drabblecast, The Dunesteef, and on the very popular Simply Scary Podcast and the No Sleep Podcast.

When not writing horror-comedy, Anderson likes to spend time at the beach with his family, attend horror cons and book festivals, work with special needs students, and write bad, corny, nerdy jokes. Dad jokes and puns with a geeky twist are his specialty, and with the help of his son, he published *The Geektastic Joke Book for Kids* under the pseudonym Giggles A. Lott and Nee Slapper. Giggles & Slapper's next book, *Jurassic Jokes, A Book 65 Million Years in the Making* will be available later in 2019.

For more information on Anderson visit KevinDavidAnderson.com

And continue your cross-country travels with...

Twisted Tales from Tornado Alley:
A Collection of Short Fiction
by
Stuart R. West

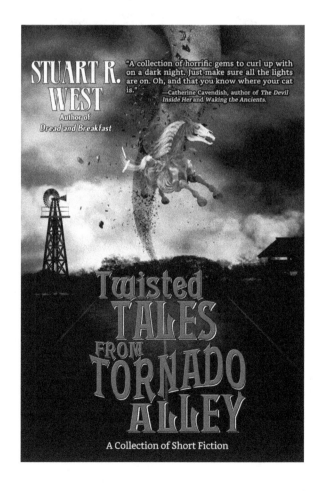

Shrouded in Mystery
The locals call it *Isla de los Perdidos*.
Island of the Lost.
According to the legends, those who venture onto the shores of
this cursed island never return.

Abandoned
Valarie DeNola and her sister Julie have chosen to ignore the
legends and the warnings. They have been selected to lead a team
of explorers to the island to discover the mystery surrounding it.
But once ashore, they become cut off from the outside world, and
what they discover is something they could never have prepared
for.

Inhabited by Death
Now they must fight against an unknown presence that is picking
them off one by one. No one can be trusted, and when even nature
rises up against them, all seems lost. Their one hope is the
extraction team they know is coming.
But will any of them survive to see it arrive?

PETER N. DUDAR

The GOAT
PARADE

"A darkly absorbing journey into
evil with a decidedly human heart
beating at its core..."
–Ed Kurtz, author of *The Rib From Which I Remake the World*
and *At the Mercy of Beasts*

"...frightening, and a whole hell of
a lot of fun to read...horror the
way it is supposed to be written."
–Tony Tremblay, author of *The Seeds of Nightmares*
and *The Moore House*

**Suffer the little children to come unto me...
and be like goats in my parade**

The city of Portland, Maine, is preparing for a parade to end all
parades, one that will usher in a thousand years of darkness. The
only thing is, they don't know it.

Four strangers will engage each other on the Devil's battlefield and
fight not only for the future of the city, but for the entire world.

Will they be able to defeat the Devil and stop the Goat Parade, or
will the world be plunged into an age of darkness and endless
suffering?

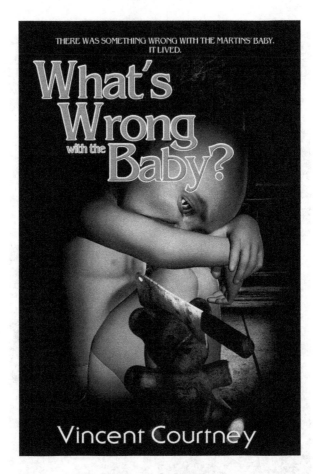

THERE WAS SOMETHING WRONG WITH THE MARTINS' BABY.
IT LIVED.

What's Wrong with the Baby?

Vincent Courtney

THE FEAR IS GROWING

From the moment he saw the ancient castle rising out of the picturesque Scottish countryside, filmmaker Dan Martin knew he'd found the ideal location for his vampire horror movie. And nothing could make him leave. Not the eerie legends of soul-stealing beasts of the night...nor a bizarre series of freak accidents. Not even his pregnant wife's tragic miscarriage.

THE TERROR IS BORN

Except that now there is another fetus growing in Vicki's womb. But little Darian is not going to be a normal baby. The Martins' adopted ten-year-old son Marty will soon find that out. In fact, Marty will soon know exactly what his new brother really is.

CPSIA information can be obtained
at www.ICGtesting.com
Printed in the USA
LVHW042337141019
634128LV00007B/2421/P